BIRKEBEINER

A Story of Motherhood and War

✛

JEFF FOLTZ

✢✢ ABOUT THE COVER ✢✢

The cover is a portrait painted by Knud Larsen Bergslien in 1869. Its title is *Skiing Birchlegs Crossing the Mountain with the Royal Child* (Norwegian: *Birkebeinerne pa Ski over Fjeldet met Kongbarnet*). One version of the saga that Bergslien portrays says that only the two soldiers and the baby made the journey. Many Norwegians believe an alternate version, that Inga was brave, an excellent skier and refused to part with her child. I join those who think that Inga accompanied the two soldiers for every harrowing step and that is why she's the main character in this story.

✤ ACKNOWLEDGEMENTS ✤

I raise my glass to the education and inspiration I received from the University of Southern Maine's Stonecoast MFA in creative writing. Then I toast the supreme mentors I found there; Michael C. White, Dennis Lehane, Roland Merullo and Suzanne Strempek Shea. Besides teaching me the nuts and bolts of competent writing, they demonstrated the palpable joy of embracing the craft and its challenges. Thanks also to the students at Stonecoast. I treasure the friendships and acquaintances that I made during those two years, most particularly with Bonnie Smith, Ben Luce, Tara Thomas and Shawna Galvin Rand, the members of my writers' group who pored over the pages of *Birkebeiner* until they knew them as well as I did. Jessica Walter was the first to read and critique the entire manuscript and I owe her one. B. Lee Hope will always have my gratitude for founding Stonecoast.

Bless Elizabeth Cooke for nurturing a "non-traditional" student in her undergraduate creative writing course at the University of Maine, Farmington. She infected me with the bug that propelled me to Stonecoast.

Thanks to Jonis Agee and Nicholos DelBanco, both wonderful writers, for their help at the University of Nebraska Writers' Conference.

For their indispensable assistance with the Norwegian translations, I must recognize Lone Jespersen, Albert & Charlotte Skurtveit and the St. Olaf's College Norwegian Language Department.

The Cornell University Nordic History Library, the Oslo National Library and the Holmenkollen Ski Museum were each instrumental in helping me understand how the Norwegian culture might have looked and thought in the 13th century.

Shellie Milford of the American Birkebeiner Ski Foundation and Silja Lena Løken of the Norwegian Birkebeiner Federation arranged for the use of a digitized print of Bergslein's portrait for the cover and it turned out beautifully. Thanks also to Terri MacKenzie, a member of my writers' group, for her efforts on behalf of the cover.

Finally, but far from least, thanks to the staff at Maine Authors' Publishing Cooperative, in particular Jane Karker, Genie Dailey, David Allen, and Cheryl McKeary, for being a great group of professionals who bolstered my confidence in them with each cheerful answer they rendered and each important task they checked off as they pieced together the final offering - a finished *Birkebeiner*.

✛✛ AUTHOR'S NOTE ✛✛

A mother's instinct to protect her child is timeless. The urge is primal. War, unfortunately, is ageless and enduring. It doesn't matter when the mother in this story, Inga, lived, or when men fought the war that surrounded and threatened her and her child. Suffice that it was long ago. Most of us, as we realize her motives, choices, conflicts, and reactions, will feel that nothing much about motherhood has changed.

The dialect of that time would be unintelligible today, even to a Norwegian.

For both of these reasons, I make no attempt to have the language sound period based. I don't want to distract those who read this story with a resonance or rhythm that might be uncomfortable and is unimportant to the characters or their plights. Instead I use an occasional Norwegian phrase to help create a flavor of the location.

Birth was an animal of prey. The only birth Inga had ever been part of, other than her own, brought pain and suffering to everyone she knew and death to many. Water ran down her legs, first gushing and then slowing to a sticky trickle. She gasped for air, each wheeze thicker than the one before. The reindeer-skin walls of the lodge closed around her. Inga groped for the door between the *soverom*, where she had been resting after she stoked the breakfast fire, and the *stue*, but the changing shape of her home disoriented her. She needed Heiki. Slow, awkward steps tangled Inga's feet. She stumbled when she reached the large hearth in the *stue*'s center, dropped to her knees and leaned against the bottom bench of the tier that lined the wall. The heated air over the long fire distorted the rows of benches on the opposite wall and added to her confusion. "Heiki, Heiki!" she called as she pushed up and staggered the rest of the way to the entrance at the far end of the *stue*.

Heiki's lodge was beyond a small knoll, on the far side of the compound. Inga heard her before she saw her. "*Jeg kommer, Inga, jeg kommer, kjære deg.*" Bounding across the packed snow, Heiki looked like a young woman. She said the deliveries kept her young. When she got close, Inga could see the valleys and ridges that defined her features, their ends nudged upward by her smile. Long silver hair reflected the sun and framed her face. The effect made her eyes bluer than the merging of the sky and the *fjord*. Often Inga thought what a beautiful maiden she must have been. Outstretched arms encircled Inga, and took her weight from the door frame. Heiki's cheek felt soft against hers, and her hair smelled like the sweet tallow that she used to make candles.

"*Det skal gå bra, kjære deg*. Everything is going to be just fine, dear," Heiki said, cupping Inga's face. Her hands were cold, but Inga's gasping slowed.

"But Hakon's not here."

"That's all right, dear. We know that's the way it is." She added a little squeeze before she released Inga's face. "Sometimes our men are away. The Croziers see to that, don't they?" She circled Inga's waist with her right arm and nudged her left hand under her elbow as they walked back through the *stue* to the *soverom*. "Besides, we don't need him right now." Heiki warbled a laugh, a sound as light and warm as her smile. "Good King Hakon has already done his part, now hasn't he?"

"But what if..."

"*Ja*. You know better than that." She wagged a finger. "Torstein and King Hakon protect each other like brother wolves." Reassured by Heiki's support, Inga, legs quivering, managed to reach the bed at the back of the *soverom*. She hung limp as Heiki lowered her onto the fur covering, and then lifted her legs so she could recline. Inga tried to hold onto Heiki's hand as the midwife turned and walked toward the small cooking hearth, where a fire burned all day. She heard the crackling rush when Heiki added a log. She could see Heiki dip water out of the large storage basin into a clay pot. The stream from the gourd ladle sounded like the crash of a waterfall. The rustle of cloth in Heiki's quilted vest was louder than the snap of the fire. Inga's world assumed the proportions of her pain, every sensation more intense than anything in her experience.

Without warning, Inga's body knotted and the pain tried to fold her in half. Her scream frightened her as much as the pain did. Heiki came back to her carrying a large red clay urn. Steam, sweet with herbs, swirled over it like morning fog over an autumn lake. "Breathe deep, Inga. Scream if you want. That's going to happen." Heiki put the urn down by the bed and knelt. She wet a piece of *vadmel*, squeezed it into the urn and used it to brush back a tangle of blonde hair from Inga's forehead.

Inga gasped, digging fingers into the fur bed covering.

"Don't tense," Heiki said, using the cloth to catch a trickle of perspiration as it moved toward her patient's ear. She soaked another piece of *vadmel* in the water and let it cool a little. Then she lifted Inga's robes and spread the coarse loomed wool on her domed stomach. Its texture reminded Inga of a dog's tongue, only warmer. "That will help. Mostly you just have to bear it, but you've got good hips for birthing. It shouldn't take too long. Our women have good hips. I think our men are attracted to that. It's a good thing. Easy birthing means our people live on."

Inga grunted a guttural cry as she doubled over again, longer this time, and she thought she wouldn't like this birth any better than the one she knew. How many more times the torture returned, she didn't know. She stopped counting sometime before she smelled the dinner fires. Thin shafts of morning, and then afternoon light, which filtered through gaps in the alder branch door, retreated into evening darkness. Other women, she thought, drifted in and out, but their presence was like a whisper to the deaf. Inga was aware only of her pain and fear, and of Heiki.

Soft bear and rabbit skins cushioned her back, absorbing some of her torment. The urn of herbs and water beside the bed spread the aroma of balsam and dried flower petals. The fragrance of that blended with the scent of lentils and scallions boiling with reindeer somewhere. But none of it chased her tormentors away. "*Tiden er inne.* It's time."

"Good. Not too long now until you meet your child." Heiki made Inga kneel on two stacks of skins and hold onto a horsehair rope she had looped over the lodge's main roof beam. "Push now, Inga, push as hard as you can."

The rope cut into her hands, but what hurt was the tearing and stretching and agonizing muscle spasms. She screamed and pushed and was sure her teeth would shatter and spill out. When she pushed, the knotting stopped and she wanted to push more. She couldn't keep from pushing. The more pressure she exerted, the less pain there was and she had an exhausted sense of nearing the finish. In one instant, she felt like her body would split and in the next, all of it stopped and she let herself fall backward into the softness.

At first she heard the cry as though in a dream, elongated, from somewhere else, somewhere distant. Then she heard the melody in Heiki's voice, "You have a son! A prince is born!"

"A prince?" She hadn't thought about her child that way.

"*Ja*, a prince! Perhaps he'll be the one to unite our country... bring our people together."

Inga's head rolled from side to side. "Please not." Her lips trembled and she dabbed at the corners of her eyes while she watched Heiki use gentle strokes of a soft cloth to remove the waxy gore and expose her son's perfect new skin. Then she laid him on Inga's chest and he found her breast. Inga absorbed him with her arms and her eyes, and paid little attention to Heiki as the midwife delivered the afterbirth, gently wrapped it in soft *vadmel*, and offered a quiet prayer.

"He's so alive and perfect and beautiful," Inga said. "Look at him. He's so magnificent, so...so perfect."

"He is, dear." Heiki covered both of them. "And so are you. Forever you'll have a bond with him that nobody else can have and nobody can break, not even you."

Now that Inga had met her baby, seen him and felt him at her breast, she thought about what Heiki had said. She whispered to him, "There's nothing we can do about that."

"What, dear?"

Inga smiled at Heiki. "I said, listen to Heiki my little one. You are a prince...*the* prince. We'll live with that, but most of all, we'll live."

Heiki's eyes narrowed and she smiled. She touched Inga's cheek and swept her hand back over her hair. She nodded as she and Inga held each other's gaze. Then both of them watched him for a while as he nursed.

"What will you name him?"

"Hakon and I decided before he left that if it was a boy, we would call him Hakon. Hakon Hakonsson."

"Perfect," said Heiki. "I'll tell everyone. The new prince is Hakon, son of Hakon."

Inga pressed her lips into thin bloodless lines. She reached for Heiki's hand without taking her eyes off her baby. She squeezed. "*Ja*," she said. "Tell them. Tell them all that Prince Hakon is here."

Heiki stayed for a while, making sure Inga was comfortable and the bleeding controlled, but they said little. Inga couldn't help but think as she lay there feeding little Hakon that things were…different now. She smiled and swallowed. She watched his soft mouth advance and retreat as his cheeks expanded and contracted like tiny bellows. That's what they reminded her of - tiny bellows fanning the flame of a new life. My baby's new life, she thought. She put her hand under the blanket and caressed him from his neck down his back and over his bottom to each of his feet. She counted his toes and wrapped her hand around the left foot and then the right. They fit with ease and warmed her palm. He responded to her touch, sucking faster and taking a deep breath, followed by a little murmur. Inga breathed in the scent of his perfect new skin, the softest, cleanest fragrance God ever made.

"*Ja*. Listen to Heiki," she whispered.

Time, Inga thinks, is both a friend and an enemy. Can he really have finished his second autumn? She is in the *soverom* preparing breakfast for herself and little Hakon when she hears the familiar rap, a sound like a woodpecker. Since there are no trees inside the compound, she knows who the bird is. Whenever Heiki visits, she bangs a wooden spoon between the antlers on the reindeer skull perched next to the threshold.

"May I come in?" Heiki yells so that Inga can hear her through the *stue*.

"Of course. I'm getting ready to eat and feed Hakon."

"I can come back later."

"No. I want to talk to you. We're in the *soverom*." There's lightness in her voice, pleasure at the last words. The bed in the *soverom* is at the back wall, and single benches, not layered rows like in the *stue*, line each of the other walls. It's where she plays with little Hakon and prepares food. It's where she and King Hakon sleep, eat and talk. It's the warmest place in the lodge, except when the *stue* is full of men in council and the fire there is roaring. When she has the chance, like now with Heiki, it's the place she can relax.

Heiki smiles. She likes Inga's spirit and her curiosity about the old ways. She walks down the right hand side of the great hearth that runs through the center of the elongated room. The fireplace measures more than the height of two men and is set between the steps of benches that line the two long walls. When she reaches the door of the *soverom*, just past the storeroom, Heiki says, "*God morgen, kjaere deg.*"

"*God morgen,*" Inga says, as she ladles reindeer and lentils into a birch bowl and hands it to her friend. "Fresh lentils.

Picked the last of them day before yesterday. Barely beat the hard frost."

"I love them. Eat them all winter. Last thing to spoil before Ull and Skade take their summer nap and I can grow more." Heiki laughs.

Inga chews her lower lip for a moment, scrunches her eyes at the corners, and then says, "Why do we still revere them? Sometimes I wonder if we offend Christ with our references to the old gods."

"Did your parents ever tell you the story about the trolls who threw rocks at the first church?"

"*Ja*, of course."

"I doubt that story would offend Christ. The old gods are just stories." Heiki takes a bite of her meat as she sits down. "Mmmm. Tastes good." She grasps her wooden spoon, sweeps it away from her into the lentils, and starts to raise it. It's not far from the bowl when her hand stops. She looks up, at nothing in particular. The lentils remain suspended for several moments and then complete the route to her mouth. She raises the spoon as if to fend off any comment while she chews. After she swallows, she lowers the spoon and says, "Their place...the old gods...in your life will be less important than when I was a girl." She pauses again and shakes the spoon for emphasis. "And much less important than they were to my grandfather."

"That's the same thing Hakon says, that it's our heritage, not our religion."

"Part of our past, no more or less. I remember my grandfather called on Thor and Odin. Not just using the names, like we do today, to curse. He thought creation sprang from Odin's loins. When thunder rumbled and lightning flashed, it was Thor. If a bear or wolf attacked, it was a *berserker* or a shape-shifting demon of some sort, sent to do Odin's bidding on Earth." She shakes her head at the notion.

Little Hakon squeals, "*Mamma, Mamma.*"

Heiki smiles at the child. "There's a sound Christ likes." She ticks her head in Hakon's direction. "Take care of him and you'll never offend God."

Inga nods. But how do I protect him from being a prince?

They watch the child's tentative waddle as he scurries out of the *soverom* toward the *stue*. They follow. "Heritage is a growing and changing thing, isn't it?" Inga says.

"This really disturbs you, doesn't it, *kjaere deg*?" Heiki says.

Inga's mouth draws into a pinched line. She looks at the dirt floor, her head hung so that her chin touches the top of her chest. She glances up at the baby to check his path, exhales a deep sigh, and looks back at Heiki. "There's so much I don't know, especially about the men's business, the war and..." Her lip trembles. She looks away and swipes the back of her hand across her eyes.

"*Het! Het!*" Hakon says, pointing to the fire at the room's core.

Inga looks back at him. She lunges two steps and grabs his arm. When she sees that she has startled him, she hugs him and rubs his back. Then she kneels and says, "That's right, Hakon. *Het. Kokhet!* Don't touch." She pulls her hands up tight against her chest and shakes her head. Part of the morning ritual with him now is to let him throw some sticks on the hearth. He loves it and it allows her to caution him not to touch *het*. His little bottom juts out as he squats to assault a full-size log, then looks back at her, sheepish at being unable to budge it.

Heiki laughs, and Inga smiles at her son. "Hakon, let *Momma* do that one. You help with this one."

The child abandons his labor with a big, open-mouthed smile, and wraps his tender fist around the twig Inga extends to him. He throws it on the glowing coals and turns to her with the face of a cat that has caught a mouse.

"*Tusen tuk*, Hakon. Thank you so much for being *Mamma's* helper." She picks up the log he abandoned, grunting to remind him how heavy it is, and tosses it into the center of the coals. Crackling sparks flare all around it, and he claps at the excitement. Several more follow that one and she lets him throw another stick.

As Inga tosses the third log into the hearth, Heiki says, "The war is what bothers you. That isn't our heritage, but I can tell you more about its history, things you may not know, if that will help."

Inga nods, but keeps her eyes on Hakon. As fast as his fascination with the fire flared, it cools and he wants to pull himself up onto the benches that line the room. "No you don't, young man. We've got to get your cloth on." He protests with a screech, but then cooperates with the familiar process as they retrace their steps to the *soverom* and she puts him on his back on the bed. She grabs a piece of *vadmel* from the supply that she has cut and pounded smooth.

Hakon rolls over and crawls toward the far side of the bed. She stretches across and snatches his ankle. It feels small and smooth in her hand. "You want to play, don't you?" She and Heiki laugh at his giggling as Inga drags him back across the bed. No sooner are her hands reaching for the cloth than he is on all fours in a hasty retreat.

"You imp. You're faster than a wolf cub. I'll get you!" Inga runs to the other side of the bed with exaggerated motion, cloth in hand this time. "I'll get you!"

The chase adds urgency to his playful flight and he giggles himself into a frenzy. She tickles his ribs as he squirms and laughs and pushes her hand away only to have the other dive in to take its place. When he has his hands around fingers on both of her hands, she picks him up and hugs him and rubs his back to calm him. "Enough now. Let's put your cloth on. Then we'll play some more. All right?"

"Play more now."

"As soon as we put your cloth on." Inga's voice is firm, not scolding, but matter-of-fact. She puts him on his back. He raises his pudgy legs, and she slides the doubled-over cloth under him, folds it through, rests it on his tummy, and ties off braided *vadmel* thongs on each side to snug it around his waist. She slides *vadmel* booties around his upturned feet, a warm gown over his head, and stands him up, pats him on the bottom, and kisses his cheek. "Now do you want to play or eat breakfast?"

"Bekfast," the child says. Easy choice.

Inga looks at Heiki. "I'm so lucky to have him."

"And he to have you."

Inga nods, picks up the child and all three move to the fire. When they're seated, Inga begins to feed Hakon. He quiets down, and she says to Heiki, "We love the Church, but we continue the war?" Inga's expression is the same as that of a farmer who believes that he has all his sheep in the stall, but keeps coming up one short on the count. She has heard Hakon and Torstein talk about the war often enough, and respects their perspective, but it affects her life, all their lives, more than drought affects crops. She longs for all the answers and probes whenever there's an opportunity. She knows Heiki will fill the gaps; explain what she never knew.

"That's the Croziers' doings, Eystein and Magnus, not our people. We can love the Church but not tolerate the bishop's authority over the way we choose our king."

Inga knits her brow, squints and shakes her head. It's something the men would never say.

"*Ja*, you're too young to remember." Heiki begins the story. She tells Inga how Crooked Neck, Magnus's father bought a crown and coronation for Magnus when the boy was five. Heiki turns up her nose when she gets to the part where Bishop Eystein anointed him. "It was later that we learned how Crooked Neck paid Eystein."

"Land?" Inga says.

"Power. Power to pick future kings if there is no heir of legitimate birth."

They both look at little Hakon, and Inga feeds him another mouthful. Then, her jaw slack, she turns to Heiki.

Heiki nods confirmation. "And that takes away the right of our *Lagtings* to choose from all heirs, born of a church wedding or not."

Inga's eyes widen as if she has met a wolf in the woods. "That's why my father was so concerned."

Heiki holds up a finger and wags it. "*Ja.* He was eloquent before the *Lagting* when the decree came down. Hakon, Torstein and so many of our people were there when he said, 'If the Assemblies have no voice, we have none. It is up to us to protect the voice of our lawmakers, to hold sacred the decisions of our Assemblies.' "

This history has moved Inga's life down paths she wouldn't have chosen, some of which she hates and fears. She looks at her child, a lingering look like you would give someone you may not see for a while, bites at the forming frown, and drops her head. In a small voice, she says to the floor. "The birth of the Birkebeiner." She looks back at Heiki, stronger now. "Still, it's hard for me not to admire the effort, what Hakon and Torstein and the others sacrifice for their people."

Heiki nods, and touches her arm.

"Why couldn't they tell me this? Why can't they reveal anything?" She pauses to push the anger back. "I was with Hakon and Torstein, having dinner and talking about the Birkebeiner, and I asked Torstein about something I remembered from when I was a little girl," Inga says. "Men, Birkebeiner, came to our village, fleeing from Magnus. I told Torstein that during dinner the men mentioned a great victory, one where he killed so many Croziers. I asked him if that was the day things changed." She looks back up at Heiki and her voice strengthens. Lines crease her forehead. "Their bearing..." she pauses, searching for the word she wants "... altered, more rigid, heads thrown back. Actually held their breath. They exchanged a look that concealed so much I wanted to know."

"Like a wall surrounded them and within it they kept a secret," Heiki says.

"*Ja.*"

"And you wondered if anyone else could pass the gates and

share their treasure?" Heiki laughs.

"*Ja, ja.*" Inga's brows arch and her head snaps back. "I felt like I had trespassed on sacred land."

"And it wasn't Torstein who answered, was it?"

Inga's mouth falls open. A spoonful of meal and lentils stops halfway between the bowl and Hakon's mouth. "How'd you know? How do you know any of this?"

"Brother wolves," Heiki says. She nods with the confidence of absolute knowledge. "They even protect each other from having to boast. What did you do then?"

Hakon squeals at the delay.

Inga watches the spoon to his mouth and says, "I held silent for a moment but let my look tell them the question stood. This was something I wanted to know. Needed to know. Something that affects my life, and my son's. I wanted to understand."

Heiki snaps a curt nod. "With that question, you went beyond the birth of the Birkebeiner. You stepped onto the battlefield, set your feet in their domain." She wags a finger. "You talked about the Great Battle."

Inga shrugs, and forces a sigh.

Heiki strokes Inga's arm. "Patience. Listen." She settles back like she needs to find a comfortable position. "In the early battles, the Croziers hurled insults at our soldiers. Time and again Magnus's superior troops routed our men. The Croziers would yell, 'Run Birkebeiner, run Birchleg. They made fun of the birch bark that wrapped our men's legs to keep the snow out." Heiki pinches her lips and shakes her head, as if someone has insulted her and she refuses to dignify their comment with a response. "Little did they know that they were giving us our name, the name we became so proud of." She reaches for Hakon's curls and twists them with a thin, chapped finger.

Inga frowns. Hakon told her of the humiliation that he and his men felt, at first, when the Croziers chanted that oppressive and denigrating tag. She misses Hakon's mouth, puts the spoon in the bowl, and fingers the food off of his cheek onto his lips.

"*Ja*," Heiki says. "Scurrying in disgrace on birch legs." She emphasizes *disgrace.*

"Crozier slurs. I guess I knew that. But then it began to change?"

"Our men gained experience, fought with more confidence, until the battle where Torstein killed so many Croziers. The one they call the Great Battle." There's more pace to Heiki's speech now. She thrusts out her chin. "What the Croziers had left at the end of that day was a lone voice, stripped of ability to act. Our men robbed them of strength, reduced them to an anonymous shout from the safety of woods on the distant side of the battlefield. "*Vi skal nok komme igjen og knuse dine birkerbeinerhær.*" She says it again with a disdainful snarl. "We will return and crush your Birkebeiner army." Then Heiki stands and raises a fist over her head. "That was when Torstein laughed, laughed so loud that the sound carried to both sides of the arena." She raises her right leg and touches it with her spoon. "Then Torstein raised his leg and touched the birch wrapping with his axe that still dripped Crozier blood. 'Birkebeiner!' he yelled. And he did the same with the other leg and at that moment," Heiki nods, "what had been an epithet became a badge of honor."

Inga's hands are still. She concentrates on Heiki, fascinated.

Heiki nods several more times. "That's right. Our soldiers began to call each other Birkebeiner and point to the birch bark wrappings on their legs. Our boys started to say, 'I want to be a Birkebeiner.' Suddenly, it was a rite of passage. Women began to say, 'My husband is a Birkebeiner,' or 'I want to marry a Birkebeiner.' " Heiki flails both hands and bounces, speaks with her whole body. "My grandfather told me that his great-grandfather told him that Odin traded an eye for wisdom. After that battle, I would tell my grandfather's story and add that if Odin visits Norway today he will have to wear birch leggings as a display of that costly good sense. Our people started to repeat that." She cackles at her mischief.

"Hakon did tell me that after that day, Birkebeiner was no longer a term of derision," Inga says.

Inga's expression and tone tell Heiki that the story has opened a door to the past. "It was incredible, *kjaere deg*. Hakon disbanded the *Leidang*, because recruitment was no longer necessary. Volunteers came from even the smallest *bo*. Everyone knew that now we could move out of the shadow of the Crozier. They were anxious to serve. The bishop had dubbed us Birkebeiner. He and those who followed his Crozier meant Birchleg to heap disrespect on us like...like..."

"Sheep dung." Inga says and smiles.

Heiki laughs. "*Ja, ja*. And after our army won the battle that day, the enemy continued to taunt. But our men touched weapons to lifted legs and shouted it back. 'Birkebeiner.' They began to like it."

The smile slips off of Inga's lips and she is silent, taking time to think. A loud snap from the fire makes her jump. She tries to laugh at her reaction, but only forces a smile. "I should love that story." She sighs, her eyes fixed on her child. "I could, if it weren't for him."

Heiki moves closer, sits again, and puts her arm around Inga. "Eystein and Magnus changed everything."

"So Hakon and Torstein made it better...for almost everybody." The baby is sound asleep. Inga picks him up and hugs him against her. She looks at Heiki. She looks at the fire and all around her *soverom*. "I wasn't even alive when some of these things happened." She kisses Hakon's cheek and he stirs a little. "But they're clear now, so very clear."

Heiki takes her hand from Inga's back and strokes Hakon's hair. "He's so beautiful. I hate to leave, but I have some chores." She rises. "He'll be all right. I'm sorry if I've caused you pain."

Inga leans and kisses Heiki on the cheek. "*Tusen tuk*. You've filled so many gaps for me. I must know these things if I'm to do the best for him." Now she strokes Hakon's head. "You're a dear friend." She feels older than before. She thinks for a second and whispers in Hakon's ear, "More experienced."

Heiki smiles, takes Inga's hand and gives a gentle squeeze. They rise together and Inga walks her out.

"Look," Heiki says as she steps outside. "Starting to snow. Good you got those lentils in."

* * * *

Little Hakon reaches up, wraps his soft hand around Inga's finger and stares out the door, transfixed by the whiteness. They've had two more heavy snowstorms since her conversation with Heiki, and several lighter ones, so for this early in the month of *Ylir*, the snowpack is deep.

"*Mamma*, Tors' play wi' Hakon?" he says as he pushes his free hand out, points and bounces against her.

Torstein Skevla strides across the well-trodden snow of the compound. Women, stirring the meager supper fare, snatch a glimpse of him through hazy smoke and freezing breath. Children scurry behind to get a closer look at the battle-axe in his right hand. The broad arched blade glints late afternoon rays from its honed edge and pulls the children along, fish following a lure. One reaches to touch the weapon's stout oak handle, but stumbles, recovers and scampers away, his day's courage spent. Dogs skulk from the warrior's path, tails held low.

The scar that angles from Torstein's left temple to the bridge of his nose doesn't diminish his features. Inga doesn't see the old wound as an intrusion, but rather as part of Torstein's identity, like the hint of silver in his golden beard and hair. The story is that the Crozier who inflicted the gash saw his last sunrise that day, as did a dozen - some say fifteen of his comrades.

That was the day he earned his name, Torstein Skevla, Torstein the Scrapper. Skevla was the only surname that Inga knew for him. One time she asked Hakon if it was true that King Sverri had sired, but not claimed, him. Hakon shrugged and said, "Whether he is Sverri's son or not, he will always be my brother." Then he laughed. "And it would be difficult for anyone, Birkebeiner or Crozier, to deny that he is a scrapper."

Hakon had mentioned the tale of Torstein, so Inga believed it, but, until her chat with Heiki, questioned whether she had heard it all. The men keep too much to themselves, she thinks. The battle had happened long before she met the king, when she was in her eighth *sommer*. She remembers that the men who sailed into the *fjord* that season and talked about the *Lagtings,* also boasted of the valor of the soldiers, about how their bravery had altered the enemy.

Springing off his haunches toward the cooking fire, one guest said, "Torstein turned this way and that, fending off those who joined the attack, stacking Croziers like cordwood." Fervor for the story spun him around like a man who had lost his senses. "As the last one started to turn, intent on running, Torstein's axe caught him below the nose, striking off his jaw so it hung from one side by a sinew. His tongue hung next to his neck like a swollen crimson slug. He ran in circles 'til he fell." Inga's sisters' faces contorted, their noses scrunched. Their mother clutched her long blond braid with both hands. "Yes, but it's true. I swear it." He touched his heart. "Torstein stood looking at the carnage." He wagged a finger as his voice tapered to a whisper. "Mind you now, after the din of battle it was quiet enough to hear the trees grow." His voice rose. "From beyond the woods line on the far side of the battleground a single voice echoed, 'We'll return and crush your Birkebeiner army.' Torstein smiled, then grinned, then laughed. He raised his left leg straight out from his body, as high as he could, and touched his battleaxe to the birch bark wrappings below his knee. Then did the same to his right."

That brought smiles and nods from the whole group, even Inga's mother. Her father clapped the guest on the back.

* * * *

Inga likes the memory...and now that she understands its

significance, fears it.

As Torstein reaches the door of the lodge he nods to her. "*God kveld*," Inga. Day's over early this time of year, isn't it?" He reaches out and tousles the baby's curly hair. "*Hvordan er det med den lille prinsen i dag*?" He says it more to Hakon than to his mother.

"He's well, Torstein. Hungry, like his father. Will you join us for supper?"

The boy reaches out. "Tors'old Hakon high," he gurgles.

Torstein puts down his weapon and reaches for the giggling child. "Up high," Torstein roars, as he hefts Hakon over his head, the baby squealing a two-year-old's approval. "King Hakon asked me to discuss the movements of the Croziers and our defense of Lillehammer," he says as he brings Hakon back to his chest. "I'd love to bless the meal with you."

"More high," begs Hakon, extending his arms over his head.

"Once more, then I have to go inside and talk to your father."

Hakon nods and screeches as Torstein drops him to knee level and catapults him in one motion over his head. "More high 'gin!" Hakon adds a more vigorous nod as if to stave off the real answer.

Torstein tickles the boy's ribs to make him release a handful of beard and gives him back to Inga. She likes the way he is with her child. With a smile, he shakes his finger and says, "No you don't. I said once more. We'll go high later."

Hakon nods and puts his face next to his mother's. Torstein ducks through the lodge door and removes his cape of bearskin. Inga helped Hakon make similar ones for both of them. He wears a vest of beaver pelts over a *vadmel* shirt that matches his leggings. The thick cloth, pressed from sheep's wool, is good for this time of year, warm and dry, its natural oil wicking away moisture. From ankle to knee, he wears the birch-bark wrappings tied with strips of rawhide, as do all the Birkebeiner men, and many of the women. His own hair is enough to keep his head warm on the walk across the compound. He raises his hand and smiles when he sees King Hakon come through the doorway from the *soverom*. He waits with Inga as Hakon makes his way from the far end of the *stue*.

"I heard my son," says Hakon, as he strides along the hearth in the center of the hall. "You're the only one other than Inga and me who can do that without scaring him." Torstein starts toward him and the two men grasp each other's right forearm as they meet.

Beautiful brother wolves, Inga thinks, remembering Heiki's gentle reassurance. She draws a deep, cleansing breath and controls its release. All three walk abreast back through the *stue* with room to spare, until they reach the fire. Torstein and Inga walk to the right between the fire and the tiers of benches along the wall. King Hakon follows an identical path to the left. He stops halfway along the fireside and picks up a long pole propped against his rows of benches. He hoists the rod hand over hand up into an opening in the roof. The gap runs the length of the fire and is the only thing that breaks the solid look of the ceiling. Poking and prodding, he bangs pieces of jagged, sooty ice and snow off the edges of the vent. He brings the pole down and brandishes it. "A *lurk* works for more than pushing yourself on skis," he says, and thrusts the shaft up against the edge of the vent again. The fire jumps and hisses when the chunks hit, and a sizzling cloud of steam billows back toward the roof. Hakon turns back to where he started and continues the procedure to the other end. Smoke mingles with the aroma of the packed earth floor and thatch from the roof, giving the room a dusky, tangy smell.

The sounds of fire and steam echo off the high timber framework that supports the roof, and Torstein watches young Hakon's delight at the commotion. "When he's excited, he can make almost as much noise as when those benches fill with men."

"He loves to be around you and Hakon. You two can churn him up to where he sounds like a small army." He loves you men, she thinks. But do you love him or what he represents? She can't help her thoughts. She tries to tell herself that she shouldn't be angry with them for not understanding something they can't fully experience. They didn't hold him in his first minutes of life, count the tiny toes and watch his mouth draw nourishment with a rhythm that, in an instant, bound her to her baby as if they were still one.

Icy snow scrabbles of its own weight down the thatch roof, tumbles onto the sloped part of the sod and stone walls and then slides to the ground. The rumble scares little Hakon.

Torstein sees him start to cloud up, throws his arms up in an exaggerated posture of fear, then points at the roof and laughs.

The boy smiles and imitates the soldier.

Inga mouths *tusen tuk*, and Torstein nods. "We'll eat in the *soverom*. There's no fresh salmon, but I'll get some *røkt laks* to add to the stew, if you'll wait for me." She hands Hakon to his father and ducks into the door to the storeroom and finds her way past the barrels of grain and lentils, and the bins of beets, scallions and potatoes. Before she reaches the back, she smells the smoky tang from the strings of *røkt laks*. The scales feel rough and leathery against her hand as she pulls three large pieces off the line. Not as good as fresh, but it will add flavor to the lentils and grain.

When she emerges, the men follow her into the *soverom*. Aromas of boiling grain and lentils, and the heady, pungent smell of *røkt laks* mix with the sweet smell of the fur and hay that makes their bed. Inga moves to the small hearth in the center of the room, uses her hands to scrape golden scales from the *røkt laks* into the fire and drops the fish into a pot of boiling grain and lentils. She takes the child from his father and moves to the bed to feed him. The men stop at the hearth.

"Sit, eat," Hakon says, ignoring the benches, and gesturing to bearskin mats. The two men sit cross-legged next to each other, angled toward the fire, where the large clay crock of food sits steaming.

Torstein unties the leather lace around his ankle, peels back the birch bark, and removes his moccasins. Holding them both in his left hand, he brushes against the grain of the beaver fur with his right, knocking off loose snow and droplets of water. Then he pinches the toes where they flare to secure his braided leather ski bindings.

"Wet?" Hakon says.

"Damp. Need to work on them tonight."

"Reminds me," says Hakon. "I've got beeswax, but need some pine resin. Spare some?"

"Give me your shoes when I leave. I'll treat them when I work on mine." He reaches into one of his shoes while he talks and pulls out a fistful of soggy-looking hay, tossing it on the edge of the fire where it starts to smolder. "I'll reline them too."

"Bring 'em back in the morning?"

"No, my king. I thought I'd let you prance across the compound in your bare feet to get them."

Hakon picks up a large hollow gourd and clunks his friend on the head with it, then uses it to heap stew into his bowl. He nods toward the hay Torstein threw on the fire. "And pull that grass out of there before the fumes kill us all."

Their banter makes Inga think of winter days when the Croziers were not camping at their door and they could enjoy being out on their skis. Inga and her sisters skied as soon as they could walk.

Women who can handle themselves on skis join the winter hunts. Inga remembers one hunt when Hakon, Torstein and she climbed high above the tree line, snow yielding to the climbing skins laced to the bottoms of their skis. They worked hard, breath short and labored, but they didn't waste any energy slipping back. Even on the steepest slopes, the grain of the hair on the pelts beneath their skis gripped the snow and set firm. Hoarfrost covered Torstein's beard, and perspiration icicles dangled from fur hats. Warmed by exertion and exhilaration, they stopped to remove their waist capes. When they reached their vantage point, they put the capes back on and removed the skins from their skis. They crouched low like wolves and watched the tree line, waiting, patient. Soon, the reindeer, feeding on the tops of small trees and pawing up the moss and herbs under the snow, crossed below, majestic and unsuspecting. The three swooped down toward the herd, making wide, silent turns. Plumes of powder sprayed and landed like clouds colliding. Inga felt the wind redden her cheeks and bring tears to her eyes. The breeze was right and they skied well, their skis so quiet that their prey didn't sense their presence until the hunters were upon them. Archers waited for the animals as they bolted into the woods. After the hunt, others, soldiers and women, congratulated Inga on bringing home food and staying with two excellent skiers to do so. Pleased with the praise, she answered that it was beautiful to ski with them, gratifying to know she could, and she would do it again.

The child's whimper stifles Inga's musing. As the men sit cross-legged and begin to eat from their carved birch bowls, she stays in the back of the *soverom* to feed her boy. Each man spoons a mouthful of stew. Torstein puts his birch utensil back into the bowl and waits for Hakon to speak.

The bed, covered with stitched fur, feels soft to Inga, like a luxury, but it's not. Just comfortable. She pulls the blanket King Hakon's mother made from lamb's wool around the baby and herself and watches the fireside silhouettes of these two guardians. Scents of dried grass, earth and bread drift with the heat of the flames and ease her like the sound of a mother's voice.

To her, Hakon and Torstein look much alike. Hakon shaves his beard, but his hair is the same golden color as Torstein's, perhaps a shade more red. Both men have summer forest eyes set above high chiseled cheekbones, straight noses and strong jaws. Hakon has a cleft at the chin and Inga would wager that Torstein has its twin hiding in his beard. Maybe the stories are true.

Hakon's words interrupt her reverie. "The Croziers' fires

grow in number. I counted almost a hundred last night." The transition to talk of war, to their business, sounds so easy for them. They don't see the shock course through Inga, like she's been dragged from a warm bed, across cold stones.

"You know they build extra fires to make us fear there are more of them than there are." Torstein sneers.

"And we both know they need Lillehammer. They'll attack us soon and their numbers are greater than ours. Thor's curse to the campfires."

Torstein looks up from his bowl without moving his head. "Tomorrow morning."

Hakon rubs his chin and pinches his lips into a thin straight line. "Yes, knowing Eystein."

"We packed down the snow trenches last night. Skjervald Skrukka and ten men did the left, and fourteen more of us did the right and center."

"Skjervald did well leading the men?" Hakon's eyebrows arch.

"He completed the task."

"But?"

"He's brash, acts like a bull reindeer in rut. Instincts only."

"You mean like you when you were his age?"

"Or like you maybe. I was too busy actually rutting to be brash."

Hakon laughs through a fresh spoonful of stew and has to put his hand over his mouth to keep it from spilling out, which makes Torstein laugh too.

As their guffaws dwindle, Hakon says, "Shh. Inga might hear you."

"Don't talk about me like I'm not here," she says. "I know what rutting is."

"We'll be polite, Inga," says Torstein. Teeth, whiter than most, show through his beard.

"Not you boys. Not 'til you grow up." She says it with a smile, joining their banter. "Words or winter trails, I can stay with you." Under the blanket she curls her fingers into fists, then relaxes them and strokes the baby's back.

"We've met our match, Torstein," Hakon says. "We'd better stick to our planning. And you should admit that Skjervald is as good as any of us on skis."

"Better. Faster up and more skillful down. Like he was born to it and the skis are part of him." Torstein smacks one fist atop the other and holds them.

"And he can work. Do you think the trenches will be effective?"

Torstein nods once. "The snow is soft and waist deep. We got within a long bow shot from their nearest campfire."

"And they heard nothing?" Hakon's eyebrows arch.

"Wind was blowing toward us."

"Have they seen the trenches today?"

"No. Haven't strayed but steps from their campfires."

"How close are the lateral trenches to our ramparts?" Hakon's forehead tightens into thin ridges.

"Their arrows'll fall short, but their catapults can reach us if they get them there. The trenches will keep them from reaching the walls, and they won't realize it until too late. You made the right decision."

"And your surprise?"

"Over one hundred buried and anchored."

"Total?"

"On each flank."

"Excellent," Hakon says.

Inga watches the ridges on his forehead relax and thinks she sees the corners of his mouth turn up.

"Should slow them down," Torstein says.

Hakon's smile turns to a laugh. "Finish your supper and get some rest, my friend. Those with more gray in their hair need extra sleep."

"Then you'll doze off in your chowder." Torstein reaches across and slaps Hakon on the foot.

Hakon grabs his hand before he can snap it back. He wraps his other hand around Torstein's forearm, slapping Torstein's hand against his own forearm. "Never fall in flight, my loyal friend."

"Those that do never gain renown, my king."

Inga rises with Torstein and Hakon as they push away their bowls and stand. Young Hakon is asleep, his head nestled on her shoulder. She walks to the fire. Both men touch the baby's blond curls. "My hope," Hakon says.

"Our future," Torstein says.

My child, Inga thinks. She pulls him tighter as the men turn toward the door.

She and the king watch Torstein as he walks toward his lodge. It is much colder now, and they can hear the packed snow squeak beneath his feet. Darkness has fallen. The glowing embers from dying dinner fires give snowmelt steam the rose hue of clouds at sunset. Yellow-orange shards of light from fires flickering inside lodges throughout the compound pierce sporadic gaps in thatch. The combination of colors looks like their ancestors's ski god and goddess, Ull and Skade, playing with their heavenly lights close to earth. They watch until Torstein blends with the darkness. Inga is glad he's such a good friend, pleased Hakon has such a loyal lieutenant, but she knows his interests are the same as Hakon's and the Birkebeiner's. Accession and defeating the enemy are what they think about. Norway can't have two kings is the men's song, on both sides. And it makes her wish again that there was just one other person in the world who put her child first and all the rest after.

As they turn to go in, men begin to stoke and fuel the campfires. Under his breath Hakon says, "Croziers aren't the only ones who can build extra campfires."

She puts the baby down, covers him, strokes his hair, talks to him and watches him sleep for a few moments before she goes to the fire and sits next to his father.

"Boy can sleep through anything," he says.

Staring at the fire, she doesn't answer.

"He was good tonight, wasn't he?"

She looks at him, but can't answer. She wants to pummel him with what she thinks, make him sting with the venom of her concern. But she doesn't want to lose control. She bites the inside of her lower lip. She doesn't want to rage, or worse, cry.

"You're upset? With me?"

Still she can't answer.

"Kidding with Torstein about reindeer rutting? You were laughing, too."

Blood rises into her face, and she turns away.

"Well, what?" he says.

She stares at the fire, and waits. She thinks back to Hakon's birth and remembers Heiki's words of comfort about King Hakon and his men being away. They were away battling Bishop Eystein, his toady, Magnus, and the army of those who follow the bishop's Crozier.

So many died to defend the birth of their rights, the birth that spawned Inga's fear of birth. She remembers again that summer when the Birkebeiner rowed all the way into Oslo *fjord*. As her mother, sisters and she fed them, they talked about how the *Lagtings*, the farmer's district assemblies, were being reborn and with it their people's right to elect a king from all royal sons.

She was only in her eighth *sommer* and didn't care who was king or how he ascended. She only wanted to stop being scared. She wanted to stop hearing women cry every time the men left and sob when not all of them returned. Now her son is here and she understands even more their anguish. It's profound sorrow, reared from the dread of what might happen in war, and then does.

Inga finally answers him. "You and Torstein laugh facing battle. Good. Fine. If that's the way you handle it, it's not my way to object."

"I don't mind. You can object if you..."

"I'm not finished." For a moment, she looks at him, not speaking. His mouth freezes open and he pulls his chin in. She sees the cords in his neck as his mouth closes. She waits until they disappear. "It's Hakon. You say he's your hope. Torstein calls him our future. He's a baby. Our baby, our little boy. Is battle what awaits him? Is that what he's to live for? To feign bravado on the eve and fight, kill or die in the morning? He's my baby. You can't think of him that way. You can't. I won't..." Her voice catches. "I won't..."

She struggles to go on, but this time it breaks and hard as she tries, she can't hold back. Sobs come in waves, retching from within like a riptide that's futile to resist. Hakon reaches for her. As she lands a feeble fist above his elbow, he pulls her toward him and holds her head against his neck with one arm, his other hugging tight around her heaving shoulders. She's not sure how long he holds her that way, but he doesn't let go until she moves her face up to brush against his and feels the tear on his cheek. At first she thinks it's her own, but when she pulls back, she can see the dampness and the lines pulled deep to his temples.

"Eystein's Croziers." It comes out like he spat it. "Magnus and the men around those campfires we watch from the ramparts are there to kill me and then they would kill Hakon without a thought. Because he's my son, Sverri Sigurdsson's grandson, the rightful heir. Eystein will enforce his decree and hold power any way he can."

"What can we do?" Her chin trembles again.

"Fight. Try to keep them from overrunning Lillehammer tomorrow. Somehow keep him safe. If I can persevere and unify the crown, then our son will live in peace."

There's a silence that's too heavy, too long. "And if not?"

"If I fail, Arne will..."

"The Earl of Nidaros?"

"*Ja*, he will become prefect for Hakon until he's old enough to accept election of the *Lagtings* and then it will be Hakon who'll have to bring peace. He and the Birkebeiners and their sons won't be safe until he does."

"Pray God keeps that burden from him."

"I hope He hears you. But if any child could grow up to possess the necessary qualities, it would be Hakon."

"I believe it, but why do you think so?"

"They called my father fierce as a lion, mild as a lamb. Sverri arrayed both animals on his crest and shield. Only his family ever saw the lamb, and we knew his gentleness and wisdom far outweighed the ferociousness for which he gained the most renown. Our people have always recognized that a child inherits qualities from both parents. And Hakon will have yours as well as those from my family."

Inga wipes her eyes and says, "Are you saying our son will be a sniveling crybaby?"

Both manage to laugh.

"No." Hakon's smile disappears. He slips his right hand from her back and, with a curled forefinger, raises her chin. "Like his mother, he will hush a king if someone he loves is threatened." He arches his brow. "Hakon will inherit honor from both of us, but more generosity," he pauses, looks up for a moment and then brings his eyes back to hers, "and more courage from you than me."

Inga hugs him tight.

He whispers, "So, try to see Inga, that when I say he's my hope, it's a hope of peace for him. When Torstein says he's our future, it's because of the future he wants, to worship a god and follow a king by his free will. Neither of us wishes for Hakon what we've endured."

"I'm glad our thoughts face the same way," she says. She pauses, staring at him. "But understand, Hakon, now and forever he will be my child first, and rightful heir after that. Don't ever think otherwise." There's no tremor in her voice now.

Hakon says nothing for a few moments. Inga doesn't take her eyes from him, not even to blink. His nod, when it finally comes, is slow and deliberate. "As it should be," he says, "but Magnus, Eystein and those who pay homage to Eystein's Crozier have as much to say about it as we."

"Not while I breathe." Her eyes still don't stray from his.

He's either content with her declaration or devoid of any answer for it, so they fall silent as they lie back on their bed, facing the dying fire. He encircles her with his arms and she nestles back against him. As she watches the embers flicker and spark, flare to flame and diminish again, like the ebb and flow of the *fjord*, she wonders if Hakon feels the shudder that runs the length of her spine. Lord, she prays, I cannot guarantee peace for Hakon, but please give me the strength and courage to do whatever is necessary, to oppose whomever I must, to assure him life.

Can what is lost be regained? Magnus labors not to think about last winter's battle of Nidaros Bridge, distracting himself by surveying the six sides of Eystein's spacious yurt. Double-layered reindeer skin provides good insulation from the numbing cold and wind that stab at the outer walls. A large fire blazes red and orange, burning hot enough that only a wisp of smoke rises from it. Even at the tent's perimeter, a body length and a half away, the air is warm. Rugs of animal skin covering the floor of hard packed snow provide further insulation.

The flaps of the yurt fly open. A frigid breeze sweeps over the fire, causing it to flare and crackle. Through the opening trudges His Eminence, his head clearing the top with room to spare. He looks more pallid than usual, especially considering how the bitter cold reddens everyone elses' complexions. When Magnus looks at that face, those chins backing up on one another and overhung on each side by jowls that would be the envy of a breed hog, his stomach sours.

"Damn this cold to hell," Eystein says, his voice as shrill and irritating as an ungreased wheel. "Magnus," he says, and fixes him with a withering glare of some duration. "We must attack in the morning —at first light. We have Lillehammer surrounded. No escape. Even a fainthearted attack cannot fail to reach their ramparts." He shakes his head hard enough to make his jowls slap, and throws his hands up, pudgy fingers thrust out.

Magnus raises his face toward the ceiling, clasps his hands behind him and turns in place with such measured deliberation that any observer would think him deep in meditation over the comment.

His eyes settle for a moment between the fire and the back wall where resides an altar with a gold chalice, a crucifix and two gold candlesticks most prominent amongst the adornments sitting on the snow-white *vadmel* vestment. Before the cross rest leather-bound scriptures, opened to nurture the perception that Eystein reads them. Next to the altar, inert in its golden stanchion, is the bishop's crozier, the good shepherd's staff, symbol of humility and protection. Ornate gold and silver form the curved head, and a straight oak shaft supports it. On the opposite end of the altar sits an oak throne carved with intricate Stations of the Cross, the handgrips and headrest also in gold. Skins, stitched with painstaking precision, fur-side up, cover the seat.

"Your Holiness," Magnus says with the best affectation of deference that he can muster, "if we wait just two more days, Erling will be here with nine hundred men. We double our strength and assure ourselves a crushing victory." He sets his jaw and bears down on the bishop with dark green eyes.

"Your father moves his men too slowly," Eystein rails, hands still flailing above his head. "He coddles them, makes them soft. We already number twice those birch-leg beggars." His hands come to rest across his mead-and-grape paunch. His voice is quieter now, but still grates on Magnus like sand in his leggings.

Eystein leans forward on his cushioned chair until it seems the momentum of his bulk will roll him out of it, spreading him on the floor like butterfat from a spilled churn. "You, of all people," deep crevasses form at the corners of his eyes as they narrow, "should be eager for the demise of that infidel Hakon Sverrisson and his bastard pretender. Your father bought your crown, but you must still earn it."

Magnus stares for a moment, scrutinizes the bishop's girth and, at the same time, turns his hand around the handle of his sword. "Your Holiness, our objectives are the same and serve each of us equally," he says. "The Birkebeiner have proven on occasion to be resourceful and unorthodox in their strategies, and..."

"No, you have proven to be an incompetent, leading curs and cowards, good only at running backwards. You must lead your men in the name of our Lord. Lead them with design and fervor, and the day will be ours!"

Magnus glances at his right hand, knuckles squeezed white. He turns away and loosens his grip. The bishop continues his diatribe. Magnus paces the perimeter of the yurt. He watches his shadow as it accompanies him along the walls. He looks back at the fire, then at the altar. He walks toward the left side of the tent, past the altar, where he comes to a pine bench. Its slats run lengthwise, and exceed the height of a man if his hands were stretched overhead. At each corner woven rawhide restraints, rough, frayed and stained, hang to the floor. The slats themselves bear similar stains, reddish-brown in color. On a leather mat next to the bench is a bulky package, the shape of a bedroll but longer and thicker. Its exterior is hide, the type indiscernible because it, too, is mottled with stains. Leather thongs tie each end. Several tubes of dried hyssop reeds, the hollow cores of which are broad enough to accommodate an object thicker than a man's thumb, rest atop a wooden box that sits beside the roll. Amongst the hyssop a large rock sits on top of the box. A rustling noise, ominous in its refusal to cease, comes from inside.

As he completes his circle, Magnus feels more than hears a pause in Eystein's harangue and says, "Of course, your expertise is in the ways of the Lord, and ultimately, as you say, He will prevail. I only suggest that perhaps He will prevail sooner and more surely if we employ the wisest military strategy at our dis..."

"Nonsense!" Eystein shouts. "Sitting here is no military strategy at all, since our enemy, your enemy, is over there." He stabs a finger toward Lillehammer. "Go and attack them. Now!"

Magnus's eyes fall again on the Crozier, the symbol of the bishop's power. He reaches out and touches it, wraps his

crawled to the top of the bank. Disbelief in his voice, he yelled, "*De birkebeinerne stå faste som trær.* Like trees."

"*Gi signal å krysse over. Bruk brua og strømmen,*" Magnus said. Sturelsson signaled the troops to cross the bridge and the stream and the charge began. Magnus scrambled up the bank next to his lieutenant to watch the Birkebeiner reaction. Still, they did not move. As Crozier troops poured over the far bank and onto the bridge, the arrows flew again, but only from one rank and only at the bridge. Two ranks on skis broke to each side and sped to the river, showing great skill as they hurtled down the bank to the snow beyond the ice. Men in the remaining rank dropped their bows and took up pikes, stout poles three times longer than a man's height and tipped with a fierce barbed point. They ran toward the center icy part of the river. Magnus's men could make little progress on the bridge, strewn as it was with corpses of men and horses. Those few that made it across were met by several of the Birkebeiners, pikes ready. He watched one man flipped over the side, run through by a pike in such a way that his arms could reach neither end of the weapon through his midsection. He fell to the ice, impaled, the honed head of the weapon pointing down. The tip buried itself in the ice and the soldier's body formed a grotesque arch as his spine snapped. He screamed and flailed arms as blood spewed from the wound and then from his mouth. Then he was quiet, suspended over the ice.

One of the Birkebeiners ran toward Magnus's position, spear raised to hurl down on Crozier troops. Before the soldier saw Magnus, Magnus's blade caught the man hard across the belly. He fell and was up before Magnus could strike again. Ropes of innards spilled to the ground. Without a sound, he gathered his guts in his hands and fled. Ten strides away he fell dead.

Most of the Croziers had reached the ice. With snow packed on the soles of their leather footwear, they were out of control and slipping. The cadre of Birkebeiners without skis was having no trouble on the ice and was decimating Crozier troops who were helpless to gain traction. Those who achieved balance would only lose it again when they swung, thrust or dodged a weapon. That was when Magnus noticed the clogs of char-hardened wooden spikes strapped to the feet of the ski-less Birkebeiners. Some of Magnus's troops scuttled to the edges of the ice to gain footing in the snow. But it was soft and deep, making them slow and easy prey for the Birkebeiners waiting for them on skis.

Several Croziers struggled to reach the little islands of snow on the ice, only to find another deadly trap. The Birkebeiners had covered fresh holes with skins and spread snow on top. As soon as an unsuspecting soldier stepped on one of those islands, he plunged through the thin ice. Magnus watched one pull himself from the water, blue and gasping. The poor soul uttered a noise, somewhere between a hiss and a shriek that started deep in his viscera and escaped to places only the evil gods know. Then, flopping on the ice like a landed fish, he froze rigid trying to draw his sword and end his agony.

"*Dra!*" Magnus said to Sturelsson, pushing him over the lip of the bank. "Go!"

Sturelsson reached back for his commander's hand and pulled him up, and they fled back across the bridge. They found an unwounded horse, and riding double, managed to escape the trap.

Later Magnus returned to the bridge. Hundreds of men… no, what once *were* men, formed mounds of tangled bodies, many inexorably joined by rock-hard crusts of frozen blood turned black by the cold. Those lying separate from others would hold into spring whatever obscene posture they offered in their final death throes. One Birkebeiner soldier lay on his back, his blood-blackened hands forever clutching the sky and contrasting with the pale whiteness of his face. A twisted lump of frozen blood sat over an open gash in his neck and rose up his chin, like fungus on a rotting log. One of his spiked clogs lay beside him.

Magnus bent and picked up the empty clog. Then he cried

for them, all of them.

* * * *

Through clenched teeth, Magnus hears himself say, "*Hva du gjør birkerebeine jævler n*å*?* What do you birkebeiner bastards plan now?"

"What, sir?" It's Sturelsson returning.

"Report."

"The troops are stirring."

"Are they in good spirits?"

"Fine, sir."

"You're a poor liar. Why would they be in good spirits, knowing that we could double our strength by waiting two days?"

"Yes sir." A meager attempt to smile falls off his lips.

"Where is that little gnome, Einar? I told you to fetch him."

"His stumpy legs can't match our strides, Magnus. He's coming."

"Einar, you obnoxious troll, hurry up," Magnus yells.

"I'm coming, my lord," Einar wheezes from somewhere in the darkness.

Then Magnus sees the dwarf's outline begin to separate from the blackness as if he materializes from the voice. He rocks back and forth, as his stiff, short legs move laterally more than forward. When Einar reaches them, he looks up, and then leans on his staff to catch his breath. Still panting, he says, "I steered wide of the bishop's tent. I don't think he likes me."

"It's your prophesying he doesn't like," Magnus says, kneeling to talk to Einar's distorted face. One eye bulges larger than the other, and his nose occupies its place like a knot on a stump. His sharp chin protrudes and is strewn with gray stubble that never grows. His ears, too large for the rest of him, appear designed to catch the wind and his mouth abides twisted brown and yellow rot punctuated with gaping black holes and expels an odor that causes Magnus to straighten again.

"I have had a dream, King Magnus," Einar says, with what passes for a smile.

"A good dream?"

"It is what you make of it, sire."

"But I want to know what *you* make of it. Get on with it."

Einar winces and grimaces as if seeking a position comfortable enough to sustain a story that is longer than Magnus wants to hear. "In my dream, you stand looking at the red sunset reflecting off the *fjord*. An orange glow surrounds you and turns you into a huge raven."

"Odin's swan?"

"Precisely, my lord. Then the raven grows. He grows so large that his beak reaches the ocean all the way to the west and the feathers of his tail spread all the way to the land of the Finns. His wings unfold to cover the whole country and more[1]."

"That's good, my small friend," Magnus says, hoping to dismiss it there.

"But that is not the end of the dream, sire."

"Continue then, but shorten it."

"An eagle appears, and while smaller than the raven, is high in the sky and even in the dim light of sunset casts a shadow on the raven, angering him. So the raven takes flight and attacks the eagle." He pauses.

"To what end?"

"They fight bitterly, with blood streaming from the wings of both, but..."

"*Helvete!* What?"

Einar winces and stammers, then spits out, "The closer the Raven gets to the eagle's nest, wherein resides a single hatchling, the harder the eagle fights." He stops.

"And?"

"That's all, sire. There was no resolution. At least not before I woke."

---

[1] *Heimskringla*, Snorri Sturelsson.

to the fire, scrapes live embers from the ash and throws on kindling.

They hear the sounds of soldiers in the compound, sharpening, honing and preparing. Whump! Whump! The sound of two axes splitting wood rolls from opposite sides of the compound. It sounds like thunder claps rumbling down a valley. Inga knows that soon the sounds will change. Wooden shields covered with reindeer or bearskin will be buffeting trees to test the straps. Pike banging against spear shaft, axe handle against halberd shaft to try strength. Archers will release drawn bowstrings. Strategies discussed, passwords whispered, families consoled, all building to a horrible cacophony before an eerie silence replaces it.

"You didn't sleep well," she says to Hakon, who has moved across the *soverom* and is wrapping birch bark and leather around his left calf.

"Our son will have peace," is all he says.

"*Jeg håper det.*" She whispers it like a prayer.

He's silent for several minutes, listening to the sounds of preparation. Inga resists the urge to intrude. As Hakon begins to bind his right leg, he looks at her and says, "Did I keep you awake?"

"No, my mind wouldn't rest."

"Thoughts of our son?"

"Your words helped me with that, but yes." She pauses, then adds, "That and knowing you must fight today."

Hakon nods, but says nothing.

When the silence begins to feel heavy, she says, "Will you be all right?"

"We're prepared and our plan is as good as we can make it."

"And that helps ease your mind?"

"Confidence in strategy and comrades always helps, but nothing eases your mind facing...well, a time like this." He hesitates again, opens his mouth, then closes it.

"Why can't you tell me? Or why won't you?"

"I just did."

"No, you started to, then changed your mind." She pauses, swallows and turns away. Then she faces him again. "Why? Don't you think I can understand? Cope?" After she says it, she starts to look away, but doesn't.

Their exchange of gazes is more a discussion than a contest. He draws a long breath. "Do you remember the battle last summer, the one on the Oslo *fjord*?"

"I remember that it was a great victory, and that you and Torstein devised a daring plan to achieve it."

"Do you remember our preparations?"

Inga recalls during the spring and early summer how Hakon and Torstein had the men fell trees and cut them into long logs and none knew the reason. Each log was twice a man's height and as thick as his thigh. They loaded them on two *skuter*, each having twenty oars. In darkness, they rowed up the Drofn *fjord* to a point where it comes closest to the western shore of the Oslo *fjord*, above the Crozier lookouts at Sloarf. By rolling the *skuter* over the logs from one *fjord* to the other, they came into Oslo *fjord* above the sentries, and escaped detection.

Hakon and his forty attacked the Crozier *skuter* at dawn. Catapults hurled barrels filled with birch bark and chips of spruce covered in flaming pitch, torching four of the *skuter* before they knew what was happening. Panicked Croziers fell from arrows rained on them by Birkebeiner bows. Many sought refuge from the flames by jumping into the water only to be pulled under by the weight of their weapons or mail coats. Those with the presence of mind to discard the weight swam to shore and were met by Torstein and his forty, who had traveled by land to come out of the hills above Oslo. Some of the Croziers fought and Torstein gave them no quarter. Others asked quarter and received it if they agreed to fight no more.

"I recall that you had a brilliant strategy and near perfect execution," Inga says.

Hakon raises his right hand, first finger outstretched. "It

was the way the parts fit together." On his open left hand he places his right fist and pries open the fingers until both hands are flush. "It was at night. It was a surprise. And it was too grueling a plan for the enemy to contemplate. As difficult a task as I had ever asked of the men, a brutal day of pushing the *skuter* and moving the logs. Our legs seized with spasms and our arms knotted so that we had to rest a day. But always I was confident the men could do it. From first light until dark we struggled, stopping only twice for food."

"And the days are long that time of year," she says.

"We drank while we heaved. But it worked." He stops again, looking at her with eyes anticipating the future, full of hope. He smiles. "How things fit together is what gives you confidence in strategy." Hakon interlocks his fingers and pulls on them.

"And you will either defeat Eystein and Magnus or deplete their army with pledges of amnesty."

He rolls his eyes and smiles at her quip. "I'm thinking we will defeat them with new strategies that build our confidence. And the men to execute them."

"And today you're ready with another innovation?"

"You heard Torstein and me last night."

"But the reason for the snow trenches eludes me." She shrugs and squeezes her hands together, then opens them and turns one in the other.

"Watch from the ramparts and pray our plan also eludes the Croziers."

"There has never been battle so close. I'm afraid to watch." She hesitates and Hakon nods. "And I'm afraid not to." She's aware he's watching her hands as she clasps and unclasps them, rubbing and wringing them in between. She tries to lay them in her lap, but they refuse to rest.

Hakon stops tying his legging and comes to her, kneels and kisses her forehead. "At least I will have weapons to occupy my hands. Watching, I think, would be more demanding than fighting."

She offers a hesitant shrug and kisses his cheek. "Whether I watch or not, I'll pray."

There's a rap at the entrance. Two quick knocks. "Enter," Hakon says.

It's Torstein and Skjervald. Inga can tell by the sound of their stride through the *stue*, in step, like a march. Both are straight-lipped and narrow-eyed when they reach the *soverom*, expressions honed for battle. Torstein is dressed as before, but has added a thick fur cap. His axe dangles at his side over a short, cruel-looking sword. He carries his birch and the leather to lash it to his legs. Skjervald already wears his birch leggings over *vadmel* pants, a skin vest, and a fur cape tied across the shoulders and thrown, from the bottom right, over his left shoulder. Mitts hang next to a dagger on a leather belt, but his large hands are bare. His hair is loose under a cap of lynx skin that falls over his ears and the back of his neck. A quiver of arrows hangs on his back so that the fletches show over his left shoulder. His bow crosses the quiver from the opposite direction, with its string across his chest from shoulder to waist. He holds a spear in his right hand. He offers a curt nod in greeting.

Torstein says, "The men prepare well. Most will eat soon, and then finish preparing their skis or snowshoes." As if the words remind him, he pulls Hakon's moccasins out from under his parka and extends them to the king.

"Half on each?" Hakon asks, as he accepts the shoes and sits to put them on.

"That's the ratio *ja*."

"You agree we should be in the lateral trenches well before sunrise?"

"As soon as we finish eating," Torstein says.

"You're on the right flank and Skjervald on the left?" Hakon looks at Skjervald. "And your men know their tasks, especially how long to wait?"

"They're well drilled, Hakon. Prepared."

"And you?"

Skjervald raises his chin and pushes his chest out. His mouth opens, but no words come out. He lifts his chin higher, and starts again. Another silence. He releases his breath as chin and eyes drop. "I've done everything I can think of, sir. And done it to the smallest detail and I want to tell you nothing can go wrong. I want to show you a man full of confidence, but I can't be less than honest with my king."

"Something wrong?" Hakon's brow furrows.

"No, no sir. We're ready. It's just that..."

"It's all right," says Hakon. "Just take your time and tell me."

"It's just that I'm...well, nervous. I feel like I'm going to throw up." His head drops again and his feet shuffle on the earthen floor.

Inga sees a look pass between Hakon and Torstein, a glance that carries more than a trace of compassion.

Skjervald is still looking down when Hakon stands, places a hand on his shoulder and says, "Son, you felt anything else, I'd relieve you of the duty. Anyone who says they feel different is a liar."

"But you, you're..."

"Nervous as a suitor at her father's door."

"But..."

"What? You think that being king, being the leader, means you're not nervous, even scared going into battle? You have to be or you won't live long." He looks at Inga, just a glance the others don't notice.

"I..." Skjervald looks at Torstein, color flooding back into his face.

Torstein nods. It's the slow, confirming nod of experience. "You'll be fine. Channel that energy into your sword and spear. The feeling disappears with first contact, believe me. Now go. Be with your men. Assemble at the gate when the bonfire is lit."

Channel the energy. Feeling of first contact. Inga wonders why preparing to kill or die is so simple and keeping her child safe is so complex? She puts two fingers on each corner of her jaw and rubs as she would a cramp in a calf or foot. She hears her teeth slide against each other. Protect my child! she wants to scream. Stop this fighting and let him live. As Skjervald turns to leave, Inga detects a loosening in his shoulders, and perhaps a slight curling of his lips.

After he goes, Torstein says, "There's strength there."

"God will that he lives to realize it," Hakon says.

"It was nice that you could give him that sense of relief," Inga says.

Torstein looks at her.

Hakon says, "Sense of relief?"

"From thinking there is something you must do that you cannot."

"He needed it."

"Some never know the feeling though." She says it with a shrug, as she takes a step to the fire.

Hakon goes back to lacing his birch leggings and Torstein sits near the fire and adjusts his own.

Inga ladles some breakfast stew for each of them and a little for herself. She spoons a taste toward her lips and puts the spoon back in her bowl, pushes it from side to side a couple of times, and puts the bowl down. She hears Hakon begin to stir in his bed, so she puts some in a bowl for him, and sets it aside to cool.

Inga sits near the men and the three of them dabble at their food and stare at the fire until it's time to leave. The men rise together and Hakon reaches for Inga's hand and helps her to her feet. He puts a hand on her waist and draws her close. She pushes up on her toes and puts her arms around his neck as he slides his own across her back and caresses. Then they step back and look at each other for a moment. Inga reaches a hand out to Torstein. He takes it and they exchange a squeeze. He turns and starts for the entrance to the *stue*. Hakon follows. Inga listens to their footsteps until she hears them close the door at the far end.

Right below the mill wheel is a large, clear pool. If you and your men would enjoy relaxing in it, I'll show you where it is. After dinner, of course." She brushed nervously at imaginary crumbs in the folds of her dress.

Hakon looked at Torstein, who smiled and nodded. "Sounds relaxing," Hakon said. "Tell me more about Borg and your farm."

After that the words flowed and so did the time. Maybe she ate, but she doesn't recall. At any other time, so splendid a meal would have held all her attention with the sweet aromas of the meat and bread, salmon roasted in butter and herbs, the fresh picked vegetables, dishes not offered every night. The fine wool tablecloth, the one that she and her mother spent a whole winter weaving and bordering with intricate stitched designs, covered the table. It came out on the most special occasions. But Inga only remembers the calm, strong sound of his voice, and the feeling that she could have talked as long as he wanted. She remembers that parts of her body tingled, but can't recall the taste of even a morsel of the food.

Hakon must have enjoyed the conversation, too, because early the next morning, before he left, he asked her father for permission to court her. Her father brought him to her and asked if that would be all right. Before the first snow fell the following fall, Hakon had asked her to go with him. When she sought permission, her family gave enthusiastic approval. She had worried, because it would be her sixteenth winter, that she might never marry. Though they never said anything, Inga believed then, with some shame, that her parents shared that concern.

The following summer, she asked Hakon about his thoughts during that dinner. "You did what the Croziers have not been able to," he said. "Left me wounded in the heart and utterly defenseless." He smiled his big smile, the one that put mischief in his eyes, and hugged her.

* * * *

Inga looks up into the gray of dawn and sees several women moving toward the ramparts. She moves, too, and finds a good vantage point. Their soldiers crouch in the snow trenches, more than an arrow's flight away from the wall.

A snow-covered field stretches far beyond the trenches. She's surprised at how gray it is. No shadows, no trees. No men yet. The featureless expanse ends at the first line of tents. They look like toys little Hakon might play with, like the wooden bowls he likes to turn upside down. Inga can tell the tents are clustered and stretch from the river on her right across the field to the edge of the forest on her left. Smoke rises, innocent in its laziness, from more fires than she can count. The wispy columns appear all the way to the woods line behind the Crozier camp.

Inga looks back at the main trench, hoping to find Hakon. She asks herself when she will hold him again, while her eyes scan the main position. It runs parallel to the wall, and is broad enough to hold three ranks of men. A perpendicular channel, so narrow it prohibits more than two abreast, breaks the main furrow into two sections, and extends to a small rise near the front edge of the Crozier camp. Birkebeiner soldiers don't cross the perpendicular line.

The second rank, two hundred men, hold bows. In the front rank, half that number has swords and axes laid at their feet. In front of each of them is a platform the size of a shield, and secured to each platform are the thick handles of two pikes. An arm's length in front of the platforms, away from the men attending them, thick logs support the pikes, and function as the pivot of a lever. Inga can see that in front of the logs, the barbed tips of the weapons, longer, she knows, than three times the height of a man, disappear into the soft snow. Several of the men manning these weapons test the bindings that hold the pike handles to the platforms, and check the balance points where the pikes cross the logs. A shorter third rank consists of two dozen archers, half on each side of the perpendicular row. There is little motion anywhere, as if the cold has frozen men in place.

Unwilling to sleep, Magnus leaves his tent. He walks toward the back edge of camp. Not far from where he starts, he sees her, the woman they call Strange One, the one the camp followers protect from the men. She's ragged and unkempt as always. Some of her hair sits in tangled clumps and the rest hangs in oily strings. She must have wandered away from the others or they would have her in a warm cap. Puffy, reddened cheeks reflect the firelight, but her eyes are invisible, sunken deep in the shadows of their sockets. Scrawny, bare fingers on her left hand tug at a thick cord of hair, starting at her scalp and running the length until she holds the tip of it in front of her face as if she is just discovering it. Her right hand holds tight to as much of the side of her shabby, sooty fleece vest as will fit into her fist. She's never still, rocking from the waist when her feet aren't moving.

She runs a few stuttered steps and stops, switches hands, the left now seeking a grip on her garment and the right finding a different twine of hair. She turns a full circle, rocks for a moment, and scampers toward a campfire where four soldiers sit. "Who has seen Erik?" she says, not screaming, but in a piercing voice, shrill as someone in a panic. "Who's seen my son? Where is he?"

The soldiers stare at her, but don't answer.

"Is he hiding in your tent? May I look in your tent?" Her eyes widen now, pushing back much of the murky outline around them. "He must be in your tent. Please. Where is he?"

The soldiers lean away from her and still say nothing. Magnus walks over and takes her by the arm. "It's all right, Strange One," he says.

She jumps. "Have you seen Erik? Erik. Erik. Erik. Have you

Magnus reaches the edge of the camp just before sunrise. He watches the glow of a large fire that burns inside the birch-leg compound, when a sound like a thunderclap rises over their walls. "So, you Birkebeiners let us know you are ready," he whispers. "You're my enemy, but you may just be the difference between me and Strange One." He turns and hurries back toward the core of the encampment, where Sturelsson is massing their troops, hurling his commands with the power of a catapult. Magnus hears him before he sees him, on the other side of a rank of cavalry, shouting the final details of formation. On his way through the mounted ranks Magnus watches two of the horsemen as they help each other tighten the straps that hold the woven sapling shoes on their horses' feet. The air is still and laden with the smell of hay and sweaty leather and four hundred skittish beasts that sense the tension. They nicker and twitch with anticipation.

He moves on and listens to the squeak of the snow under his feet. At least his troops won't have to deal with the effort of wet, heavy snow.

Magnus reaches Sturelsson, who holds the reins of both their horses. As he lifts his mount's right foot to be sure the snowshoes aren't so wide that they impede the animal's gait, he says, "The horsemen are in position for the first wave of the assault?"

"Two ranks. Two hundred mounted in each."

"Twenty ranks of twenty infantry in the center, behind the horsemen?"

"*Ja.*"

"Move them forward with dispatch."

"I heard the clap of their weapons, sir. We needn't worry about stealth," he says.

"Oh, they know we're coming and they're ready. Speed. As much as the conditions will allow. We will attack as soon as there is adequate light."

"Yes, sir."

"Sturelsson."

"Sir?"

"*Kjemp hardt og lev vel.*"

"And you too, Magnus."

Magnus sees the first glimmer of morning behind him as he swings up into his saddle. In less time than it takes to consume a scanty meal, he will once again be delivering death, or facing his own. He has often pondered this cycle, unable to end it, but accepting it as part of being a soldier. A tug on the reins starts his mount turning a tight circle, allowing Magnus to survey the troops he will lead. While the horse turns, Magnus asks himself if today will be the day. He wonders if Einar's prophecy of the screaming eagle will prove true before nightfall. He wants to know if he will win this battle and be able to tell the dwarf again to have dreams with more satisfactory outcomes. With each battle these kinds of questions plague him. It isn't his own death, but death all around that burdens him. Constant. Unending. He wonders, If I cared less about death, would that lift my yoke? Would my effort be more effective if I could order death without caring? Would that bring an end more quickly? Am I determined enough? Will Einar's prophecies defeat me? Or a better prepared enemy?

"Magnus! Why the delay? The sun rises at your back. It's time to kill those brazen infidels!"

He stares down from his mount into that repugnant face. "Aren't you cold, Your Holiness? Perhaps you should retire to the warmth of your yurt as we begin our charge."

"Your concern for my comfort is touching, Magnus," Eystein says. "But I fear if I fail to offer my encouragement, the attack may languish into slumber."

"No fear of that, Bishop. Not amongst soldiers." He holds Eystein's eyes and adds, "Everyone's salvation is different, isn't it?"

Creases on Eystein's forehead gather and he opens his mouth. The furrows deepen but no reply comes.

Magnus spurs his horse and feels the animal's strength, the chest and shoulders swell with the thrust of the first stride. In rhythm with the steed's motion, Magnus raises his hand. For the moment, his mind focuses more on a hope that Eystein will not be able to get out of the way than on death. Then he hears four hundred riders on his right thud heels to beasts' ribs, four hundred weapon handles scrape against mail, boots chafe against wooden stirrups, mounts whinny and grunt. All move as one. A battle cry generated in the center of the infantry spreads forward into the cavalry. At the far end of the column he sees Sturelsson, his hand raised, and all thought but the execution of the battle plan leaves him. Magnus drops his hand, and Sturelsson his. The cavalry columns move against the resistance of the deep, soft snow like a wave whose energy is spent, covering the beach but lacking speed.

Even with the oblong snowshoes on the horses' feet, they penetrate the snow almost to their knees. A trot is all they can manage. A few lose their shoes and sink to their haunches, falling behind, helpless to do anything but turn back. The rest, whose shoes are effective, reduce the snow's resistance for the ground troops. When they reach a point little more than an arrow's flight from their encampment, and the mounted troops begin to spread out, Magnus sees many of the infantry file into a snow trench that heads toward Lillehammer. Sturelsson sees it, too, and signals them to stay out. Because this new path offers little resistance or because they fail to see the signal, many continue to charge two by two down the corridor. He shouts warning, but it drowns in a sea of other screams and battle cries. Flanks of horsemen on both sides of the channel accelerate. The infantry in the trough is too far ahead, running down the corridor now, and in danger of isolation. The two leaders have no alternative but to keep pace with them. Both of them watch the center. At the end of the long trench, Magnus sees an intersection with much larger trenches spreading left and right. Birkebeiner archers, too many to count, form a phalanx at the intersection and loose volley after volley of arrows down the passage at his men. He can only watch as his soldiers topple like chaff before the scythe. Dying fingers clutch the embedded shafts, and gaping mouths feed mortal shrieks onto a blaze whose only fuel is horrified wailing. Others flail back into the deep snow, spending the last of their strength before they collapse.

No sooner do those men fall, than a barrage of arrows flies from both the left and right of the Birkebeiner lines. A dozen horses tumble and more men fall as the Croziers bear down on their enemy. A horse topples with a shrill death cry. The rider lands clear, and rises next to Magnus, only to be struck by three arrows, the last piercing his forehead. Magnus hears the sickening sound of the strike, like it has hit a tree, a dull thud followed by the rattle of the vibrating shaft. Zfft, zfft, zfft. Arrows whistle past his head. Screams from behind tell him some find marks, but the sounds are too strident, too entangled in one another to recognize whether man or animal utters them.

Ahead of him, two horses, one riderless, converge on a third, causing the animal to stumble, throw his master, and roll over him. The horse struggles to its feet and joins dozens of others with empty saddles. They careen through the troops, nostrils flaring and eyes wide with panic, disrupting the line of the charge. Several have blood pulsing around protruding shafts. One snorts crimson foam from mouth and nostrils and collapses, a cloud of white billowing along the furrow he plows. Magnus's eyes dart back and forth across the battle, registering the action, measuring his moves. His mind absorbs what he sees and tries to filter out the torment around him. Many riders are still abreast of him and Sturelsson, pushing their mounts to the limit.

Magnus is close enough now to see the back edge of the right-hand trench. What looks like a hundred archers are poised to fire again. He watches the arrows spiral toward him, catching two on his shield, hearing two more sing past his head and strike behind him. Another shriek of agony. Cries of men and animals fly at him faster than the arrows, and land with more impact.

Waiting birch-legs ambush the men who have run the length of the perpendicular trench, striking them down from each side with swords and axes. But Crozier cavalry is close enough to leap the last measure of untrammeled snow, and deliver some pain to the enemy. Magnus gives his horse one last spur as the barbed tips of pikes, hundreds of them, burst through the snow's surface. Like a pouncing lynx falling on his prey and realizing too late that his target is a porcupine, the mounted soldiers try to take evasive action. But momentum has sealed their fate, and half of the horses impale themselves on Birkebeiner quills. Several riders lurch over their horses' heads to land on a second echelon of protruding spikes. The sound of the pike piercing his own horse's chest bears the innocence of a child slurping porridge. The animal and Magnus hit the ground. Many in the line between him and Sturelsson go down, and those able to rise have no choice but to press the attack into the trenches on foot.

A woman near Inga asks, "When will it start?" In the frigid air, her breath floats like thick fog. A whisper of it crystallizes on a lock of hair that escapes her hat.

"Soon." Inga moves closer to her and takes her hand. The woman tries to smile at Inga, but it looks heavy on her face and quickly sinks.

The ramparts offer Inga and the other women little protection from the cold, but they can see the full battleground, an expansive snowfield, whose drifted contours are broken only by the trenches. More women, some carrying their children, take up positions near Inga. The lines around their eyes and down-turned mouths are severe, as if the burden in their hearts is pressing all its weight against their faces. Some struggle to keep their heads up, their eyes forward. Some move their heads from side to side, perhaps trying to recognize a loved one in the mass of soldiers below.

"Look. The horses." The woman who'd spoken to Inga points at the far end of the field.

At first the noise reaches them like the distant thunder. As the lines of cavalry gain speed, the clamor grows. Individual sounds exist only as part of an overwhelming cacophony, a din that buries sane thoughts. Words are indecipherable.

Foot soldiers reach the long trench that moves away from the ramparts toward the Crozier camp. Inga can see Hakon, his hand in the air, waiting to signal his archers. His hand falls and a force of bowmen step from each side and loose arrows down that long, narrow shaft from which there is no escape. Croziers fall so fast they appear attached to one another. Noise that Inga thinks can get no louder, increases. More archers, perhaps a hundred, send volleys into the charging

The sounds of a battleground in the aftermath of combat are unendurable. In combat Magnus's concentration blocks battle sounds like his shield deflects blows. He hears noise, a screaming dissonance, but the chaos engulfs him so that he cannot distinguish individual sounds. The tumult is gone now as he makes his way across the snowfield. The silence is eerie and complete. Croziermen and Birkebeiner, those who were able, have withdrawn. A weak cry for help intrudes but disappears too quickly to detect its source. A spear, leaning in the snow, topples from its soft support and clangs against a helmet, a single toll from a phantom bell. A horse whinnies, convulses in agony, and also falls silent. Magnus consoles himself with the reminder that he's a soldier. He's used to this. He watches steam from fresh wounds rise like departing souls, while blood turns dark and freezes on older ones.

Just as the carnage and sounds of the abandoned battlefield remind him that he is a soldier, he reminds himself that without Gudrun and Jorund, all he *has* is being a soldier. Otherwise, he has nothing. His only real choice is to be the soldier he knows he is, determined to unite his country and end the war. Objectives larger than that are of his father's and Eystein's choosing, not his own. There will be but one king in Norway. There cannot be two and have the country survive threats from the south and east. Sverrisson and his infant son will die. Someone will see to that soon. Perhaps that will satisfy Crooked Neck and he, in turn, may be able to keep Eystein at bay. Magnus curses aloud, thinking of how close they came today to being rid of the Birkebeiner leader.

Magnus's worst fear is that even when his father recognizes

his sovereignty and he no longer dwells in his shadow, he will still wear the harness of the bishop. Next to leading his men in honorable military pursuits, the one thing he wants is to cast off Eystein's shackles, even if it takes forever.

Birkebeiner women and old men watch from their ramparts as the last of their soldiers return to the gates. Magnus can't see their expressions from this distance, but that's not necessary to know that they reveal anguish and fear. His army has just been forced to retreat, but perhaps those poor souls on the ramparts are worse off than he is. At least he can fight and feel that he has some control over the outcome. And this defeat is temporary. He'll fight again.

He turns and trudges back toward his camp.

"Thank you for coming, Torstein," Hakon says.

"You don't need to thank me. You're my king and lifelong friend. I thank you for summoning me."

"How does my wound look?"

"Be a while before you walk on that leg again."

"You got the arrowhead out. Inga tells me it penetrated to the bone."

"*Ja*. While you were unconscious, she and I cleaned the wound." He cocks his head toward Inga. Then he moves closer to the fur-covered bed and sits cross-legged on the floor, so his face is level with Hakon's. Hakon looks at Inga and smiles. She brushes at a stain on her shirt, returns the smile and bends at the waist to pick up the large bowl of reddish water and the bloodstained *vadmel* clumped next to it. She steps to the fire and puts the damp bundle of cloth into it. It hisses and smokes as she returns and picks up two small bowls and empties their contents into the fire. This time it flares almost waist high.

"Wine and boiled pine sap?" Hakon says, looking at the eruption.

"*Ja*," says Torstein. "Then we had to cauterize it."

"And I thought that aroma was Inga burning dinner."

"How often have I burned your dinner?" she says, holding up the fire-blackened knife they had used.

"Not nearly as often as I have burned yours."

"You see, Torstein," Inga says. "he has a full grasp of reality."

"Ah, you thought I was delirious, my friend," Hakon says.

Torstein shrugs. "No more so than usual. How does it feel?"

"Well, you're right. Walking is out of the question. But it's with you."

"*Pappa* 'old Hakon high?"

"Either he or Torstein will hold you high," she says.

As she walks back to Hakon's side, the baby gurgles and wriggles. "Here's *Pappa*," she says, and hands him down to Hakon who holds him up over his face, the child whooping like a wolf cub.

"Up high!" says Hakon, straightening his arms and bouncing his baby.

Torstein takes the boy, drops him between his legs and then catapults him up over his head. "Up high, young prince!" he shouts, and the baby yelps a laugh, one that Inga likes better than the men's. Torstein hands the child back to her, but little Hakon stretches his arms back toward Torstein.

"More 'gin high Tors."

"I have to talk to your father right now. We'll go high again later, all right? He strokes the baby's cheek.

"I think he'll sleep for a while if I put him down," Inga says. Save him, she thinks. Don't just play with him. Can you men do nothing but banter?

"Come right back, please Inga. You and Torstein and I have to talk." As she walks to the far end of the lodge, she hears him say, "Torstein, it is he that we must plan for, assuming Lillehammer is lost."

She wonders what Hakon's thinking. She blushes as if Hakon has overheard her thoughts. As she carries the baby back to his bed, she looks at the child's face and then over her shoulder at his father. Several times before she puts the baby down she glances back. This has to be what I want, she thinks. They're going to talk about how to save my child. Muscles in her jaw relax, but her hand goes to her stomach and presses.

"Are we to assume that? I want to fight them," Torstein says.

"So do I, but I need to ask you to fight them in a different way."

"Different? We've outwitted them with clever strategy

before. We can devise a..."

"Torstein, I want you to run. Take the prince and run for Nidaros."

Torstein glances at Inga as she moves forward, and then directs his attention again to the king, his expression that of a man caught in an ambush. "I...I can't leave you and abandon the men in the face of battle."

"He's the prince, the heir. If Magnus and Erling overrun Lillehammer, Eystein will order them to kill me. Then without hesitation they will also kill my son and with him any chance of securing future succession from the bishop's grip. Do you want our people serving Magnus under the twisted shadow of the Crozier?"

Inga watches Torstein's face. The lines around his eyes tighten like bowstrings and his lips press white against his teeth.

"No."

The simple reply echoes in her brain. At least they speak of saving her son. Not her reasons, but they'll do, if they save her baby. On the heels of that thought, she shudders at what the decision means for her king, for the two of them, and what she must do. Color drains from her face.

"Then the plan we must devise is for you to go. Get Skjervald. He'll go too," Hakon says.

"Why them?" Inga says. Both men freeze. Heads snap around and jaws drop, but she doesn't flinch or look away.

Hakon winces as he starts to answer. "Torstein is our best warrior and second only to Skjervald in his skiing abilities. And I'm convinced Skjervald can fight with the fiercest. Had he and Torstein not stood their ground and driven the Croziers back when I went down, I wouldn't be here."

"Why just them is what I meant." Her tone says clarification, not apology.

"Who else?"

"Me. I'm going too."

"Eystein won't kill you if we are overrun tomorrow. Only

me and our son."

"If Eystein catches the three of them, will he kill our son?" Her outstretched arm points a rigid finger in Torstein's direction.

Hakon moves his hand to his wound and looks down at it.

"Will he?" she says.

"Yes."

"So you're going to make me stay here to watch your execution, instead of letting me try to protect our son." He continues to inspect the wound. She can feel heat rise in her face. As he looks back at her, she sees it rise in his, too.

"Inga, you'll slow them, cause them to protect you as well as Hakon."

"*Helvete!*" She has never been profane with him, but she screams it. Makes no attempt to temper her words as her rage gushes over them. "You know I have kept pace with you and Torstein on reindeer hunts, or when we had time to just climb and glide. I will throw myself into Magnus's path before I let him catch my son! You're king, but you are not God! You can't tell me not to go with my son. If you must send him, I will go."

Silence, blanched lips and narrowed eyes tell her what he's thinking.

Her lips tremble and she swallows hard. She starts to say something and has to swallow again. She drops to her knees beside him and takes his hand between both of hers. "Oh God, Hakon, I want to be with you. Please know that I do. You're my life's love. But if what you say comes to pass, you can not… you *must* not make me choose between watching your death and trying to save our son. Send me with them Hakon, please." She looks from Hakon to Torstein and back.

After quiet longer than the grave's, Torstein says, "Hakon will need milk. We may not have time to stop and thaw goat's milk."

Inga seizes Torstein's thought like a drowning person grabs for a rope. "My God yes, Hakon. Torstein's right. Our son will need my milk. Of course. He will have to have my milk.

Certainly you can see that I must go. You must see that?"

There is another interminable pause, as Hakon stares at something the other two don't see. When he finally focuses on her, she perceives deep pain, more than the leg wound could induce. "Inga, go to the *skihytte* and get Skjervald. The four of us must decide your route."

She cups his face while she kisses him. As she pulls back she sees the redness in his eyes. She rises and sets out for the ski lodge to find Skjervald.

.

Magnus can do nothing now but wait. Wait for Eystein to unleash another tirade. Wait for his father and his father's troops to arrive. Wait to be king. He used to think waiting required only patience. Now he recognizes that it wants a large measure of humility as well. As he leaves the battlefield, he decides to sidestep Eystein in order to avoid the rant and the humiliation.

The wounded are on his mind. He looks toward the only lodge in the encampment, near the center. The Birkebeiner had built this large structure before they built the rest of the compound, to house those involved in the construction effort. It is not as sturdy as the permanent lodges inside the compound because it has no heavy stone foundation. Roof support consists of pine timbers that hold woven alders and thatch. Alder walls, insulated with skins, hang from the roof's framework. With the reinforcement and insulation that the Croziers added, the structure provides more warmth and space than the tents. Wounded receive treatment there, and Magnus knows that is where Sturelsson will go to assess casualties. He's anxious to get there himself. A grimace creases his face as he considers the misery that awaits him. He knows he can't alter the suffering in war, so he endures it, but he still sighs, closes his eyes for a moment, and says out loud, "Tend the wounded."

Magnus tries to grab a fistful of the snow that is piled high against the building's walls to provide insulation. It's like rock. He stares down the only path that cuts through the high banks to the entrance and listens to the sounds funneling through the narrow corridor from inside, a horrible dissonance of moans and cries. The sounds have a mournful quality, similar to those he has heard around the funeral pyre of a leader, but these are salted with cruel screams of fear and physical pain. The noise causes Magnus to linger a moment more before moving toward it.

When he enters, there are at least a hundred men lying in rows on the floor, some on mats, others not. Several fires throw off comfortable warmth, but his eyes burn with the reek of smoke that mixes with the smell of lacerated bowels and the acrid, metallic odor of blood. Some of the wounded can't hold back their water and that adds to the stench so that he has to force himself not to bring his hand to his nose.

He sees Sturelsson, across the shelter, rise from beside one of the men, shake his head and gesture to two able-bodied soldiers who pick up the poor soul by his arms and legs and begin carrying him to the door. Several of the camp followers aid the wounded, and Magnus notices that one near the dead soldier sobs. Sturelsson touches her shoulder, says a few words, and she nods. They turn in opposite directions, seeking others in need. Sturelsson spots his commander and begins working his way toward him through the sickening labyrinth. Magnus weaves his way around the broken, slashed and punctured bodies. Some of the wounded groan and writhe as he passes. Curse you, Eystein, for not waiting until we were at full strength, he thinks. Curse me for not defying you.

"Ugly, sir," Sturelsson says, as they meet near the hub of the misery.

"Worse than ugly, Sturelsson. Stupid. Stupid and unnecessary."

"We had no choice, sir."

"You had none, my friend. Let's look forward to the time when the bishop will hold no sway." He pauses a moment after Sturelsson nods. "How many did we lose?"

"Hundred-twenty-three dead that we know of, at least that many wounded. Half of them will die or be unable to fight."

"For not waiting two days!"

Sturelsson says nothing.

Magnus looks around again. "You have men fetching bedrolls for the wounded without them?"

"*Ja.* Won't stop till they're all protected from the ground."

"I want you to…"

Eystein's rasping voice, spewing Latin, intrudes from outside the lodge.

"Is he doing what I think he is?"

Sturelsson nods and shows his teeth.

"Fat swine hasn't the decency to come inside and say it over one man at a time?" Magnus bites down on his lower lip until he almost draws blood. "Go to him. Say you have something to tell him in confidence. When you've gotten him away from here, inform him of the casualties."

"If he asks for you?"

"You haven't seen me."

"If he asks about the battle?"

"Tell him we lost."

* * * *

For a day and a half, Magnus avoids Eystein by staying in the lodge with the wounded. Several men die while he's with them. Each time, it pulls at him in ways he hasn't expected. One goes, and he wonders if the soldier will see Gudrun or Jorund. Another very young soldier dies while Magnus is with him and his father, who is also a Crozier soldier. The father, whose name is Vegard Larsson, is a rugged, strong man, as good a fighter as any. Years ago he suffered the loss of his wife to a fever, but continued to raise his boy. Magnus watches him shrivel with grief. Even as he tries to console him, he knows he can't. Losing a child is beyond the limits of tolerance, and he understands that the man will never feel as whole as he did yesterday.

By high sun two days after the battle, a forerunner from Crooked Neck's army arrives, and Sturelsson brings word.

Crooked Neck and his men will reach camp before sunset.

"Does Eystein know?" Magnus says.

"He was there when the forerunner came in."

"Fetch me as soon as Father is here." He decides not to eat until his father appears.

"*Ja*," Sturelsson says.

A wait nearing its end. Sadness over his dead and wounded comrades dulls his concern about his own dignity. When Sturelsson alerts him, Crooked Neck is already on the edge of the encampment. Magnus lengthens his stride as he weaves through the pods of tents to where his father is. He draws a deep breath from the first air in two days that doesn't reek of death. The aroma of roasting meat drifts past him. He stops, bends and picks up a fistful of snow, looks at it for a moment, hurls it to his feet and stomps it as he walks on.

As soon as he sees his father, Magnus realizes that Eystein is already with him, facing away from his approach. Once within earshot, Magnus catches the last few words of his father's question.

"...attack without waiting for me?"

"The boy is impetuous, overzealous," Eystein says. "I beseeched him to wait for your strength."

"Father. Welcome," Magnus says.

As Inga approaches the *skihytte*, she watches the cloud of steam hovering over the back of the building where the ski wood is cambered and shaped. There's a shiny glaze on the snow covering the roof. Though still several strides away, she sniffs the tart scent of pine tar sweetened by a whiff of beeswax.

Inga finds Skjervald where Hakon said he would be. She has always felt he is at home here, working at his craft, surrounded by all the necessary tools and, of course, the skis. As she enters, Skjervald looks up and lifts the broad draw blade off of the new ski. A coiled peel of wood falls from it and joins a growing mound around his feet. His left hand releases its side of the tool and he lays it on the bench. "How is the king?" He cocks his head and the furrow of his forehead reaches down to his brow. His eyes widen. Fingers of his left hand move back to the ski and float along it as if he's unaware of the stroke.

Inga walks over and touches his cheek. "Thanks to you and Torstein, he's alive. His leg causes him pain, but still he jokes."

"Good sign." Skjervald smiles. "Needn't thank me. I couldn't have done less. I'm a soldier." He shrugs and wipes his hands on his shirt several times, as though he wants to say more, but can't find the words.

"He asked me to bring you to him. Are you able to stop what you're doing?"

Skjervald looks awkward, embarrassed by the question. "Of...of course. This work is of no importance if King Hakon calls." He puts down the tool, throws on his vest and hat and they walk without speaking.

Half way across the compound, they pause at the long lodge

where women are treating the injured. Family and friends of the wounded gather in front. One large group stands in a loose circle near the entrance. Some shake their heads. Vacant, exhausted eyes stare at the snow. Their murmurs rise and fall, like swells on open water. A woman steps from inside. Her clothes are so splotched that unstained cloth appears as a random pattern. The reddish-brown stains covering her hands and forearms match her clothes. Her chin is down and Inga detects a trace of head shake as she speaks to the group. A horrifying, tormented wail crushes the murmurs. One woman falls away from the group and leans heavily on the wall, her face buried against her raised forearm. Her shoulders tremble with her sobs. Several people clutch each other as if they haven't strength enough to stand apart. Inga can't keep her eyes away from the one who cries alone, only the building to support her. She wonders if it was her husband. Her son? Grief and fear churn in Inga's stomach. The shiver that follows has nothing to do with the cold.

They move on, saying little until they are several paces beyond the sickroom. Skjervald looks at Inga, draws a deep breath and releases a sigh. "There is honor in being a soldier, but that doesn't mean it's good, does it?"

"You mean easy?"

"*Ja*, that's better. It's not easy, not comfortable."

The word strikes Inga as odd at first, but as she ponders it, she thinks, What better way for a soldier to look at what he must do? A warrior can't torture himself with revulsion or he'll go mad. He can't walk away or he abandons his people and his values. He can't complain or he will drag down the morale of others. So he says it's not comfortable, like a pair of shoes that you're used to, but whose worn spots allow a stone to intrude. Like that, except not so easy to change.

"Someday it'll be better," he says.

"*Ja*." But she fears what lurks between now and then.

They arrive at Inga's lodge and she pushes back the door and holds it as Skjervald follows her in.

When Skjervald enters the *soverom*, Hakon sees him and extends his hand. "Your valor, and Torstein's, saved me."

Skjervald walks to his king and bends at the waist, as much to show deference as to reach Hakon's extended hand. "The troops rallied around you and Torstein. I was simply there."

"Son, your modesty is commendable, but your words belie what all saw. The only question is whether you or Torstein reached my side first. I give you my thanks."

Skjervald starts to smile, but catches it, nods, and steps back. Inga's not sure what it is, his youth perhaps, his quiet modesty, but she's sorry he has to be a soldier. She's sorry any of them have to be soldiers.

"I've called you because I need for you to join Torstein and Inga in a task that will be most difficult. They know what I ask."

Inga sees Skjervald glance at Torstein and then at her. His expression reminds her of a little boy about to get his first lesson on skis, anxiety tinged with excitement. She watches the look change to astonishment as Hakon tells him their plan.

"But sir, they will not overrun us. The men will defend. We'll fight harder than ever." He labors to keep protest from creeping into his appeal. "I can't abandon you and my men."

"You will not abandon us. You will follow the orders of your king to protect our cause in the event we are unable to defend Lillehammer. I know you would fight to your last, but what I ask is even more important. The prince must survive if our people are to have peace. It is up to Torstein and Inga and you, Skjervald, to assure that."

Skjervald swallows, rubs the back of his hand across his mouth, and looks at each of them. He nods once.

Hakon grabs two short scrolls of birch bark that lie beside him. "Torstein and I have drawn some maps." He struggles to sit up and unrolls the charts. He points to an X and says, "This is Lillehammer." His finger runs along a line. "And this is the river at our backs, running into Lake Mjose." He moves his finger away from the river and touches a second X. "This is Nidaros. You must reach the regent, Arne, there. The rest of our forces rally around him. There will be safety there."

"Why is there safety with him?" Inga asks.

"Because he has pledged before the *Lagtings* to uphold the rights of succession and protect any heir to the throne who has not yet reached maturity."

Torstein adds, "And he is dedicated to the defeat of Crooked Neck and Magnus, as well as the death of Eystein. What's more, he has over a thousand men with him."

The last is the only answer that matters to Inga.

Hakon continues. "Between here and Nidaros, there are two possible routes, one through the Gudbrans Valley and its surrounding peaks and the other through the Oster Valley and the mountains around it. We must decide which valley to follow." He pauses as they study the series of overlapping wedges he has drawn to represent the long mountain ridge between the two valleys.

"Gudbrans catches all the weather from the west," says Torstein. "A storm moving from that direction is usually more severe there than in the Oster."

"But Gudbrans is the shorter route. Less climbing. And at the north end, where the trails widen into the Old King's Road, it's easier to travel." Hakon says it as if he expects Torstein to challenge the statement, as if he wants him to.

Torstein shakes his head. "If there aren't many storms, you can reach Nidaros a half day, maybe a day sooner through the Gudbrans. In either valley, we will have to follow game trails and trading routes until we reach the King's Road. But the weather is less stable in the Gudbrans."

"So if we choose Oster, my son will be safer?" Inga says.

Torstein looks at her. "Unless the Croziers pursue us on a parallel course through the Gudbrans, and get good weather. Then they could reach the north end of the Gudbrans," he fingers a spot on the map, "block the road and wait for us to come over the mountains from the Oster."

"Why couldn't we take the Oster and cross to the Gudbrans

at a different spot near the north end, to evade them?"

The men think about that. Inga takes the moment to remind herself to keep desperation out of her voice.

"How do those two crossing points compare?" asks Hakon.

"The most northern pass is the easiest and the one they will most likely ascend from the Gudbrans in an attempt to intercept us, but if they take the more difficult one, we could…"

"Run right into them." She doesn't mean to say it out loud. Then she's glad she did.

The men nod their agreement. Hakon looks at Inga, then at the men, and says, "Take the safer route through the Oster. Hand me the candle."

Inga reaches for the stub of tallow and hands it to him. He touches the corner of the maps to the flame and she feels her shoulders twitch. He drops the burning birch to the floor. She watches the bark curl in the flame. When the sap-blackened smoke reaches her nostrils, the shudder from her shoulders travels through her entire body.

"Now, to get you out of here and past sixteen hundred Croziers," Hakon says.

"Magnus's troops are at the river, ready to flank from the north. Half of Crooked Neck's forces are in front of us. The rest are on the southern perimeter," Torstein says.

"On three sides of us?" Hakon says. "None behind us, across the river?"

"Few, if any. Afraid to cross the river this early."

"With good cause," Skjervald says. He reaches for charcoal and a blank piece of bark, and sketches the river in larger dimensions, showing the back wall of the compound flush against the water. "Here's the island, near the middle." He draws a small circle. "It's tiny, but ice is thickest between it and both banks. The water is shallow, and the current slow. I've made it across on skis. I can pick a route for us."

"So the three of you and my son could slip out the back of the compound and get across?" Hakon says.

Skjervald hesitates before he nods.

"At night?"

This time he shows less hesitation. "From the rear tower, I can survey the ice while it's light, select the best route. Even if the moon is behind clouds, there'll be enough light for me."

"Keep watch for any Croziers on the far side," Torstein says.

"Is there any way we can distract them?" Inga asks.

The men look at her, surprised that she would ask a tactical question. "A decoy?" Hakon says.

"Would it give our son a better chance of getting away?" Inga says.

Hakon looks from her to Torstein.

"It could work, but it puts more men at risk."

"Or more men to help us, should they make it across and into the woods," Inga says. "Skjervald could pick a place on the far side where we can meet them."

Torstein pauses. "They'd have to understand that we won't wait long for them. And they must not know which valley we'll travel."

Again, they wait for Hakon.

"They'll understand that it's their job to draw attention away from you." He pinches the bridge of his nose and rubs his eyes. "Any that I ask will have the choice to stay if they wish. We will meet here well before the moon sets. Prepare your supplies and equipment. Get some rest."

After Torstein and Skjervald leave, Hakon turns to Inga and says, "Go get Sigurd Fuselang, Bjorn Tolefsson and Erik Holstrum."

* * * *

After sending the three soldiers to Hakon, Inga decides to return to the *skihytte,* in part because she wants to help Torstein and Skjervald prepare the skis for their journey, but more because she understands how difficult a conversation Hakon will have with the other three. Her presence would help neither him nor them. And she feels responsible for their situation and not ready to face them.

Torstein looks up as Inga enters, but Skjervald keeps his eyes on his work. Even though he's closer to the entrance than Torstein, Inga feels he's unaware of her or anything other than the skis he bends over. The residue of steam, used to warp camber into the wood, hangs in the air of the workshop and makes it warm and sticky. Both men have their *vadmel* shirts hanging on a wall peg and wear only pants and open beaver-skin vests. The birch leggings are never off.

Two skis are strapped upside down to a contoured workbench that holds them secure as Skjervald applies his skill. The fingertips of his left hand glide over the wooden surface in harmony with his gaze. Inga has the sense that if he were struck blind, the fingers would continue their task uninterrupted.

For a moment she watches him trace the gold and russet lines of grain in the polished wood. Some of his best memories must ride there. She would wager that he's certain his skis have saved his life more than once. There's more than pride there, but what? Torstein is looking at him too, shaking his head in wonderment.

Finally, his diligent inspection concluded, Skjervald looks up. "Oh, hello Inga. Have you been there long? I was... uh..."

"Absorbed."

"*Ja*. It's easy for me to get lost when I work on my skis."

"Why?"

He looks confounded by the question. When he squints, he has the thoughtful, experienced eyes of age trapped in the smooth face of youth. "Hmmm? I'm not sure. Trust, maybe? Can you trust or distrust things like you do people?"

He appears to be asking himself, so Inga doesn't respond.

"Kinship, perhaps that's it, like a faithful dog." He looks at Torstein. "Not so much like a comrade, like Torstein, but something...a relationship?"

Torstein nods at Skjervald, but doesn't speak.

Inga can tell by the way Skjervald's eyes drift along the wall that she hasn't heard all the answer yet. I hope he puts the same concentration into saving my son, she thinks.

Torstein interrupts. "How about helping Inga with her skis?"

"Glad to. To get past the Croziers, we're going to have to dash." He dips his fingers into a bowl of black goo as if it is honey and he's a bear. Scent of pine, already strong in the *skihytte*, swells to a tart pungency, almost overwhelming. He spreads the pine tar thin in the middle portion of the ski, takes it from the bench, replaces it with one of Inga's and gives it the same precise attention that he has given his own.

At least she's sure their skis will be good. While he and Torstein attend to the skis, she focuses on other preparations for their departure. Fire is the most important. They'll need a fire at least once a day, more if the air turns colder or they face a storm, so she plans to take a supply of tinder to last eight days, hoping the journey will take only five or six. She stuffs a beaver-skin pouch, from a store of tinder that has dried all summer and fall in the *skihytte*, with as much as will fit. The combination of shredded birch bark, dried grass and lichen is easy to ignite. She crams the small bow and friction dowel on top. The pack smells like autumn.

They store frozen meat and dried vegetables and meal in separate storage rooms adjacent to the *skihytte*. The rooms contain all the supplies the Birkebeiner would need for hunting trips. She retrieves four chunks of frozen reindeer, each the size of her upper arm and aligns them on a bench. She goes back and gets two pouches of dried lentils, and two each of oats and cornmeal. The bags are large enough to hold a half dozen fish and made of sewn pieces of *vadmel*, tied off with rawhide laces at the top. Next to them she puts hooks and wool line for fishing, even though she knows that fish don't feed much after the streams freeze. Skjervald's spear or arrows more likely will account for any fish they catch. For fear they won't have time to fish, she puts out six pieces of *røkt laks*, each almost as large as the reindeer roasts. She rolls six large sewn furs, their bedding, two at a time, and ties the ends of each with rawhide thongs. The bundles are bulky, but not too heavy.

For clothing she adds three pair of *vadmel* leggings and three pullovers. Two small *vadmel* blankets go on the bench for young Hakon. She runs her hand over the soft garments as she looks at the collection. Their security will depend on these things. Survival has never been a guarantee in Inga's life. Even as a little girl, she knew that the whimsy of nature or the Croziers could do them in at any time. Two or three items can make the difference between life and death. Her baby will live or die because of what she does, because of her judgment. She wipes her palms on the front of her leggings and thinks, Where will I get the strength and resolve I need?

Inga's not sure how much time passes before she returns to her task, but terror hasn't frozen her yet. When she's satisfied with what she has gathered, she begins fitting it into three backpacks woven from split alder saplings and covered with birch bark. She checks the leather shoulder straps and the bindings that go around the waist. When she's comfortable that they are sturdy, she ties a set of furs to the outside of each pack and hefts the smallest of them onto her back. When she straightens her neck and arches it back, she can feel the top of the pack against the back of her head. It's wider than her shoulder blades and the bottom rests low in the small of her back. She tightens the waist strap and strides the length of the *skihytte* in both directions. The load's heavy, but well balanced and doesn't bounce. Both of the other packs are longer and wider, and she's sure they will fit the men's backs.

Without removing the ruck basket, Inga picks up the last article on the bench, a folded *vadmel* blanket, woven tight and dyed green. Holding a corner she flings it and lets it unfurl onto the bench. It's longer than her height and almost square. Even with the snug weave, it has a thick, soft feel. She caresses it and smiles, then folds it into a triangle and ties the ends of the longest side together, hangs it around her neck so that the knot rests on her left shoulder, and unfolds the rest across the front of her torso in the form of a sling. Her hands enter the sling from each side, spread it open and push down on it. The bottom of it lies against her pelvis, so she adjusts the knot until it is at her waist. "He'll like riding in this," she says.

She removes it and the backpack, checks everything once more, and then goes back to Torstein and Skjervald who have finished preparing the skis and are ready to return to King Hakon.

* * * *

It doesn't take Inga and the two men long to cross the compound. When they reach Inga's lodge, Bjorn, Erik and Sigurd are still with Hakon. Mourners at a pyre carry less solemn expressions. Inga looks away from them and checks straps on her pack that she's already checked three times.

"You know what you must do," says Hakon. Strained control governs his words. "After you leave and cross the river, try to reunite on the far side. Torstein, if your group is attacked, Erik and his group will come to your aid. Otherwise, they will try to draw the Croziers away from you. If you do not meet immediately after entering the woods," he says, looking at Torstein, "you are to push on. If you hear the sounds of fighting, you are to run toward your route. Stop for nothing. If neither group is challenged, the six of you continue together. Only the three of you are to know the direction." He sweeps a pointed finger across Inga, Torstein and Skjervald, and then looks at all six of them, one at a time.

Some nod. Others whisper their acknowledgment.

"Go and rest until just before the moon sets."

All but Inga start toward the door.

"Wait," Hakon says.

They turn.

"*Tusen tuk*," is all he says.

"No," Bjorn says. "We thank you," and they leave.

The sentinel that guards Inga's thoughts about the men's motivations allows an intruder. These men risk so much. Would I suffer this peril for another's child?

When they're gone, Hakon slides down, stretching his body the length of the bed, wincing as he disturbs his leg wound. Inga lies next to him and nestles into the crook of his arm, her forehead against his cheek. She takes his other hand and holds it between both of hers. For a long while, they lie that way without talking. When she senses that it will not be long before they hear the sounds of the others returning, she whispers against his neck, "Is there any other way?"

"No."

"Know that I will do all I can to..."

"I know, and I love you for it. Your courage is even stronger than the men's."

"No, Hakon. I'm terrified. Afraid to run and lose you. Afraid to stay and lose little Hakon. I make these men sacrifice so much. If not for trembling and crying, I don't think I could move at all. I feel like I want to throw up. I won't be able to fight when I have to."

"I've seen strong men vomit before battle, or actually cry with the anguish of anticipation. Some freeze in the face of a charging enemy, but most are able to do what they have to. They're the courageous ones. And these men are men I've chosen, not you. They're doing what soldiers do. If they blame anyone, it's the Croziers."

"I need to be a soldier. I hope I can."

He kisses her forehead, and they're silent again. After a while he says, "I'm sorry we never married."

They'd never talked about it before. A lump swells up in her throat and she pushes it back. "I know. I've always known. That's Eystein, not you."

"I could've gotten one of the priests who sympathizes with our cause to perform the ceremony."

"*Ja*, and then he'd have been excommunicated or worse. I can think of many who had a ceremony, but not contentment, not like us."

He squeezes her hand.

"I could not have felt more like a bride if I had had the most lavish wedding feast in all of Norway. And our child could not have had a better father."

"Or a better mother."

She props her head on her hand so she's looking down into his eyes. It brings back to her a time when they were a suitor and a maiden outside her parent's lodge, lingering in each other's eyes, their bodies close, each knowing it was time to go, but neither wanting to say goodbye.

* * * *

"Not as cold as the last two nights," Skjervald says.

"Cold enough that we don't have to worry about the ice not supporting us," Torstein says.

Inga's ski bindings are secure and her pack is in place. Torstein hands little Hakon to her, hoists his pack into place and then adjusts the child's sling over his shoulder. Inga has her pack on and helps Skjervald balance his. As Skjervald slides his arm through the wide leather straps, he says to Bjorn, "Not carrying packs?"

"No."

"We'll share what's in ours, but I don't think there's enough for..."

A puncturing glare from Torstein stops him. "We have what we need."

"On the move you don't have time to eat much," Bjorn says. He looks at the ground, avoids their eyes. "And somebody has to stand guard, so we can't all use a bedroll at the same time." Sigurd and Erik kneel and check their bindings again, careful not to look at anyone.

There's a clumsy silence. All of them avoid conversation like ice too slippery to tread. Each fumbles with tasks whose only purpose is to keep them away from further discussion.

When there's nothing left to do but go, Skjervald moves to the opening in the back of the compound and says, "Let me show you the safest way across the river before we lose the moonlight." They crowd around. "There," he points, "is the island. When the moon sets you won't be able to see it from this far. Torstein, Inga, the prince, and I will cross to it and then head a little south to reach the far shore. You see the swath of snow that looks whiter than the rest?"

"*Ja*," Torstein and Inga say it at the same time.

"It's whiter because it hasn't gotten wet. Probably means the ice under it is thicker."

"Probably?" Inga says.

He looks at her. "Well, it can mean that the snow has bridged and there's nothing under it."

"Except water?"

"Stay in my ski tracks, Inga. Holds me, it'll hold you."

"But what about Torstein and my baby?" Inga looks at Hakon, who had awakened and jabbered at the excitement when they first reached the wall. His eyes are droopy now and Inga's sure he'll be asleep again soon.

"We'll go last," Torstein says. "The danger is from getting wet, not from going under. The river is waist deep most of the way, so if I go in, I'll hold Hakon over my head until I can hand him to one of you. But then I'd have to go back. Quickly."

"Oh." The thought saps strength from her legs. She wonders if they could be lost before they even cross the river.

"Bjorn, you three go north along this bank until you're three arrow shots from the compound. You'll see a similar-looking swath of snow to a smaller island. Erik, you're the biggest, so..."

"I know. I go first." Erik rolls his eyes and his attempt to laugh is awkward and stilted.

Skjervald looks at each of them. Clouds cover the moon just as it sets.

"Ready?" Torstein says, and glances around. "Let's go."

Bjorn's group slips out first. The others let them get clear, and Inga follows Skjervald out, with Torstein and her son last. Her eyes have adapted to the dark. She can see shades of black and white and Skjervald's silhouette in front of her. She can't see the island and certainly not the far shore. As they creep toward the edge, she slides her skis into the darkened indentations left by Skjervald's. The ice moans and she thinks that she has never heard it so loud. A sharp crack and she gasps, pinches her eyes shut and waits for the shroud of freezing water to engulf her. When nothing happens, she opens her eyes and finds she's still on something solid and dry. Skjervald's there. She twists her head so fast that it hurts her neck, certain she'll see Torstein struggling to keep her son above water. But there they are, following her tracks.

Calm, she tells herself. Calm down or your mind will turn to mud and you'll start to see trolls behind every tree. It's a long journey. Stay in control, Inga. She forces the alternatives from her mind and takes the next stride. And the next. A cold breeze, carrying the sooty smell of campfires, pushes her forward. Not yet a bow-shot from the compound and she's chilled, the wind seeking new routes to her skin. But it's not just the wind. Cold is all around her, gurgling beneath her, whispering through her *vadmel* leggings, tearing her eyes and making her nose run. With the moon set, the sky offers only pinpoints of light, helpless to warm the freezing blackness around them. She hopes the baby's warm, then reminds herself that he has more layers of clothing than she does and the extra insulation of the sling. She looks back again and misses her footing but recovers. Inga knows she's got to push these things away, concentrate on the journey. Her effort to focus must help, because she begins to settle down, refuses to allow the sound of water rippling beneath to frighten her, starts to concentrate on where to place her skis and plant her *lurk*. Attention to precise movements helps to ease her fears. She considers how soothing the rippling sound can be during *sommer*. Creaks and groans are interesting, she decides, at least all but the worst of them.

"All right?" Torstein whispers.

She nods, but doesn't know if he sees. She can tell Skjervald doesn't hear him because he pushes toward the destination with no change in pace or posture. She thinks she sees the outline of the island. With each stride, she sets her skis down in Skjervald's tracks, careful not to vary a hair from his line. The island's outline fills, becoming a mass blacker than the black around it. At last, for the first time since they left the bank, she senses a rise under her skis and knows they're on the speck of solid ground.

Skjervald stops but continues to look straight ahead, as if he might lose his way if he looks elsewhere for an instant. When Inga hears her skis tap against the tails of his, she stops. Torstein crowds behind her. They wait for a few moments and she's not sure why, except that the solid feeling under them is reassuring. Torstein steps around her, taps Skjervald on the shoulder, and waves the young soldier forward. Skjervald looks toward the far shore again and slides off the island, each ski stroke smooth and gentle as it passes the one before and lengthens the darkened grooves that will guide the others.

When the gap is adequate, Inga slides off in his tracks and hears Torstein follow. She can see the shore and the tree line behind it. Now she doesn't sense the cold, not even on her face, but she's aware of that shore. She can touch that shore like it's already beneath her feet. Reaching there is her only thought, all her mind will allow. Another sharp crack startles her, but she's able to keep her eyes straight ahead this time, fixed on that shoreline.

Torstein whispers, "A little farther, Inga. Hakon's fine."

She wants to believe him.

A yelp from Skjervald and Inga watches him scrambling to his right. She can tell his skis thrust hard. Short, choppy side steps, jumping from one ski to the other. Something splashes, but she can still see Skjervald, upright. Then he's still. She's still, and hears no movement from Torstein.

After what seems like passing seasons, Skjervald says,

"Some ice broke off under me."

"Are you wet?" Torstein asks.

"No, just the tails of my skis went under. Inga, get out of my tracks and go wider to the right."

She can tell his body is twisted, looking back at her. Her skis feel like they're frozen in place, her knees locked.

"It's all right. Just take your time. Move slowly to your right. Halfway to me, stop. Give me time to move ahead again."

As if she's afraid of waking someone, Inga takes four cautious steps to her right, moving her right ski as far as she can, each time touching it down like she's on sacred ground. Don't let us break through is her silent prayer. Then she draws the left ski next to the right with the same care. After the forth step, she realizes she's not breathing. She releases her lungs and sucks in new air.

"Far enough," Skjervald says. "Now, come toward me."

With the same precision that regulated her side steps, Inga slides one ski forward, balances on it, and then slides the other next to it until she's halfway.

"Stop." He twists back around and starts forward. Much farther on, he turns again. "Come ahead."

She continues until he halts her, losing track of how many times they stop and go. She doesn't look back at Torstein, but can hear him each time he draws up.

"Reached shore. Get back in my tracks and you'll be fine," Skjervald says.

Now she takes quick, flowing strides, anxious for solid ground.

"Will it hold them?" she says as soon as she reaches Skjervald.

"*Ja.*"

She holds her breath as she watches Torstein approach. He, too, moves quickly. When he gets close, she sees that he is carrying Hakon in his hands rather than cradled in his arms, ready to raise him above his head if he has to.

"Thank God," she says. They relax a little and Torstein

hands Hakon to her. The boy's fast asleep. Torstein looks at him, then at her, shaking his head. They're both able to smile.

"Get to the woods," Skjervald says. "Could be a patrol on this side." The woods is a few strides away and Skjervald heads straight for the trail. Once certain no one can see them, they stop.

"Can't wait long," Torstein says. Moments later, shouts and the sound of clashing weapons come from north of them. Men's screams rip holes in the night.

"*Dra! Dra!*" rasps Torstein through clenched teeth, and the three of them bolt down the path as fast as skis will carry them.

Magnus's father struggles with a thin-lipped smile. "Son. The good bishop and I were talking about you."

"His Holiness and I have had some interesting conversations in your absence. He has a way of holding one's attention, doesn't he?" Magnus smiles at Eystein. He knows the bishop suppresses his glower at the thought that Magnus may have overheard him, and he enjoys the frailty of Eystein's glare as he watches the man's weasel eyes dart to the ground.

"I'm hungry enough to eat Birkebeiner cooking," Crooked Neck says. "Let's discuss the next siege over some roasted reindeer. The bishop has informed me of the results of your initial foray."

"I'm certain the bishop was much too generous with tribute for the attempt. His plan was bold and he really should offer me no credit for it."

Erling's brow pushes his eyes to slits as he tilts his head. The angular prominence in his throat bobs and grows more pronounced. Magnus smiles.

The two of them leave Eystein and make their way toward Crooked Neck's yurt. It is Crooked Neck's habit to put his tent at the back edge of an encampment. He claims it causes him to travel through camp when he wants to survey a battleground or front lines, and gives him a sense of the men's morale. Right now it causes Magnus and his father to wade through hip-deep snow. When they reach the entrance, they're both breathing hard. Magnus wishes they had invited Eystein to eat with them. Watching the fat man struggle would have been entertaining. Perhaps he would have suffered a seizure.

Erling yells to two of his men as he pulls back the flap, "Several of you tramp the snow from here to the pathways."

He ducks and Magnus follows him inside. The sweet scent of roasting meat fills the tent. They go straight to the fire at the center, where a soldier turns a spit.

"Done?" Crooked Neck says.

"Yes sir. May I carve a piece for you and the king?" the man replies.

Father nods. "Then carve some for yourself and take your leave."

Magnus looks around the yurt. Sparse, as usual for Father. A bedroll on a base of dried grass near the fire, a bow, arrows, axe, and sword and shield propped in a straight line against the wall nearest the opening, a mail coat hanging from a roof support and next to it an extra parka. The shield displays Crooked Neck's emblem, a standing bear with lightning bolts over and under the image. Despite its many scars, it looks sturdy enough to fend off a blow from a catapult. Near the bedroll sits a small oil lamp, a handful of map scrolls and a small keg. When the soldier hands Erling and Magnus each a wooden bowl full of reindeer, Erling sits in front of the fire and crosses his legs. Magnus starts to do the same, but his father puts his hand out, palm first, and says, "Go to that keg and draw us each a gourd of wine." Crooked Neck reaches for Magnus's bowl and puts it down while Magnus fetches the drink.

As Magnus returns, the soldier says, "Unless there is anything else..."

Father is negotiating a chunk of reindeer with one hand and waves the soldier off with the other. Magnus sits down on the opposite side of the fire on a single skin. He stokes the fire and adds a log.

He has a mouthful of food when his father says, "What compelled you to attack without waiting for my troops?"

Magnus gets most of it down and says, "Eystein."

"Eystein?" The doubtful brow intrudes again.

Magnus nods.

Crooked Neck is quiet for a moment. Magnus suspects he

is considering whether to reveal what the bishop said. Then he says, "Why must you blame Eystein for everything?"

Magnus shrugs, knows there's no answer that will satisfy him.

"You're the king. You must start to act like it." He waits to see if his son will reply. When he doesn't, he says, "Exercising good judgment would be a start."

"The choice was defying the Church or mounting the best siege I could. Now that you're here we'll shatter their defenses. Let's put together our strategy."

Erling starts to say something and thinks better of it.

Magnus believes he wants to argue, but knows they have to tend to the business of the Birkebeiner fortifications.

Crooked Neck drops his head and shakes it slowly in both directions, then looks back up at Magnus, lips pursed straight and thin. "As you wish. Let's devise our strategy. I suggest my troops mount a direct assault. Keep yours in reserve on the northern flank, next to the river, to sweep across their lines as mine penetrate from straight on."

"Did Eystein tell you about the pike traps?"

"No."

"Probably doesn't know about them. Never got too far from his hearth and wine."

Crooked Neck's upper lip tightens across gritted teeth and he rolls his eyes. Magnus can't tell whether his father is annoyed at Eystein for his laziness or at him for talking about it. "The Birkebeiners had buried pikes by the hundreds, rigged to spring up along the front margin of their trench line. I doubt they'll repeat the ploy, but sending infantry behind a line of shields, with mounted troops backing them would be a more effective way to penetrate."

Crooked Neck ponders this for a moment and says, "Very well. I feel your army should still take a flanking approach from the river."

It makes sense and Magnus nods.

"Have any of the birch-legs tried to break out and run for

it?" Crooked Neck asks.

"None that we've seen. I've had patrols across the river. They tend to run only when their strategy calls for it."

"And right now, that's exactly what I'm afraid of," Crooked Neck says.

Magnus furrows his brow.

"You do understand, don't you, that either Hakon Sverrisson or his bastard son must survive this siege or they have lost Norway?"

Magnus holds a handful of meat out between them. "The man who skewered this meat understands that. The man who shoes your horse understands that. The camp followers probably..."

His father throws up his hand, palm out. His head is down and in a slow, measured cadence he says, "Then why have you done nothing about it?"

"You mean like waiting for you for two days and mounting a successful siege rather than venturing forth without the advantage of overwhelming force and suffering an embarrassing debacle."

"An explanation would be helpful." Color rises in Crooked Neck's face.

"Only two explanations are possible."

"Go ahead."

"Either I enjoy watching my men slaughtered and humiliated, or someone whose authority I can't challenge ordered me to attack."

Crooked Neck's hue darkens. "Even if it's true, you can't say that about Eystein."

"Even to you?"

"The wealth and power of the Church buys ears and minds, even when hearts don't follow."

Magnus heaves a sigh. "Which is why I didn't defy him."

Erling takes his time digesting that and then says, "Sverrisson was wounded in the last siege. Tomorrow, when we swarm over them, we must finish the task."

Magnus nods.

"That includes his son."

Magnus hesitates and nods again.

"I don't sense resolve."

Now Magnus's face flushes and he averts his eyes.

"Well?" his father says.

Magnus looks at the tent ceiling and draws a deep breath before speaking. "I have no problem with Sverrisson. No problem at all. He's an enemy soldier." He lingers on that statement, and then sees that his father expects him to continue. The pause is heavy enough to crush a warhorse.

When Erling understands that his son is not going to add anything more, he says, "Sverrisson is half the problem."

"And Eystein is the other half," Magnus says.

"That thinking is not only dangerous to our future, it's militarily incomplete. Unsound."

"I don't intend to deal with the second half of the problem with a military solution," Magnus says through clenched teeth.

"Your second half or mine?"

Magnus opens his mouth to respond. Shouts of men and the clash of weapons reverberate from across the frozen river. He breaks off his thought and the two men race each other to get outside. Three soldiers run toward the river as Magnus emerges from the yurt. He stops a fourth. "What's happening?" he yells.

"Not sure," the soldier says. "Fighting across the river."

Torstein goes to the fire and puts a finger into the water. Satisfied, he pours some into a gourd and puts it to the boy's lips. Hakon slurps and looks content. Torstein passes the gourd, and holds the pot for each one of them, then finishes what is left.

Skjervald leans on the shaft of his spear as though he wants to drive it into the snow, and relaxes on his skis. He looks up the slope that runs the length of the valley. "Let's climb, and then move along the ridge until we find a good trail to return to the valley."

"That'll take extra time," Torstein says. "We run the risk of letting them get ahead of us and then having to go through them."

"But if they follow us, we'll gain time," Skjervald says. "We're better climbers and have more control in the descents."

"If they follow, that's right. We'll gain time. But they won't," Torstein says.

"How do you know?"

Torstein is steadfast. "Two reasons. You said yourself that they don't climb well, so they'll stick to the flats in the valley where they think they can outpace us. Also, they know that the valley is the shortest route to Nidaros, and by now, they know that's our destination. If they can avoid climbing and end up between us and our objective, where do you think they'll go?"

Skjervald pauses, then opens his mouth.

Torstein cuts him off. "They'll stick to the valley, and that's what we're going to do."

turelsson's men push and shove the two Birkebeiner prisoners toward Eystein's yurt. In the dim light provided by the campfires they pass, Magnus sees that one has a long, gruesome gash across his swollen forehead. Fresh blood runs over that which has already caked and dried around his eyes and across his nose, mouth and cheeks. The Birkebeiner's eyes look huge, as if pried open beyond their normal dimensions. Magnus wonders if it's fear or just the contrast of dark, crusting blood next to the whites.

The other one limps, falls when his guard pushes again, and cries out in pain as he struggles to get up using the damaged leg. The man's hands, bound behind him, are useless in relieving the wounded leg from the exertion of rising. He gasps and grunts, tries to hold his balance, but the pain weighs the prisoner down as he crumples onto his side and rolls to his back. An impatient captor grabs a fistful of the Birkebeiner's hair and forces him to twist back onto his stomach. Then the Crozier pulls upward, using the hair to steady the prisoner until both legs support him again. The Birkebeiner's gritted teeth reflect light from the large fire outside of Eystein's tent, as if this time he refuses to let himself scream.

Brave men, Magnus thinks.

Sturelsson opens the flap and his soldiers throw both men through the opening onto the floor. Magnus stands in the entrance, watches Eystein survey them with an expression one might have after stepping in sheep dung. Saying nothing, he spreads himself into his throne, puts his elbow on his knee and rests his chin on the bridge formed by his thumb and forefinger. Fully half of each digit disappears into his chops. Both prisoners glare back at him, their expressions a blending

Lord will grant you mercy when you do His work," Eystein says. "And right now His work is to tell who escaped from Lillehammer and where they are going."

"I'll tell you nothing, you fat sow." Tolefsson hisses it through grinding teeth and labored breath.

"You will tell me everything," Eystein says. The whisper turns raspy and his face crimson. His tongs rip away another toenail.

Still, Tolefsson refuses to answer.

The blood doesn't bother Magnus. The screams penetrate, but he's used to hearing men scream. What's repugnant is the base indignity. It's one thing to face a soldier on the battlefield and kill him in combat, but quite another to strap him to a table, helpless to defend himself, and slowly rip him to shreds.

"We can do this all night!" Eystein rants.

Magnus moves toward the entrance, then steps back and out of the tent, weary of watching the Birkebeiner's agony and knowing Eystein can, indeed, continue all night. He walks back to his yurt, hopeful of getting some sleep, but the distance fails to mute the soldier's cries. Magnus's mind churns past and future while his fire's light flickers on the ceiling. A piercing scream from Eystein's victim causes Magnus to groan. Dying in battle is harsh enough, but at least there is honor for the victor and for the dead. Eystein cares little for honor, he thinks. Ha! I doubt he knows the meaning of the word. Could I find a horse that would support him, I'd lash him into the saddle and drag him into battle just to watch his face. Just to see him experience the helplessness of terror. And when I see the fear etch its way into his face and when I'm sure that the look is as hard as kilned clay, I'd let him go just to see him run.

Magnus lies on his bedroll and, for several hours, watches shadows trace along the ceiling while his thoughts continue in this vein, punctuated by a soldier's cries for mercy. Finally, near dawn, the cries cease.

Feeling more fatigued than when he lay down, Magnus drags himself out from under his sleeping skins and scavenges through leftover bread and meat for his morning meal. He finishes the skimpy serving and slams his wooden spoon against his plate in frustration. No matter what I turn my mind to, I can't purge Eystein from my thoughts any more than I am able to eliminate him from my life. Someday, though. Someday.

Wishing he had not tried to sleep, Magnus sets out for Eystein's tent. The camp is stirring now. Men stoke their fires, prepare their morning rations. He sees one honing the edge of his axe. Next to him, another wraps new rawhide on the shaft of his spear where his hand will grip it. Magnus stretches his stride and turns toward the back of the camp, content to avoid Eystein for a while longer.

Near the far edge of the camp, separated from the other shelters, stands a large yurt. There's a sizeable fire in front of it, hot and giving off little smoke. Several cooking pots, steam rising out of them, hang over it or sit near it. Even though the tent is isolated from the others, the path coming and going is well trodden. Magnus is about to cross the pathway and set his course back toward Eystein when the women come out, ten or twelve of them, the camp followers. All of them have good footwear, but are otherwise disheveled and ragged. There is little color to their garb, browns and grays for the most part, designed for warmth. The women vary in size from tall and scrawny to short and stout. Most have camped with Magnus's army before. Some look as if they have marched too often and too long. He doesn't see Strange One, but another stands out. She's new this campaign, Magnus thinks. Her red hair is tied back and disciplined as it hangs down her back. The tie is a strip of green cloth, the only color he sees in the whole lot. The woman looks up and smiles and Magnus nods. She reminds him of Gudrun, because of the hair, he supposes. He looks away as soon as he nods, but it's already too late to avoid thinking about his family again.

When he married Gudrun, he didn't think that he would love her as much as he did. As much as he does. And when she gave him Jorund, Magnus knew his life was complete. With a beautiful wife and perfect son, he wanted nothing more from his days than to be a soldier, to command soldiers. But he knew he could forsake the life of a soldier if he still had his family. The crown mattered little to him. That he rules had been his father's quest, and Eystein's, not his. As long as he had Gudrun and Jorund, he kept Crooked Neck at bay by feigning interest in the crown. Now all he has left is his army. If I have to be king to keep command of my army, he thinks, then so be it. I believe I hold no more sway over the Norwegian succession than I do over tomorrow's sunrise. But I have to be a soldier.

These are thoughts Magnus doesn't want right now. He forces himself to return his mind to the errand at hand. As much as he hates Eystein, he finds that smoldering at him blocks painful memories.

As he approaches Eystein's tent, Magnus hears low, guttural moaning, but nothing else. When he throws back the flap, he sees the bloated bishop asleep in his throne, head rolled back and mouth open. His hands, streaked with stains from his night's work, are clasped across his belly. A trace of blood stains his pale face where his hands wandered to scratch or rub. Always hard about the Lord's work, Magnus thinks. Tolefsson moans again and Magnus looks over at his outstretched figure, his head rolling from side to side. The poor soul has lapsed into semi-consciousness from the butchery that has befallen him. Few places on his body are not bleeding or bloody. Fingers and toes are mutilated, some missing. His left eye is swollen closed, and a grizzled, crusty socket stares from where his right eye used to abide. Sitting at his feet, still bound, is Sigurd, his eyes fixed on his comrade with such intensity that he does not notice Magnus. When Magnus moves closer, Sigurd looks up. Magnus realizes his face must reveal his horror, because as soon as Sigurd sees him, he says, "Kill him."

"What?"

"Kill him. You're a soldier. Do you think another soldier deserves to die this way? Take your sword and plunge it into his heart. He would do the same for you."

"I…" Magnus's eyes return to the tortured Birkebeiner.

"Do it, please. Don't let him die like this. Kill him like a soldier. Coyotes kill a wounded reindeer with more mercy than this."

Magnus begins to draw his sword just as Eystein stirs.

The bishop looks at him and then at his hand on the sword. "I assume you are drawing that to use on him?" He nods toward Tolefsson.

"He is spent, Eminence, and beyond helping you."

"Don't be absurd. I will get my answers." He leans forward, hefts himself out of his seat and walks to where Magnus stands. The bishop doesn't let his eyes stray from Tolefsson while his hand walks at random over his ugly tools until one is in his grip.

"Bishop, need I remind you of the Church's ban on torturing the same victim a second time?" Magnus says.

"Of course not. Praise the mercy of our pope. I would never disregard his decree on that matter."

"Then why do you prepare to begin again?" He nods toward the instrument Eystein holds.

"I am not torturing him again. I am merely continuing what I started last night, after offering the compassion of a rest." He emphasizes the word *continuing* with a smile and a flowing motion made with the tooled hand. He prods the man's face with the implement. "Wake up, Birkebeiner. It is time for us to continue our chat."

Tolefsson opens his functional eye, but it's clear he comprehends nothing.

The bishop's hand drops to his side. "For once Magnus, you may be right. He is spent." He pauses, thinking. "But there is another way to get the information." He looks at Sigurd.

"You'll get no more from me than you did from him," Sigurd says, determined rebellion fixing his glare.

"When you see how I shall start with you, you will change your mind." He looks at Magnus and points to Sigurd. "Stand him up." As Magnus complies, Eystein takes one of the hollow hyssop reeds in his right hand. With his left, he pries open Tolefsson's mouth. Tolefsson gags as one end of the reed reaches the back of his throat. "Get me two of Sturelsson's men."

Knowing the horror of his plans, Magnus stands fast, looks at the ravaged soldier.

"I said get me two men."

"Get them yourself."

Eystein's head snaps back and for a moment Magnus is sure the bishop's going to strike him. He hopes he does and lets an insubordinate stare say so.

Fists clenched, Eystein stomps to the entrance and screams for two soldiers who stand over the nearest fire. When they enter the tent, he growls to one, "Hold this reed." As soon as the soldier grasps it, Eystein says to the other, "Pull a burning ember from the fire." The second soldier takes a pair of tongs and selects a large, glowing chunk from the fire. Eystein reaches for a glove and puts it on his right hand, then opens the wooden box with his left. The rustling from within intensifies to an agitated thrashing as the Bishop lowers his gloved hand into the box and withdraws a wriggling garter snake longer than his arm. He holds it before Sigurd's terrified face. "Behold Satan's disciple, my friend, saved from summer, warmed and fed for just such an occasion. He will extract the information from you that I could not get from your friend, Bjorn."

"No, please," Sigurd begs, shaking his head.

"Watch as our slithering friend demonstrates his persuasion on Bjorn. Then at least you'll know what is to befall you if you don't yield the information we need." He inserts the serpent's head into the end of the hyssop tube and says to the soldier, "Prompt him with that coal." The soldier holding the ember hesitates, a grimace spreading across his face. "Hurry, soldier.

Never fear doing the Lord's work."

The soldier touches the snake's tail with the burning coal and follows him with it as the serpent disappears into the reed. Gagging and choking noises grate from Tolefsson's gullet. Eystein takes a burning stick from the fire and as the snake's tail disappears into the reed, he ignites the tube. He looks at Sigurd. "This gets him where we want him, fast."

"In the name of God, please don't!" Sigurd begs.

"It is in the name of God that we must," says Eystein, as he removes the stub of the smoldering reed from the Birkebeiner's mouth. The serpent has disappeared. "They don't like the confines of a man's entrails," Eystein says, putting his face close to Sigurd's. "Some say it's the bile that disagrees with them. Whatever it is, watch. He'll quickly find his way out, and then *you* can try this."

"No, please! Have mercy!"

"Tell me what I need to know. Who left Lillehammer and where're they going?"

Sigurd hesitates, looks at his comrade, and then closes his eyes.

"Very well then. We'll do it the hard way."

At that moment, Tolefsson screeches a sound that cannot come from a human. Every muscle in his devastated body tenses. His back arches away from the bench with such violence, Magnus is sure his spine must snap. Three more times in quick succession, the victim's body spasms. Each time he slams back against the bench with force enough to break ribs or wood. With each impact, Magnus's hatred for Eystein grows. A spot of blood appears near the soldier's navel and grows as he thrashes against the pain. A forked tongue flickers out of the hole and the top of the snout follows, twisting against the rim. As the head emerges, Tolefsson's body goes limp, his one eye fixed on nothing.

Eystein looks at Sigurd Fuselang. "Interesting how the slithery serpents seem to find their way back to the surface, isn't it? You'll last longer than your friend, as you will be rested when our helper visits your innards." He pauses and cocks his head in mock sympathy. "You needn't suffer this." If not for the cruelty, it almost sounds caring.

"You'll give me quarter if I tell you what you want to know?"

"Of course. I don't want to hurt you." Now Eystein sounds like he's the man's nurse. "But you must tell me immediately."

"It was Torstein Skevla, Skjervald Skrukka, Inga Varteigsdotir and her son, Hakon Hakonsson."

Impossible, but Eystein's already pallid complexion blanches. "Their destination?" he screams. "Tell me their destination!"

"They run for Nidaros."

"By what route, you Birkebeiner pig?"

"I don't know. King Hakon made a point not to tell us the route."

In a rage, Eystein lunges back to Tolefsson's body and rips the snake from the wound. He turns to the wooden box, throws open the lid and plunges his hand into it, withdrawing a fistful of writhing serpents. Sigurd recoils as Eystein thrusts the creatures into his face. "I swear you will eat all of these if your next words do not reveal the route they took." His jowls shake with fury.

"Before God, I swear I don't know the route!"

"Strap him to the bench! We'll see what he knows!"

"Please, no! You promised quarter!"

"You promised information."

"I have told you all I know. Please, my lord."

As the soldiers remove Bjorn and struggle to secure Sigurd to the bench, Magnus says, "You waste time now, Bishop. There are only two routes that make any sense. By the time we realize he doesn't know which one, we'll be another day farther behind them. Send two parties now, one by each route. Don't squander time on him. After all he's told you, he wouldn't withhold that detail if he knew it."

Eystein pauses, regards the fistful of snakes as if he hates to waste them. He looks at Sigurd, who is quaking beyond control. "Magnus, since you're so adept at predicting Birkebeiner strategy, get two parties together now." He throws the snakes back into the box. "You lead one, and Sturelsson the other. Review the routes with me and be ready to leave before the sun breeches the horizon."

"Father wants my army on the northern flank during tomorrow's siege."

"Your army will be on the flank, but the fact that the bastard pretender survived the first siege is your fault, and you are going to correct your error. I'll talk to Crooked Neck. Get Sturelsson and set your plans."

Each time I believe I hate this man as much as I can, I find out I'm wrong, Magnus thinks. "As you wish, Your Holiness." If he says anything else, he's sure it will be something he'll regret, so he pivots, strides out of the shelter and beckons to the men nearby. They run toward him and Magnus points to one. "You. Get Sturelsson. Have him go to my lodge." He leans close to him and whispers, "Tell him to fetch the gnome." He looks to the others and points back to the entrance. "Take the prisoner Fuselang and put him where he'll not be in the bishop's way."

* * * *

Sturelsson arrives at the lodge with Einar waddling behind. Before Sturelsson can open his mouth, Magnus says, "Sturelsson, gather sixteen men, good skiers. You and I are going to chase down Sverrisson's son."

"Chase down?"

"Skevla and a young soldier named Skrukka have escaped the encampment with Varteigsdotir and her bastard son."

"With what objective?"

"Nidaros and the safety of Earl Arne's army."

"When do we leave?"

"As soon as possible. Tell your men they have time to eat and pack seven days' provisions. Travel light."

Sturelsson turns and leaves, and Magnus transfers his attention to Einar. "Well, troll, today we put an end to Sverrisson and my succession is assured." He shares with no one his lack of enthusiasm for the crown.

"Good, my lord. It seems my dream will come to pass."

"What happened to all the trouble I was supposed to get from your eagle, Sverrisson?"

"I didn't say the eagle was Sverrisson, sire. You did."

"It's of little consequence now. Sverrisson is as good as dead."

"Why do you concern yourself so much with Sverrisson?"

"Because you said I would fight the eagle and we would both be bloodied."

"Again, sire, the dream is what you make of it, but I never said the eagle is Sverrisson."

"Then who is it?"

"I don't know, my lord."

Magnus glowers while the gnome wrings his hands and toes the snow. He hasn't looked up at Magnus since he arrived. "Then how do you know it's *not* Sverrisson?"

"Because, sire, it is a she-eagle."

Skjervald doesn't want to abandon his idea for a route and continues to try to persuade Torstein. "But if we do end up behind them, all we have to do is wait," he says. He looks at Inga like a child trying to enlist an ally in a snowball fight.

"Wait for what?" Inga says, not trusting herself to say more.

"Wait for the king to arrive with reinforcements." He says it as though it's certain. As if she should heed his word the way Magnus is said to embrace the babbling of the dwarf prophet. She wants to grab his tongue and snatch it from his mouth.

"Are you now a wizard too?" Her tone makes the edge of Torstein's battle-axe seem dull by comparison. "Do you dare me to believe what cannot be?"

"I don't dare. I simply..."

"Simply is right. Addle-minded, dimwitted simple. I'll tell you what's simple. My love for this baby is simple." She thrusts her arm toward young Hakon, now drifting towards sleep again on Torstein's chest, the warrior's shield protecting the child from the wind. "My love for his father, the king you would wait for, is simple. The fact that the valley trail is the shortest route to our goal is simple. You...your problem is that you don't know what simple is, even when it sits like a wart on the end of your nose."

He shrinks back a step, eyes glazed and wide. Inhaling through flared nostrils, he says, "What in Thor's *fyr* are you so angry about? I have an idea that I think will work, an idea that can reunite us with Hakon and his army, and I'm sharing it."

This time, Inga lunges toward him, arches onto her toes, pushes her face as near his as she can. "*Hva i helvete*? Are you deaf or stup-" The words clog her throat as if her tongue has swollen. She tries to continue and cannot. Sweeping her fur-covered hand across her face, she feels the scratch of frozen tears, and the words no longer form. Stammering, she takes the baby from Torstein, crumples cross-legged in the snow and buries her face in his soft, sweet smell.

"What's wrong? Idea's as good as any." Inga doesn't look up and Skjervald turns to Torstein.

"The idea is not as good as any and that isn't the point. Can you be that slow-witted?" Torstein says, his voice thick with anger.

At that, Inga turns her face up. The tear hits her like driven sleet. This great protector, this mightiest of their warriors, a man who has not winced from the slashes of swords or the prick of spears is crying too, sobbing like an orphaned child. Skjervald Skrukka looks from him to her and back, a man whose *skut* has sailed into a storm he wasn't expecting and who has no capacity to deal with it, let alone understand where it comes from.

Now Torstein yells, "Damn you, Skrukka. Damn you to hell. *There* is the king." He jabs his hand with the axe in it toward the baby in Inga's lap. "There is the king. He is the only king who is going to join us, and the king we must save and protect even at the cost of our lives. Don't you understand? The king you have known and we have loved," he kneels and puts his arm around Inga's shoulder and looks into her face, "is dead."

Skrukka staggers, his face as lax as his legs. Inga has seen men, thrust through by spears, hold expressions less pained. He buckles at the knees and drops like a stone next to the two of them, and his arms surround them both. Inga can feel his shoulders shaking.

* * * *

My son is all I have left of him. Once again she swears that he will have all her life's energy. I would have stayed and died next to his father, had we not created this child, but because we did, I pledge my life to him.

Their sense of danger must outweigh their sense of loss. The three of them rise, make sure the child is warm in the sling and proceed down the valley. Thick woods line the trail and Inga wishes that these narrow boundaries could enclose her mind like they do her body. The snow beneath her yields to skis she can't feel. If she sees Skjervald and Torstein and her son, it is only because of a mother's instincts to protect her child. The snow should crunch beneath her skis and the wind should make some noise, but all Inga hears is the vanishing voice of a lost love, mingled with the agonized internal scream of her denial. Her palate is numb until the bile rises in her throat and she spews vomit, discoloring the snow. Retching racks her again and again, and she's grateful to feel something, anything.

Only when she's aware of the two men helping her, one holding her forehead and the other her waist, does the world begin to emerge again. When she's able to straighten, Inga says to Torstein, "Let me have Hakon for a moment."

While he lifts the child from the blanket sling, she washes her mouth with a handful of snow.

"Here, Inga, hug him," Torstein says.

And she does and kisses his face again and again before she puts him back in the sling and they trudge on. After a few steps Inga says, "We must lose no more."

Is there any doubt that destroying Sverrisson's line to the throne is our most important objective?" Eystein says. He looks at Magnus and Crooked Neck. Emphasis on the words *is there any doubt* suggests that there is only one answer.

As Crooked Neck nods, Magnus says, "Your Holiness, I believe the primary objective is crushing Sverrisson and his army. When we do that, they have no way to support their claim to the throne."

"If the line survives, the support can arise," Eystein says. His voice is louder now and he looks at Crooked Neck.

"I agree with the bishop," Crooked Neck says. He puts his hand on Magnus's shoulder.

"I need to lead my men," Magnus says.

"You're still in command of your army, but we have overwhelming numbers. Gather Sturelsson and the other men and tend to what is most important to your future. Go as soon as possible."

"But..."

"We can't pass this opportunity to end their claim to succession," Crooked Neck says.

"Don't relegate me to chasing an infant and his mother."

"Why don't you understand the importance of this?" Crooked Neck says.

"Of killing a child?"

"Of ending the Birkebeiner succession." Crooked Neck's free hand undulates with the slow and pointed rhythm of his words.

Magnus's eyes narrow to slits. The sentence starts as a whisper. "I'll end the Birkebeiner, if you and Eystein"—"will get out of my way!"

Eystein's face reddens.

"Enough!" Crooked Neck says, yanking his hand from his son's shoulder and slashing the air with it.

Magnus glares at them. Then, fists clenched, he turns and strides out of his father's tent to find Sturelsson.

* * * *

Just before first light, as the attack begins, Magnus and Sturelsson and their sixteen men are on the river bank, on the Lillehammer side. Their main force advances and they watch. The Birkebeiners, never unprepared, have moved their pike traps back to a new trench line and filled the long, narrow trough with spears and pointed sticks driven blunt-end into the snow, leaving sharp tips up to rip the underbelly of mounts and impale fallen riders. Crooked Neck has briefed his men about the pike traps and Magnus's men don't need reminding. Crozier mounted men avoid the long furrow. They reign in their animals well before they reach the final line of wide trenches, but it makes them slow targets for the birch-leg archers. Many fall, but their numbers are so large, it's like losing a few snowflakes in a blizzard. Birch-legs reveal more treachery as a wall of fire erupts from oil-soaked snow in front of their line. More Croziers fall. Still, it makes no difference to the inevitable outcome.

As he abstains from participation in certain victory, Magnus strains to see his father in the melee, wondering if he is among the fallen. "Hoping?" he hears himself say.

"What?" Sturelsson says.

"I said, no hope for the Birkebeiner. We waste time watching. Let's get on with the task." He doesn't look up at Sturelsson, but turns on his skis and the men follow in file. As they cross the river and Magnus hears the gurgle beneath the ice, thoughts return of that day he lost Gudrun and Jorund to the cold waters. He remembers the waves washing over him to lap at his son and the pitiful fear in the boy's cries. He can't help but wonder how he will bring himself to destroy a child who must be like Jorund, the same age he was, perhaps bearing many of the same characteristics. Since he first heard that Hakon Sverrisson's woman had borne him an heir, he knew what must happen, but he never thought it would fall to him to carry out the deed. Truth is, he still hopes someone else swings the sword.

Magnus and his men ski along the bank, listening to the chaos across the river, until they find three sets of tracks into the woods. "Here," Magnus says, turning up the trail and staying in one set of tracks. His men follow.

It isn't long before Sturelsson says, "They must have run like blind rats." He holds up branches snapped off by impact. "How far ahead do you think they are?"

"Assuming they left at the same time as the prisoners we took, a half to three-quarters of a day."

"We'd better increase the pace," Sturelsson says.

"And travel by moonlight, too. Rest only when there is no light at all," Magnus says.

"Will all of us stay together?"

"Only to the trail to the Gudbrans. Then you and half the men will climb over the ridge and travel the Gudbrans Valley until you reach the last of the northern trails back toward the Oster. With luck, you will be waiting there, between the Birkebeiners and Nidaros, when they descend from the plateau. And the rest of us will be behind them, if we haven't already overtaken them."

A smile spreads over Sturelsson's face. "Then the rats will be in a trap they can't escape."

"Don't get overconfident, Sturelsson. They won't yield without a fight. Until we see which way their tracks go, we can't be sure that they aren't following the Gudbrans."

"But nine men against two? And that's only if we fail to close on them at the same time."

Magnus grabs his lieutenant's shoulder, pulls Sturelsson closer, and lowers his voice. "Remember, Skevla has killed a dozen of us in one day. I know little of Skrukka, but Sverrisson wouldn't have sent him unless he's a worthy combatant."

"Yes, but…"

"And don't forget the girl. What's she capable of?" Magnus adds.

"I fear, my lord, that you listen too much to Einar the misshapen. The woman is not an eagle and she is the least of our worries."

A flush comes to Magnus's face and he stops. Sturelsson stops, too. Magnus holds his eyes for several moments without saying anything. Then in a voice that is too much under control, he says, "Just don't underestimate them. It might kill us."

Sturelsson is a good lieutenant. He looks at his commander, but says nothing.

Then, in a tone closer to normal, Magnus says, "We can discuss strategy when we rest. We need to make up half a day. Let's move!"

* * * *

The Croziers maintain a speed so that by midday there are gaps between the men. From the front Magnus can count only twelve within his line of sight. Tree limbs heavy with snow hang low over the trail, narrowing it and blocking his view down the path. Even so, he's sure they've become too spread out, so he tells Sturelsson to stop and they wait for the stragglers. When they catch up, he puts Sturelsson at the rear to keep the ranks close, and eases the pace, but only a bit, since he has no sense of whether they are closing on the Birkebeiners or not. As the sun lingers just above the horizon, at the beginning of that gray period which is neither day nor night, he stops, but motions the men past him until Sturelsson draws even. "Dark soon. First opportunity, let's stop, eat, and rest until moonrise." Sturelsson manages a nod, as if fatigue has stolen his voice.

Skis look heavy on all the men, a burden to their legs. Heads don't even bob, but hang as if tethered to the skis. Before the final flicker of sun, each soldier is spread on his bedroll, guzzling water or rummaging through his pack for food. Over a small fire, several boil lentils, and one turns a shank of mutton on a spit. Heads and eyelids begin to droop as soon as the last morsel disappears. Magnus puts more green wood on top of the dry that is burning, assuring them of warmth until the moon rises. Even with a full stomach and the soothing rhythm of the fire's flicker, he can't sleep, his mind too much on the battle they left behind.

He considers what he would have done if he had seen his father fall. He enjoys imagining that he would return and impale the pompous bishop on his Crozier. Or he would bind him to his blood-soaked bench and help him become intimate with his tool kit. Or better, bind him to his altar to mock his service to God. Yes. Empty the chalice on him, refill it and pour it again until he is covered with the blood of Christ. Then let his candle burn down and ignite him. That's it. Perfect. He would become the Host, roiling up in clouds of smoke, blackened by an abundance of burning suet, as a perfect sacrifice to the Lord he serves with such diligence.

Magnus's fantasy causes him to wonder if he could become Eystein. God, I beg you keep me from that fate. Perverse, Magnus knows, but he feels gratified by the indulgence, relaxed by even the thought of owning that much control over Eystein. Perhaps he can sleep now. Smoky odors left from supper play at his nostrils as his eyelids grow heavy. His own breathing lengthens to the cadence he hears around him. There's no other sound in the forest.

In the western sky, an orange-and-pink smear floats beneath the descending gray that turns light into dark like a snuffer over a candle flame. Inga's hand moves to her face and finds the welts less prominent, but still a reminder of the branches slapping and stinging her skin, and her breathless run for safety.

Saftey? Five, six more days with a ruthless enemy in pursuit, who knows what kinds of weather, terrain to challenge a goat and a limited supply of food—safety has come down to the immediate absence of death.

Light from the sunset filters through a stand of spindly birch trees, lending them a pinkish cast, more like spring flowers than trees surrounded by waist-deep snow. And the snow reflects a similar tint. Fir trees line the west side of the trail and reveal no color, just enough gray contrast to outline their shapes. As Inga lowers her gaze, she sees the snow and the base of the trees become one shade, merge into one mass, and she can't tell where one stops and the other begins. It occurs to her that she is beginning to notice external things again and respond to them. She looks down at the snow sticking to her shoe, then as far ahead as she can see before the trail rounds out of sight. She takes one hand off her *lurk* and wipes some perspiration away from her eye. She looks at her glove, as if it's a new discovery, and shakes her head.

"This is a good place to stop," Torstein says. "We can shake the snow off those birches and build our fire under them." He looks at Skjervald and points across the trail. "Cut some large boughs off those evergreens while Inga and I get the area ready for a fire."

"Enough for beds or beds and shelter?" Skjervald says.

"Both."

Inga can barely see the knife Skjervald pulls from a sheath tied to his waist, and she's amazed how quickly he blends into the shadows among the firs. Even the sounds of his work evaporate, muffled by the thick woods and its snow cover.

"It doesn't feel like it will be too cold tonight," she says.

"Not too," Torstein says. "And once the moon rises we'll be moving again. So all we need is a fire to cook and keep us warm while we get a little rest."

Both of them strip bark from some of the birches, and Torstein finds a dead birch, which he cuts down to salvage the driest of it. After that he cuts limbs from some of the larger trees to add to the fire once it's going. Most of the branches come from the area which will form their shelter, giving them more room. Before they start the fire, they jostle each of the trees within that perimeter so there will be no snow left to fall and bury the flames. Inga puts her back against one of the taller trees and rocks it. When most of the snow falls on top of her, her skis skitter out from under her and she flops onto her back with the skis pointed skyward, snow pelting her face and shoulders. As she sputters and flounders in the soft cascade, Hakon, awake in the sling and watching her as Torstein treads the immediate area to pack it, begins to giggle. Hakon's carrying on alerts Torstein to Inga's ridiculous plight and he begins to chuckle. When Torstein laughs, Hakon shrieks with glee. At that, Inga throws her hands into the air and joins their laughter.

Just then, Skjervald returns with fir boughs cradled in his arms and stacked well above his head. "What's going on?" he asks from behind the load as his ski tips bump into Inga's hip. He pitches forward, covering her with his cargo and then with himself. Lost in laughter, neither Torstein nor Inga can answer him. He adds his voice to the chorus.

Inga's sure, as she lies there, that later she'll say the incident was amusing, but for now it is enough to know that there will be times when she won't cry, on the outside or the inside, and it feels good, if only for an instant. Each of them, like children themselves, forget their burden and their grief for a moment and play in the snow.

Skjervald uses rawhide strips to lash alder branches against birches and shoves boughs between them to form tight walls on three sides. He builds a fire on the fourth side. Skill and experience speed the task and Skjervald is finished before Torstein and Inga finish spreading a pad of boughs to keep them dry and warm as they sleep.

Before long, the sweet smell of the reindeer meat sizzling over the fire reminds them of how hungry they are. All drink from a pot of melted snow and Inga sighs as the cool liquid travels down and she drinks twice more. Torstein and Skjervald eat while Inga drinks and feeds Hakon. The baby sleeps again as soon as he is full and Skjervald shakes his head and says, "Amazing."

"What?" Inga says.

"How he can sleep through all of this."

"And find something to giggle about. As long as he's warm and has a full tummy, he thinks this is fun."

Skjervald nods.

"And thank God," Inga adds, as she strokes the soft blonde curls that creep out of his blanket hood onto his forehead.

"Are you ready for some food?" Skjervald slices off a generous portion of reindeer and offers it on a piece of birch bark.

"*Tusen tuk.*" With her free hand, Inga takes the makeshift plate and sets it beside her, lifting the meat to her mouth. It's too hot, but she doesn't care. It tastes as sweet as it smells. She sucks in air to cool it, and licks a dribble of warm juice before it races away from her tongue and down her chin. Warmth travels the length of her body and hunger retreats.

Torstein has wrapped himself in his bedroll, his feet toward the fire, and appears to sleep. Inga watches Skjervald as he begins to unroll his skins. "Skrukka," she says. "That means 'the short. Skjervald, the short? Why would anyone call you that? You're tall."

"I wasn't always. When I was a boy, I was short and fat. The girls my age called me short, stout Skjeri. They chanted it. Short stout Skjeri, short stout Skjeri." He curls the left side of his mouth in a mock snarl, causing them both to laugh. "I was humiliated to the point of tears."

"What happened?" she says, smiling, but trying to sound sympathetic.

"One summer, I seemed to grow faster than the flowers, but it was too late by then. The 'short' part stuck and here I am, Skjervald Skrukka—Skjervald, the short—forever." He spreads his arms as if to bow in presentation, then growls over a smile.

Inga laughs and says, "Is that why you became such a good soldier?"

He looks down, shy. "No, all I ever wanted to do was get big enough to go back and beat up those girls. Perhaps I tried too hard."

Her laugh makes him laugh. He points to her pack. "Can I unroll your skins for you, so you don't have to put the prince—uh—king down?" He looks away like a child who realizes he has said a bad word.

"That would be a big help," Inga says. Her voice carries too much gratitude. "If you have time, that is." Now she looks elsewhere.

Skjervald unrolls her covers during an awkward silence.

When he's finished, he pats it and says, "Well there, all ready for a nap."

She nods.

"I guess I'll roll up in mine and get a little sleep myself."

"Skjervald?" She says it to stop him, not sure of what she wants to say.

"Yes?"

"Skjervald…I…I'm sorry."

He waves his hand and shakes his head at the same time.

"No. No, let me finish. I'm sorry I got so angry at you."

"No, that's al—"

"And I'm sorry for your loss too. You had no idea. The thought had just never occurred to you that...that Hakon might be..."

"No, it hadn't. It was so overwhelming. A club could not have made my head reel more. I'm sorry I was so clumsy. I didn't think."

"Maybe we should hold hope. God knows I want you to be right."

"I know. I understand now," Skjervald says.

"Friends then?"

"More." His face turns serious, almost grim. "I promise you no one shall harm your child while I live."

"I know. Hakon wouldn't have sent you if it was otherwise."

He smiles a little.

"Good night, Skjervald the tall."

"Good night Inga, King's mother."

* * * *

Inga awakens not sure she's even been asleep. At best, she slept in troubled fits which obliterate the respite of earlier, lighter moods. Moonlight has restored shadows which disappeared at sunset. Since the men are already stirring, Inga assumes they are no better rested than she is. They waste no time getting on the trail. Stiffness and mind fog dissipate as they stretch into their pace. Skjervald and Torstein ski in front of Inga. She listens to their conversation and watches their faces in profile as they turn their heads to talk to each other.

Torstein says to Skjervald, "Before daybreak, we'll come to the trail that goes west to the Gudbrans. Perhaps you should take that path far enough to make the Croziers wonder which route we are taking."

"If I ski up and back, I'll leave two sets of tracks, and if you and Inga continue toward the Oster, they can't be sure which way Hakon has gone until they find where my tracks turn,"

Skjervald says.

"Exactly. And you can prepare a greeting for the Croziers on each trail as you return to us." Torstein emphasizes the word *greeting*. "Be careful not to let them slip between you and us."

"If I hurry, I can lead them a chase they'll remember and be back with you before sunup," Skjervald says. He picks up the pace and pulls away from his companions.

"Godspeed, Skjervald," Inga calls behind him.

Nobody of the men speak as they break camp, perhaps because the prospect of traveling without sunlight is daunting, or perhaps because it's colder now, much colder. Most eat a bit while they pack their gear, knowing they will have little opportunity once they start moving. Magnus slept well after his fancied sacrifice of the bishop and needs Sturelsson to awaken him.

"The men are ready, Magnus."

"Good." He sits up, rubs his eyes, rises and shakes a dusting of snow off his skins. He rolls his bedding, packs his ruck basket and is ready before the others. "Let's go," he says to Sturelsson. "Keep the men close. We'll ski until we reach the cutoff to the Gudbrans."

The pace is slow at first, as they struggle against stiffness. Magnus is soon warm from exertion and relieved that the cold is not as severe as he thought earlier. His stride is strong and consistent.

A man called Olaf One-Ear draws next to him. He has a swarm of straggly red hair that protrudes from a beaver-skin hat and meets an uneven beard of the same color. Magnus can see lines of sweat running from his forehead and disappearing into the beard. Fine hoarfrost covers the area around his mouth and small icicles dangle from matted wisps. His breathing is not too labored to talk. He says to Magnus, "How long do you think it will take us to catch the bastard and his whoring mother?"

"You mean, how long will it be before you can confront Skevla, don't you?"

One-Ear flashes a glance that makes Magnus glad he's the commander and not the reverse. "Why do you say that?"

"Because when someone loses an ear, it's unlikely he has fond feelings for the one who took it," Magnus says.

"Torstein Skevla was lucky that day. This time I will get an ear. And more." One-Ear talks with his jaw set.

"I'm sure you will, but I find it difficult to think of Skevla as lucky. He did worse to many of your comrades that day. They don't call him Torstein the Scrapper because of his talent at milking goats. Don't underestimate him or you may be reunited with your ear before you want to be."

"I'm ready for him." Olaf brandishes his axe as the words hiss through his teeth. He pulls the straps of his woven basket rucksack up higher on his shoulders and strides away from his leader.

Olaf One-Ear is a good soldier. But this is personal. Magnus saw him last summer stop his fishing to pull back his tangled hair and watch the water reflect the scarred and ugly space where his ear used to be. Revulsion was what Magnus expected, but anger was what he saw. A soldier can control strength, stamina and skills when he fights an enemy with no name. When he fights one man he hates, he may try too hard, overexert, forget a long-practiced maneuver and then...Skevla is driven for his cause, not for reprisal, like Olaf. Magnus doubts there is a better soldier than Skevla in either faction. He sacrifices no power in the focused precision of his moves. While the eyes in the front of his head engage his immediate foe, the ones in the back of his head sense the next. Now he protects his best friend's, some say his brother's, son. Erling and Eystein have, by now, killed his friend, his king, and he knows it. Magnus knows Skevla will fight with a singular purpose. He understands Skevla won't let personal vengeance grip his battle-axe. And that makes him very tough, much tougher than poor Olaf, Magnus fears. He decides it would do no good to share these thoughts with One-Ear.

And the woman, Inga. Perhaps she is a woman like any other, but she may also be a soldier or she may be the eagle. Magnus remembers Sturelsson's caution about listening too much to the dwarf prophet, but he recognizes that a female protecting her young can be ferocious. Sverrisson would not stay long with a woman he thought ordinary. Magnus wonders if his men will feel her talons or her sword, or both, before this ends, and he worries that he and his troops pursue three very good soldiers *and* Einar's eagle.

Magnus picks up the pace again and overtakes Olaf, who breathes much harder now. "The sooner we catch them, the sooner this matter ends and you get your ear back."

Inga watches Skjervald until he's out of sight. "He moves like he has wings."

Torstein says, "When I watch him ski, I believe the skis are an extension of him. So smooth and natural, it's as if his feet lengthen at each end."

The image of someone's feet expanding fore and aft and the way Torstein says it, moving his hands from close together to far apart, makes Inga laugh. "I saw his skill for the first time on a hunt and I had the feeling he wasn't exerting. That he didn't need to."

"Most of us can cover twice the ground in a day of winter travel than we can in summer. Skjervald can triple it." Torstein starts to ski again and Inga moves alongside so he can hear her. Their pace is brisk, but they are able to converse.

"You cautioned him about letting the Croziers get between him and us. Do you think they're that close?" Inga asks.

"No. I doubt they started before dawn yesterday, which gives us at least half a day's lead," Torstein says. "Skjervald knows he doesn't have to go very far toward the Gudbrans in order to confuse them. He'll turn in plenty of time to get back to us, and have time left over to create some misery for them."

"He'll be tired though?"

"He's young. The speed will stimulate him. A little food and rest tonight, he'll recover."

"You're right, I guess. I hope. It scares me to think otherwise." After that she hears no sound other than the shushing of skis and the rhythm of her breathing. The terrain is flat and their pace still moderate. There are scrub pines, not much taller than Torstein, along the right side of the trail. Moonlight casts shadows on their left. The ground rises on that side, and in the distance, where the low scrub doesn't block her view, the mountainside shines like a huge lantern burning a candle that yields silver light rather than gold. The beauty is welcoming, but at the same time foreboding, like something you want to touch, but know you shouldn't. Inga remembers her caution to little Hakon when he went near the fire in the *stue*. He knew he shouldn't touch it, but she could see he was drawn to it. Whether or not she wishes to be, and regardless of the apprehension it instills, the glowing snowfield on that peak draws her.

As the moonlight merges with the gray of dawn, Torstein says, "If the sky stays clear, we'll have nights with light like this for the rest of our journey."

"So will they." Inga says it like a challenge.

"Except that moonrise is later each night. The timing could have an influence."

"I don't follow."

"Going up the mountain and across the snowfield plateau, it doesn't matter when the moon rises. But once we're on the descent to the Gudbrans, having light will be a distinct advantage," Torstein says.

"And not having it?" Inga asks.

"Have you ever been there?"

"No."

"You'll understand when you experience it."

"Can you tell me?"

"The climb is steep, treacherous in places, and the snowfields on top stretch as far as you can see. There are timber huts across the plateau, as well as on the trail on both sides of the mountain."

"How'd they get there?" Inga says.

"People crossing between the two valleys put them up to shelter travelers. The *Lagtings* established laws for use and maintenance. Most wayfarers adhere to the spirit, since it's in their interest to keep them in good repair. Many summer days Hakon and I would carry timbers from below the tree line to use for repairs or to store as firewood."

"Hakon's been there?"

"Often."

She's on a trail he's crossed and will come in contact with things he's built, things he's touched. It will be the first time since Inga left Lillehammer that she'll see anything of his other than their son.

Inga's face must betray her thoughts, because Torstein says, "I'm sorry. Will it pain you to see a place where he's been?"

"I hope not. I need to think about him to...to keep him close," Inga says.

"Do you know he told me how you met?"

She turns and looks at him full in the face. "You mean when he visited Borg to see my father?"

"*Ja*."

Borg is so small. She remembers that Hakon called it a *bo*. She laughed and protested that it wasn't that small a village. She doesn't suppose, though, he would ever have visited except that her father is the *Lagting* representative from the district that makes up their *Ting*.

Torstein continues. "Hakon said he could not imagine Borg could contain anything of interest to him beyond Varteig's voice at the regional *Lagting*."

"Oh?" Inga raises her eyebrows.

"But that was before he got there. When I saw him afterwards, he said he would have to return soon because he'd found Valhalla and she was tall and slender with gold locks worth more than a treasury of metal the same color. And green eyes that wouldn't leave him alone when he was away from them. And skin, that if he could touch it but once, he would never want for another thing."

"That's what he told me when he came back the following spring to ask my father if I could leave with him." A tear runs down her cheek and she watches it drop to her ski and freeze. "I was barely of age, but I wanted to go more than anything I could imagine. I was excited when father gave his consent."

For a few moments they don't speak. Inga knows she should drop back and step into his tracks to conserve her energy, but the conversation is somehow soothing, something she needs right now. She looks up toward the plateau again and the reminder of the daunting task ahead makes her think she should be more prudent, so she starts to drop back.

Perhaps a slack moment is something Torstein needs, too, because he speaks again. "You made him very happy, Inga. It troubled him that he and you couldn't exchange your vows in the Church."

"I know, but I understood it was because of Eystein. It has served the bishop's purpose well to call our son a bastard. But I believe Hakon and I had a stronger bond for it." Inga pauses as the wind gusts and a tree creaks against it. It's the first time she's aware of anything more than a breeze. She shivers and wonders if it's the cold or emotion that causes it. "I hope," she says, stutters and starts again. "I hope I didn't hurt him by... you know...with my decision to leave with the baby. I didn't want to leave him when he needed me."

Torstein shakes his head. "Hakon knew your child would need you more." He pauses as if he remembers something important. Something he wants to repeat with accuracy. "When he returned from that trip to Borg, he didn't speak just of your eyes. He said 'she has spirit and the mind to go with it.' "

Inga looks down the trail while she visits with those memories. They ski on in silence for a while, until they come to a fork, one trail continuing north and the other heading west. The trails are of equal width, but she can see that the one to the west begins to climb. They stop. "Is this the first trail to the Gudbrans?" she asks.

"*Ja*. See Skjervald's tracks?" Torstein doesn't wait for an answer. "When he returns, he'll step into my tracks, so the Croziers will discover two sets instead of three."

"And those two sets will go in both directions."

Torstein nods. "Croziers won't be able to tell who went

which way." A smile creeps across his face. He doesn't linger with it, but increases the pace.

Torstein lets Inga go ahead of him and they ski single file for a long time, each with their own thoughts. Dawn's glow illuminates what the moon lit a short time ago. Inga looks up again toward the ground she will tread. Instead of silver, now it's a wall of green and white, except near the top, where the white is dominant. She can see wind swirling billows of snow and hopes it's not blowing that hard when they get there. She stares at it and slows till Torstein is beside her. "You know, he talked much of you, too."

"We're good friends." Torstein says.

"More than that, he told me. And I've heard the lore, too."

"Don't believe everything you hear." He's intent on looking straight ahead.

"He said you had a claim to accession if you wanted to exercise it. Sverri was your father too, wasn't he?" Inga watches his eyes. They refuse to stray from the trail.

"Some say it."

"But you don't?"

Finally Torstein turns and looks at her.

At first, Inga thinks his expression is a challenge.

"What point would it serve? Hakon is...was a great leader. And like a brother to me, whether we shared a father or not. I had no desire to be king and no desire to claim Sverri if he did not claim me."

For the first time in her life, she understands the fine line between friendship and resolute loyalty. "You could not have been a better, truer friend."

They return to single file and listen again to the rhythmic shushing of their skis. They cover a lot of ground before Torstein says, "Let's stop long enough to eat and drink. Give Skjervald a chance to catch us. "

They stop and Inga feeds Hakon, who hasn't made a sound through the night. He feels so good against her. "You look like your father," she says, as she looks down at his profile.

Torstein builds a small fire, melts snow for them to drink, and then mixes some meal and lentils with the water that is left. It doesn't have much taste, but it fills Inga and she feels less tired. Still, she yearns to close her eyes for a full night's sleep. She squeezes the muscles in both of her calves, then presses the heels of her palms into the small of her back several times.

Just as Torstein begins to douse the fire with snow, Inga hears something. She looks down the trail in the direction they came from.

Torstein straightens over the fire. His body tenses. He turns his head so that his ear faces down the trail and pulls his battle-axe from where it hangs on his waist. Rising, Inga opens her mouth to speak, but a finger of Torstein's free hand goes to his lips, signaling silence. "Take the baby and go," he hisses. "Don't stop until I call you."

Leaving her pack where it sits, she scurries away from the sounds, Hakon over her shoulder with the blanket around him instead of slung. Her breathing turns short and raspy. She tells herself to take deep breaths, and forces her scrambling stride into a rhythm. Hakon whimpers, his meal abruptly snatched away. "It's all right. *Mamma* and Hakon are going to play now. We're going to ski real fast and then eat some more. Will you like that?"

"*Mamma* play with Hakon?"

"Yes, baby." Don't stop, Inga, she tells herself. Don't let them catch you. She manages to get the blanket from around Hakon. The knot is still in it so she can sling it over her shoulder and put him back in it while she flees. Still the right length for Torstein, it hangs low on her and is awkward, but better than trying to keep the child over her shoulder. She puts the baby in and twists the sling twice to shorten it. Now she has both hands free, giving her more rhythm and speed.

Inga doesn't know how close they are. She doesn't dare look back. Her head is forward, her eyes on the ground in front of her. She sets her jaw and settles into a level of exertion she can sustain. She has stayed with Hakon and Torstein and Skjervald on skis. "No Crozier is going to catch me," she whispers.

"Fast, *Mamma*, go fast," Hakon says.

She still hears sounds behind her, but they're no closer. *Stay within yourself.* Still, she pushes her limits and battles the feeling that she's going to drop to her knees and wretch. She fights for each breath now, without the satisfaction of getting a full one. The front of her thighs burn and Hakon bounces against her stomach in rhythm with her strides, increasing the feeling of nausea.

Inga's not sure how far she's gone, but she has run since dawn and there is full light now. First, the sounds seem closer. Then they take form. She hears her name.

"Inga!" Then, "Inga, stop! It's me, Skjervald."

She must be imagining it and pays no heed.

Closer now. "Inga! It's us! You're all right. Stop!"

Despite her fear, Inga risks a look, turning her head in time with the backswing of her arm. On the next stride she leaps into the air, skis and all. When she comes down, she turns and drops to her knees, arms outstretched. It is, thank God, Skjervald just rounding the last bend in the trail, and behind him, Torstein. Her legs burn and go weak. She pulls Hakon to her and hugs him, disguising her sobs as she gasps for air. She hears their skis, and soon after, feels Skjervald and Torstein's comforting hands on her back.

"By Odin's sword, woman," Torstein wheezes "I thought Skjervald was fast."

Inga looks up into his strain-contorted face and smiles. She looks to Skjervald, who appears equally beaten, and begins to laugh. They lift her to her feet and the three almost crush Hakon with their hugs. He giggles at the new game.

His breathing more controlled now, Torstein says, "That's the last time I'll tell you to keep going till I stop you. Next time we hear them, we'll stand and fight. Easier to stop the Croziers than it is to stop you."

That makes her laugh and she turns toward Skjervald. "Skjervald, I'm so glad you're back safe."

"Glad, maybe," he smiles, "but I'll wager you saved me no breakfast." He hands her the *lurk* and rucksack she abandoned.

After a rest to eat and drink, the four of them continue. Torstein is carrying Hakon and the child is in a playful mood. He reaches up and tugs at Torstein's beard, trying to draw some attention. Torstein pokes and tickles his ribs, but can do little else to keep him occupied. Rays from the brightest sun they've seen since leaving Lillehammer filter through pines and bare branches of winter.

"It's colder," Inga says.

"Clear skies bring the cold. By tonight, we may need a big fire," Skjervald says. "The good thing is that if the skies stay this clear, the full moon will give us all the light we need, but..."

"What?" Inga says.

"I'm afraid we may see snow by this time tomorrow," Skjervald answers.

"How do you know?"

"Something I've observed on long hunts. Usually, if it gets cold and skies clear, clouds will come from the west a day or so later. If the sky is red tomorrow at sunrise, we'll get snow."

Inga pulls in her chin and squints at him..

"Wait and see," Skjervald says.

"Torstein, does that mean we'll be climbing to the plateau in a snowstorm?" Inga asks.

"If not, we'll be crossing it. If it's a bad storm, we'll fashion a snow cave and wait it out, or find one of the huts." Torstein looks at Skjervald. "Did you leave our Crozier friends some trail memories?"

"Two, actually. Nothing fancy, just a reminder of how much we admire them."

"Good."

Skjervald now sets the pace. Fast for Inga, but she's sure he's well within himself. He never looks back, but each time she begins to struggle, the pace slows a little.

At dusk, they gather lots of firewood, dig a shelter out of snow that has banked against a thicket, and line it with pine boughs. While Inga feeds Hakon, Skjervald cooks some meal, lentils and *røkt laks* over a large fire in front of the dugout. Eating takes time, as they have to keep putting their food back over the fire. A few bites and it's cold and will freeze if they don't re-warm it. After dinner, water thrown to the snow freezes on contact.

Torstein tosses on all the wood he can, and they put Inga's bedroll under the four of them and two sets of furs over them, huddling close to share body heat. At first, Inga fears the proximity might keep her awake, but she's weary. Next thing she knows, Torstein is shaking her back into consciousness, and she's staring at a bright full moon through the fog of her frozen breath.

Dawn has come and gone before Magnus and his men reach the Birkebeiner campsite. Skjervald's shelter is still intact. Not a wisp of smoke rises from the campfire. Magnus skis to it, kneels and bares his hand to feel its remains. The ashes are cold as the snow. Magnus looks at the packed area within the shelter, at the fir woven into the alder frame, and knows his quarry didn't suffer much from the cold wind. He looks at the tracks that wind north on the narrow trail and rise toward the plateau. His eyes follow the tracks to the first turn through the pines, near a stand of spindly white birch bent low over the trail by the weight of snow. Magnus turns his head toward the plateau. Morning sun reflects from its white edges. The snow cap is still a thin outline across the top of the forest, but it looks close enough to touch. Magnus doesn't let the illusion fool him. He knows the climb ahead is tough, for him and for the enemy.

Sturelsson arrives while Magnus is still kneeling. "Are we close?" Each word is accompanied by a foggy puff of breath. The neck of his parka is covered with enough frozen sweat to brush away.

"No," Magnus says, as the others gather. "We've gained little."

One-Ear grinds his teeth and glances about to see if he convinces anyone of his disappointment. He picks at icicles dangling from his thick eyebrows. Per Ingersson, a broad-chested, thick-limbed veteran of many battles says, "We'll have to hurry if we're to reach the Gudbrans trail before sunset."

Magnus knows Ingersson is familiar with the routes to the north. "We'll eat on the move then. A short rest to heat water and we go. Break out what you need."

Sturelsson nods and the men are quick about removing their packs and finding food. They sit back-to-back at the wooded edge of the trail, trying to reduce contact with a persistent wind that grows stronger. As soon as they finish drinking, they resume the trek at a faster pace than before. Sturelsson and Ingersson begin pushing the tempo, pulling some of the others with them. Now Magnus senses genuine urgency amongst the men. Even Olaf is beginning to convince him.

Magnus kneads the tops of his thighs each chance he gets. He can tell by his men's breathing and the amount of hoarfrost accumulating on beards, eyebrows and loose hair that they are working hard, pushing to cut their quarry's lead. For the first time the men's efforts look efficient, expended energy producing speed. Not a soldier lags. Each one exhibits determination to stay with the others. Only the sharpest twist in the trail causes the last man to lose sight of the first.

The Croziers begin taking turns at the front, letting the leader pack the Birkebeiners' tracks, so that each man in the order has a firmer, faster trail than the one in front of him. They close ranks. Each time another man assumes the lead, the pace accelerates for a period and the prior leader relaxes and falls to last, giving himself just enough respite to resume full stride and work his way back up front for his next turn. Magnus knows the Birkebeiners can't duplicate this efficiency because there are only three of them. The soldiers force themselves to finish their food, trying to chew and breathe at the same time without gagging. A handful of snow scooped from the ground or swept from a protruding limb staves off thirst.

Ingersson drops off his rotation in the lead, and grunts in Magnus's direction. "We're using a lot of energy."

"But wasting none," Magnus replies.

"Uh."

There's nothing Magnus can add to that and neither of them has breath to spare. Magnus is concerned that it's beginning to get dark, but he's aware there is only a short distance to the cutoff. As he takes the lead again he says, "We'll stop at the fork." Magnus hears the men pass it back. It gives them one last surge of energy, something they didn't know they had left. His own intensity is such that he doesn't notice the trail or its surroundings. One thing he can't ignore is the sun's reflection off the distant plateau. He knows that is where they'll close in on the Birkebeiners and where he will determine his relevance or damage his soul, or both.

Before Magnus can drop back again, they reach the Gudbrans trail. There's still enough light to see the sharp rise in the terrain to the west. Now he can see the tree line where the snowfield begin. Magnus raises his hand and hears a collective gasp as the men stop, lean on *lurks* or spears or trees and draw as much air as they can. As his own breathing returns to normal, he turns and looks at them. Fog, eerie as a morning mist, rises from each one as their bodies cool. Framed in the diminishing light, this hazy cloak makes them look like beings in a dream, not quite human, but not fearsome or savage either.

"We'd better get to our fires and dry our clothing," says Sturelsson, noticing the same thing. "When the fires are going, build your shelters. Then we'll eat."

Surprising energy and enthusiasm renew as the soldiers perform their tasks and it isn't long before they're wrapped in their bedrolls and sitting close to several large, hot fires, bellies full and thirsts quenched. Scarecrows dance close to the flames as vests, footwear, and *vadmel* shirts dry on sticks and hastily constructed racks. The sweaty stench from drying wool mixes with the lingering smells of cooked meat and *røkt laks*.

"Phew," says Sturelsson, "any animals that might be attracted by the meat smell will be discouraged from approaching by whatever died in your shirt, Olaf."

One-Ear, feigning offense, retorts, "Whatever died in my shirt, Sturelsson, was killed by inhaling your shoes."

Men already laughing at Sturelsson's remark laugh all the harder, inserting 'oohs' and 'aws' in recognition of blows landed and parried.

"Sturelsson's shoes didn't kill your shirt. They were trying to escape it and got sucked in," says another, evoking more participation from the rest.

On they go like that, in good spirits, until they exhaust an abundant supply of barbs and banter. Then Sturelsson says to no one in particular, "Clothing aside" he holds his nose. "what did you draw from the diverging sets of tracks at the fork?"

"You mean that two sets go in each direction?" says Ingersson.

Sturelsson nods.

"That two of the birch-legs went one way and two the other," Olaf says.

"Dolt, there are only three of them!" Sturelsson says.

Everyone laughs and One-Ear turns red, throws his birch bark plate at the fire, and mumbles something the others can't hear.

Sturelsson answers his own question. "It means that they are trying to confuse us, make us wonder who went what way."

"Which means they are all continuing together," Ingersson says.

"Yes, but which way?" Sturelsson says.

"We won't know until we find a set of tracks that reverses," Ingersson says.

"So they're making sure we have to split our pursuit," Magnus says.

"But we were going to do that anyway," Olaf says. He still mumbles, as if not confident he has a valid observation.

"Right," Magnus says.

One-Ear looks up, snaps off a nod, and reaches for his shirt.

Magnus continues. "So if they didn't do it to split us, then why?"

One Ear, checking his shirt for the smallest wet spot, doesn't reply, so Magnus leaves him with a small victory and answers himself. "Two reasons. First, to keep us from knowing before we split, who of us is following *them*, and who is following no one."

"To what end?" Sturelsson interrupts. He slices a piece of mutton from the spit and gnaws on it.

Magnus holds out his hand and his lieutenant hacks off a piece for him while he answers. "To force us to form two strategies, one for the pursuing group and one for the intercepting group. And we don't have the opportunity to coordinate those strategies since we won't know for half a day which is which."

"You said there are two reasons. What's the second?"

Magnus starts to take a bite, but pauses with the mutton halfway to his mouth, "To slow us down."

"Traps?" Sturelsson says.

"With that thought, will you ski as fast as we did today or will you be more cautious?" Magnus asks.

Sturelsson puts a thumb and forefinger over the bridge of his nose for a moment and says, "So whether they have left a snare or not, the possibility slows us?"

Magnus shrugs. "Depends on our attitude." He looks around at the group.

Blank stares respond.

"Either we concede their escape by slowing and checking every bend and dip in the trail, or..." He shrugs.

"Or?" Three of them say it at the same time.

"Or we proceed as we did today, each taking a short turn at the point, and hope they haven't had time to build any effective device."

"Giving each of us a one in eighteen chance of being at the front at the wrong time," Sturelsson says.

"One in nine," Magnus answers. "We'll split into two groups and there can be a trap in either or both directions. Or more."

Jaws that are busy chewing stop. Hands lifting drink or fumbling with drying clothes hover in midair. The only sound is the crackling of the fire. No one looks at anyone else.

Sturelsson breaks the din of silence. "Catch them." His opinion cast, he circles the group with his eyes. Each man nods in turn. One-Ear hesitates, but conforms.

Magnus says, "Let's sleep, then. We need to make up time when the moon rises."

Half the force—Gunnar, Jorund the Quiet, Thorgeir Hullisson, Vegeir, Bork the Stout, Bjarni Flat-Nose, Grim No-Hair, and Hrolf Thorisson—prepares to leave with Sturelsson. A bright moon lights their way across the foothills toward the Gudbrans Valley. Ingersson, Olaf One-Ear, Sveinn, Ulf, Egil the Thin, Askell, Lars Nellsson, and Thorvald Ericsson will follow Magnus farther into the Oster. The groups face each other as they mount their skis.

Magnus presents the strategy. "Follow the snowfields across the top all the way to the Gudbrans Valley. Then follow the valley north until you reach the northern most trail coming from the Oster," Magnus says. "If the weather is good, you should reach there well before they do."

"Assuming they follow the Oster," Sturelsson says.

"Assume that. You'll know if you see that there is one set of tracks that returns here. Put yourselves across the valley trail, so they'll descend from the plateau right into you. Then do what you must, but don't harm the woman."

Sturelsson's look makes Magnus regret that he said the last, but all the lieutenant says is, "What if we are delayed?"

"Stick to the plan. We'll be closing from behind. It'll be perfect if we can pinch them between us as we follow them off the mountain."

"And if they have taken this trail to the Gudbrans?" Sturelsson cocks his head toward the trail his men will follow.

"Then you're the pursuer," Magnus says. "If we get to the top and see no sign of them or you, we'll descend the most northern trail and hope to intercept them with you at their heels. Under any circumstance, they mustn't slip through. One of us must get between them and Nidaros." Raising his voice, Magnus says, "Two sheep and a ram to the one of you who brings me Skevla's axe." He pauses for a moment and adds, looking at Olaf, "And his ear."

One-Ear's jaw muscles tense and he tightens his grip on his own axe. "In less than two days we will have them."

Magnus thinks that's optimistic, but doesn't say so.

"What about the child," one of the men asks.

Magnus stays silent as all their eyes come back to him. He doesn't avoid looking at his men, but he delays until someone has to speak. "While we travel, keep in the rotation," he says. "Don't overexert. We'll close on them faster that way." He pauses a long time, long enough to look at each man. "Is anyone unclear on our pursuit strategy?"

One by one, every soldier responds by checking his bindings or footwear or by studying the ground around his feet.

"Good. We have to catch them before we can do anything."

Frigid air has made the snow hard and abrasive. All of them know that this will reduce glide and increase exertion. Each has wrapped his face and spread tallow on any exposed skin. Some toes and fingers will blacken and die before daylight. Necessity is the only reason to travel tonight, and Magnus knows some will pay a price.

Ingersson comes forward for his turn as Magnus drops back. "Bitter," Ingersson says.

"Have adequate protection on your hands and feet." Magnus makes sure his tone is more warning than advice.

Ingersson replies, "So far I'm good, but if we stop..."

"We can't stop. Not till the sun warms the air," Magnus says.

"And it may not," Ingersson says.

"Storm?"

"I fear."

As Magnus drops to the rear, he asks each man about his extremities.

Only Thorvald Ericsson, the man behind One-Ear,

complains of any problem. "Thumb and forefinger on my left hand," he says.

"Just cold?"

"Can't feel them."

"Carry your spear in your right hand for a while and swing your left in a circle over your head. Then tuck it inside your vest until the feeling returns." Ericsson does it. Magnus reminds himself to check him later, certain the soldier has more pain to come. For the sake of pursuing a child who has yet to see his third spring, some of his men will die and others lose...who knows what. He wonders why he shouldn't turn back, kill Eystein and strike a treaty with Sverrisson. "Ha." He says it loud enough that Ericsson turns his head and looks at Magnus as if he wants him to repeat it. Magnus waves him off and thinks, I don't do it, I suppose, because I would have to kill my father too.

* * * *

For a moment Magnus remembers his fifth birthday, when Crooked Neck signed the pact with Eystein to bless the boy's ordination and promise his *Kroning*. Since that jubilant coronation, Crooked Neck has obsessed over the unification of the monarchy with his son on the throne.

"You are the one to unite Norway, the only one," he told Magnus. "You must be the one, true and only king." It was Magnus's birthday message each year, and most days in between.

So often since Eystein lowered that crown onto his head, Magnus has wished he had the ordinary torments of men to grow weary of, like the nagging of a wretched wife or a festering skin disease, instead of this millstone of succession that he carries. Besides, he assures himself, Sverrisson is already dead.

Each time Magnus is with Eystein and his father, they talk about how Sverrisson and his bastard child must die. In the fall, before they began the siege at Lillehammer, the three of them dined with a few of their most trusted lieutenants. The conversation turned, as always, to the topic of extermination of the Birkebeiner and, in particular, their leaders.

"We show them too soft a hand," Eystein said, his jowls quivering with conviction.

"Not by design, Your Eminence," Crooked Neck said, his throat bulging more than usual with the strain of being on the defensive. "They are loathe to stand and fight, preferring to take their toll in snatches, using ambush and harassing attacks as the pillars of their strategy. Three days ago, a group of no more than fifteen of the beggars killed twelve of Magnus's men," he ticked his head in his son's direction, "as they traveled the road to Oslo."

"Magnus had two hundred mounted troops. Why didn't he pursue and obliterate the drooling bunch of them?" Eystein said.

Eystein spoke to his father as though Magnus wasn't there. Magnus maintained his expression as if it were carved in stone. Before Erling could answer, Magnus intervened. "The woods are too thick there to penetrate on horseback. Had we dismounted and pursued on foot, they would have picked off more of us at opportune spots that they know and we don't. For all we knew they had a larger force waiting for us to leave our mounts so they could rush out of cover, kill the guards and help themselves to the horses and any weapons left on them."

Eystein said nothing, but the mockery in his look would have caused the bishop's death, were he anyone else.

"I see that Your Excellency is not familiar with conditions at that point along the way to Oslo," Magnus said.

"What I do know," the bishop said, face red and eyes angry, "is that we need two things in order to unify Norway: the demise of Sverrisson and his lone descendant, and a courageous and innovative leader to become the one true king when that happens."

Before the last word left Eystein's mouth, Magnus started. "Courage and innovation flow from…"

His father interrupted. "From the spiritual leadership and forthright intervention on our behalf to God, which only Your Eminence can provide."

Eystein seemed to like that, and deferred further comments.

* * * *

A jagged scream breaks Magnus's thoughts, a scream so horrible and convulsive, he knows it can mean only one thing, somebody is dead or soon will be. He races for the front of the pack, where others have already gathered around a soldier who is draped over a birch sapling that angles across the path. It's Lars Nellsson. His left arm hangs limp on the other side of the tree from his body, and his right hand grasps the trunk in a feeble and useless attempt to push it away from him. An ugly, sharpened bolt of wood protrudes from his torso. Blood runs down the front of the shaft and pulses from his back where the point exits. The front of the spike is lashed across the stem of the birch where it would be centered as it whipped across the path. Two more barbs flank the one through Nellsson. Either would have impaled him if he had been more to the right or left. The springy trunk, which hung low in the trail in its relaxed state had been flexed forward until it was parallel with the trailside. A trip line buried just beneath the snow held the trap in place until Ingersson, skiing just ahead of Nellsson, skied into it.

Poor Nellsson's head rotates in agony as he emits a slow, gurgling groan. In the moonlight, they can see froth around his mouth that would be red if there was more light. Before any of them can do anything, his whole body shudders and a column of blood spews from his mouth and he hangs limp.

There's not a word for several moments.

"Would that *Odin's* sword take all the birch-leg vermin," Ingersson yells.

Magnus puts his hand on Ingersson's shoulder. "He was

your friend. I'm sorry."

"What will I tell his wife? She's with child, their first. He was about to take his turn at the front. A few more strides and he would have sprung the trap on me or Olaf, instead of me on him."

"Or it would have gotten both of you as you dropped back even with him." Magnus grabs one of the other spikes to illustrate his point. "It isn't your fault you were where you were or that he was where he was. Remember, we thought something like this might happen to the leader, not the second in line."

Ingersson nods and hangs his head. Magnus hears another oath under Ingersson's breath.

Two men hold the sapling tight while One-Ear and Magnus pull Nellsson from his death snare. They bury him as deep in the snow as possible, hoping that the coyotes won't get to him until after he freezes. That way there might be something left to take home on their return.

They push on and Magnus falls in at the rear, thinking perhaps he should worry less about what Eystein says.

Inga has known since childhood that numbing cold and its brothers and sisters of winter, snow and ice, are the seasonal companions of the Norwegian people. Her parents taught her, and their parents taught them, and it has been that way for as long as the old have taught the young. Inga, and her family before her, learned to cope with winter, even enjoy it, except in its most vicious moods.

"Keep one of the bedrolls open," Torstein says "so I can line Hakon's sling with it. Tonight, he'll need the extra insulation."

"Even my bedroll won't fit," Inga says "not and leave any room for the baby."

Torstein nods, and tightens his lips in thought. He takes off his bear-skin parka and the beaver-skin vest under it. He takes Hakon, already wrapped in a *vadmel* blanket and his own small bearskin, and layers on the vest. "That should hold him," he says as he puts his coat back on.

Hakon says, "You play with me Tors'?"

"We're playing animals, and you're a bear that just got eaten by a beaver." He arches his eyebrows and sticks out his tongue, while he pokes a finger in Hakon's ribs. It makes the boy laugh out loud.

"What sound does a bear make, Hakon?"

Hakon looks puzzled.

"Rooaar," says Torstein, holding his hands up next to his head in an imitation of bear paws.

"Rooaar," Hakon mimics.

"Won't you get cold?" Inga asks Torstein.

Torstein puts a finger in front of his face. He takes her bedroll and throws it up over his shoulders so it falls over his pack in back. With a leather thong, he ties two corners of the fur together at his neck so it hangs like a cape. He puts the blanket sling around his neck. He pulls a corner of the fur cape up from his feet and drapes the bottom of it into the cradle of the sling. He holds the sling open. "In you go, Your Majesty."

"Wonderful," Inga says, as she sees what he plans, and puts Hakon into the fur-lined carrier. Then she pulls the other edge of the bedroll cloak up and through the sling, covering Hakon except for a small breathing space. Torstein now has the fur wrapped all the way around. Inga's hand probes the breathing space, pushing the fur back so Torstein and she can see Hakon's face. He beams an opened-mouthed smile, delighted at the prospect of yet another game.

Torstein presses a finger to the tiny nose. "We're snug as can be." Hakon laughs and Inga closes some of the hole again. Torstein looks at her. "This will allow enough air to circulate, so I don't overheat and both of us can stay warm. Are you warm?"

"Not right now, but I will be once we get moving."

"Skjervald?"

"I'm fine, but like Inga says, we dare not stop."

"Anybody feels a hint of frostbite, let me know. Won't take long to build a fire," Torstein says. "Once the sun is up, perhaps it'll warm."

"Will we get to the plateau before sunset?" Inga asks.

"Doubt it. Lots of climbing between here and there."

Winter elements have conspirators in the terrain. "Is it as difficult a climb as the one you and Hakon and I did when we hunted reindeer?"

"Harder."

So they start. Exertion melts icy thorns of cold pricking at hands and feet. Each time they stop, those thorns will reclaim extremities thawed by effort. Keeping a balance between fatigue and warmth will require good judgment today. Stop too often or too long, and they run the risk of freezing toes or hands or more. If they overtire, the body won't have the energy to warm itself, even in motion. "Torstein, what happens if we stop to build fires? Will they be doing the same?" Inga says.

"If they don't, they're going to get tired or cold, or both."

"Which is better for us?"

"If they have as much ground to make up as I think, I hope they try to do it without warming and resting. It'll cost them in the long run," Torstein says.

"And if they're closer than you think?"

"Then our stops put us at risk of being overtaken."

Inga doesn't say anything. Every time she begins to feel the least bit confident of seeing Nidaros and safety, something unanticipated happens. The weather turns bad, the hills get steeper and the snow deeper, they don't have time to eat, drink or sleep enough. Whenever she and the men consider their situation, the assessment ranges from disaster to the thinnest knife-edge of survival. Determination is the closest they come to optimism.

Inga can't escape her fears for her child's safety or her grief for his father. What keeps her from bogging down in a quagmire of worry is that she told him nothing would happen to their son while she breathes. She embraces the memory of that pledge. It's the best she can do.

"We'll go as long as we can," Torstein says.

Skjervald nods.

"*Ja,*" Inga says.

* * * *

By sunrise, Inga is leaning into the tips of her skis.

"We're beginning the climb," Skjervald says. "Is the pine tar gripping when you press the camber down, or do you want me to put more on?"

"Mine are good," Torstein says.

"Until just now, I wasn't aware of the slope. How long before we need the climbing skins?" Inga says.

"It doesn't get much steeper than this for a while. Let me

know when you start slipping," Skjervald says.

She's aware of feeling the center of her skis gripping the snow as she puts her weight on them. Skjervald has done a skillful job with the pine pitch, giving each ski enough adhesion to avoid slipping backward, but not so much that it keeps her from sliding the other ski forward with little resistance. She doesn't think the Croziers are as skillful. She hopes not. She reminds herself again not to fret. She'll need her mind as much as her body.

"Anybody cold?" Torstein says. "Hands, feet? We can have a fire going before we cool off, and rest long enough to eat."

"Let me go ahead," says Skjervald. "I can have a fire going when you arrive."

"Are you warm enough to wait, Inga?" Torstein asks.

"Sounds like a good idea. I'm fine for a while."

Skjervald's long, graceful strides conceal the power necessary to push up the hill. Torstein and Inga maintain their pace, and Hakon sleeps. Not much time passes before Torstein points and says, "Smoke. Our fire tender is just ahead."

Waves of heated air above leaping orange flames make the trail beyond look even steeper. Looking up through the distortion causes the new sun to ripple as if reflected off the *fjord*. The image warms Inga while she's still too far away to feel the heat. When they reach the fire, mitts, shoes, coats and vests come off, the smaller items set to roost on the sticks Skjervald has pushed into the snow close to the flame.

"Good job, Skjervald," Inga says, as she revels in the warmth. She watches tiny streams of vapor rise from the gloves. The fire is so hot that it carries away the smell of drying sweat.

"I was lucky. Someone left a large stack of well-dried wood right here. I suppose most travelers would stop here to camp and rest before assaulting the long, steep terrain."

Warm now, Inga gets up and starts back down the trail.

"Where're you going?" Skjervald asks.

"I've got to wash my ski bindings."

"Wash your ski...."

"Skjervald," she says, rolling her eyes.

"Oh. Hurry back."

"On a day like this? I won't be long." Both men laugh.

When she returns the two men are playing with Hakon, one sweeping him up in the air and passing him to the hands of the other.

"Look, Torstein, it's Hakon the hawk," says Skjervald, careful not to release his grip until Torstein's hands are in place.

"Look how high he flies," says Torstein, while Hakon howls his delight.

Inga glows, and whispers a prayer for these two men who keep some boyhood in their hearts.

They drink the rest of the water and finish the hominy of meal Inga has mixed. She's about to throw snow on the fire.

"No, don't," Torstein says. "Throw the rest of the wood on instead."

"Why?"

"Because you'll get your hands cold putting out the fire, and burning the rest of the fuel deprives our pursuers of it, and if tonight a few smoldering embers make them think they're closer to us than they are, maybe they'll waste energy."

"Or better yet, maybe they'll relax," Skjervald says.

They toss the rest of the logs on the fire.

"That'll burn most of the day," Skjervald says "and they may really need that wood by the time they get here."

"Why do you say it that way?" Inga asks.

He nods toward the east, and she looks around. The sky is a vibrant rose.

Open-mouthed, she snaps her head back around to face him.

His eyebrows are arched, and he nods once, confirmation, not swagger.

Why does one death unnerve me when I have seen so many? Magnus keeps asking himself that question, unable to suppress visions of Nellsson's horrific death. All he can do is order the men to bury their comrade in the snow and help them console one another. Vehement oaths that followed Nellsson's impalement have died away, and the men move along without words. Magnus makes it a point to ski abreast of each one for a while. Expressions range from anger to gloom. Magnus's legs feel weak as he struggles to pull alongside Ingersson.

"Snow's slow," Ingersson says, looking over at Magnus.

"Glad I'm not the only one who feels it. Perhaps we're both carrying Nellsson."

Ingersson draws a deep breath and releases it in a sigh. "Before that stake punched through his body, I felt strong. All of us did. I've lost friends before, but always in battle. Even if I saw one of them fall, I could fight on. My legs stayed under me until the fighting ended. Last night, when I heard Nellsson's scream, my strength deserted me. Still hasn't returned."

"Maybe we gird ourselves for the worst when we face battle," Magnus says "not with just helmets, mail and shields to protect our bodies, but with weapons to protect our minds."

Ingersson gives him an odd look, somewhere between confusion and doubt.

"Sounds strange, but think," Magnus says. "Don't you anticipate, before you run into combat, that some will die?"

Ingersson nods.

"Don't you hope it's not you?"

"Not like that, no." He pauses as they look at one another.

"You don't hope that you won't die when you go into

battle?" Magnus feels the ice crack on his brow as he arches it. At the same time he thinks of Eystein and how, never facing battle, he can order men into the fray without a thought. He doesn't care if the force is at full strength as long as he knows he's beyond the range of arrows and spears. At least Magnus's father understands what it is to be a soldier. Magnus can admire the soldier in him, but not in Eystein. Never in Eystein. There's no soldier there. Never known the longing to return to a family. Who would have him? Magnus is not surprised when the soldier inside him burns with the ambition to destroy the shell that the bishop's black soul occupies.

Ingersson finally replies. "*Ja*, when you say it that way. Facing battle, I hope not to die."

"But you know somebody will die?" Magnus holds out one hand in a half shrug.

"Certainly, but..."

"So when somebody else falls, you're glad it's not you?"

No answer.

"Right?" Magnus says. "You're glad to be alive, glad you're not the one maimed and bleeding?"

"I don't want to see my friends fall in battle!" The protest in Ingersson's voice is evident.

Magnus shakes his head. "Of course not, but when they do and you don't, you're glad it's not you. That's the armor you put around your mind. When your shield deflects an arrow, you're grateful to have it. The mind's armor works the same way. When it protects us, we're glad."

"Why didn't it work last night?"

"Because we didn't have time to put it on. We weren't going into battle. We were in pursuit."

"So I was only able to say, 'I'm glad it's not me'?"

"And you had to say that without having time to say 'some of us will die. I hope it's not me.' And that leaves us feeling like we're glad Nellsson died. The thought pierces us and makes us feel weak because we didn't have time to gird our minds."

Ingersson hangs his head. "Why do we do this, Magnus?"

"This? You mean fight?"

"*Ja.*"

"To control land? To control men? To unify our country? I don't know for sure."

"I have my little farm. I'll never control any more land. Most of my men don't even have that. They're only under my control because they're soldiers. When they return to their homes, I won't control any men either."

Magnus looks away, pretending to be distracted by something off the trail. Gudrun would help him separate the soldier from the realm-seeker if she were still with him. He'd be playing with his son rather than pursuing someone else's. Heeding Eystein and my father may cost me my army and my soul, he thinks.

"Are those the reasons you do it Magnus?"

"*Helvete!* I don't know! I told you I don't know!" The vehemence of the outburst startles them both.

Ingersson looks away and drops his head, like a man ashamed or afraid, or both. After a time, he says, "I'm sorry. I had no right to question you. Nellsson's death disturbs me more than I thought."

"It's all right, Ingersson. You're a good soldier. We were pondering a mystery, man to man. You weren't disrespectful to your king."

"Thank you."

Magnus nods, too much aware that he doesn't make eye contact. What can he say? That his father bought his crown and paid for it with their souls? That he has to be king, though he's only a soldier? That they track down a child at the cost of men's lives and in weather he wouldn't even wish on the bishop? No, he tells Ingersson that he's a good soldier, and that he's sorry his friend is dead, and then he does what he has to do. "It's ordained," He says it out loud and laughs.

"What?" Ingersson says.

That's when Magnus sees the thin lines of smoke and seizes an excuse to change the topic. "Is that their campsite?" He points ahead to the left of the trail.

The men draw swords and axes or notch arrows. They advance to where the signs are clear - charred coals, packed snow, and a snow dugout. Magnus bends over the makeshift hearth and feels heat rising. "Some of the coals are warm." The men sheath their weapons. "If we sustain our pace, we'll reach the hills by sunset. We've gained ground." He looks around for an indication of how much lead the three may have and notices Ingersson massaging his fingers through his mitts. "Are they frozen?"

"Not yet."

Magnus nods. "We're in for a storm. We'll continue till last light, dig in and build some strong fires."

Whiteness dusts their shoulders well before dark. Not long after that, the wind swirls thick snow. Pellets sting Magnus's eyes as if someone is throwing sand in his face. Even though he wants to press on, his instincts tell him to stop. "Ingersson, take three of the men and make a dugout. I'll cut saplings for the face of it. One-Ear, Sveinn, Lars, gather firewood."

The men's jaws are rigid as they attack their tasks. They have to lean into the wind. Fresh snow covers the tops of their skis even while they move. It would accumulate even faster if it weren't pounding sideways, obliterating vision and battering exposed skin.

A deep burning in the front of Inga's thighs refuses to let up now. Her muscles quiver like they're only moments from spasm. She fears they'll cramp, rendering her helpless to go on, and she can't control it. The back of her calves, the thin part just above the heel wants to snap away from her foot if she leans any harder from the ankles into the increasing pitch of the hill. Her head is down to help keep her body weight forward and over the center of her skis. Skjervald's skis and feet are in her normal range of vision, but she has to tilt her head back to see all of him.

There are still plenty of trees along both sides of the trail, but none are as tall as at lower elevation and they're mixed with scrub. Overhead, the covering thins, and there are only pines, no hardwoods. Inga doubts the trail is as wide here as it has been, but the open canopy, even with the dark overcast, makes them feel wider. The wind is picking up and the smaller trees offer little protection. Cold coils itself around Inga's body, snaking its way through every small opening in her clothes and squeezing away any remaining warmth. Breath drawn through the nose freezes the walls of her nostrils. Panting like a long-haired dog in the summer sun is the only way to get enough air.

Even with his weight well forward, Skjervald starts to lose traction. No sooner does he slip than Inga's left ski loses its grip and shoots backward from under her. She's able to catch herself on a right ski that holds, but the left ski fails again. This time, she drops to one knee and punches her *lurk* into the snow to stop the retreat. The extra effort of catching herself causes her to breathe even harder, rasping on the icy air. Skjervald splays his ski tips toward each side of the trail, forming a wedge to get traction. Inga mimics him, but the terrain pitches steeper yet and the tactic doesn't help much.

Behind her, Torstein says, "We're all slipping. Let's stop and put on the climbing skins."

While their breathing recovers, each of them turns skis across the trail, using the edges to keep from sliding.

Skjervald shouts down to them, "There's a small flat area up here, not far off the trail. We can build a fire."

Inga sidesteps up the hill until she reaches Skjervald's path into the woods. Torstein does the same, and all of them pack an area too small for someone to lie down with legs straight. Frigid air has robbed the snow of its moisture and it's difficult to pack.

They start a blaze using dead limbs until the green wood finally ignites. There's a great deal of smoke, but enough warmth. Inga pulls her mitts off with her teeth, breathing in the pungent stink of sweaty leather and tasting the sooty flavor of the smoke. When their hands warm, they pull the skins from their ruck baskets and secure them to their skis.

"This will allow them to gain some ground, won't it?" she asks. She knows that skis with skins on them don't glide much. They'll be walking on them. It's the best anyone can do up a steep hill, but the thought of slowing for any reason terrifies her.

"Maybe," Skjervald says.

Inga knows they're about to lose the advantage they have when they can glide. And she knows that the Croziers will know they've gone to skins, because the tracks are so distinctive, blurred at the edges like a log that's been hacked instead of sawn. New snow will cover the evidence for a while, but eventually the enemy will know. She tries, but can't keep the apprehension from her face.

"Don't worry," Torstein says. "We have no choice and neither will they. The important thing is to maintain a steady pace and conserve energy. We'll glide again on the plateau and down the other side."

Skjervald squeezes her shoulder, and she nods. As they set off, a few snowflakes drift around them and Inga looks at him, shaking her head. "How did you know?"

Skjervald shrugs a kind of apology.

"Do you think it will be a bad one?" she says.

He looks at her for a moment, then at the sky as if he expects it to speak to him.

*　*　*　*

Her hands are still warm from the fire, and already the snow swirls around them, driven by increasing winds. If not for the protection of the woods, they couldn't see more than two or three body lengths.

"We'd better stop and make camp while we're still able," Torstein says.

"Look at the pitch," Skjervald says.

"No choice. Find the flattest spot we can."

"Might as well leave the trail here," Skjervald says. He's yelling now so they can hear him over the wind. "I see snow banked against some trees." He cuts into the woods.

"I'll gather wood," Inga yells.

"Keep us in sight," Skjervald says.

He shouts the words but it sounds like he's yelling from the next valley. Inga nods and starts looking for dead trees and branches, lucky to gather an armful without losing sight of the men. When she gets back, Skjervald has made the snow bank into a dugout, deep enough for all of them to sit against the back wall with their legs outstretched. It's two body lengths long. Torstein is cutting saplings and pine boughs to cover the front. Inga puts the wood into the dugout to keep snow from burying it, and starts out for more.

"You warm enough?" Torstein hollers as she passes him.

"Wind's starting to go through me. How about you?"

"*Ja*. Fires'll be going in no time."

Soon, Inga has another partial armload, and thinks she

sees more up the hill. She drops the load to mark her spot and climbs to gather the new. As she trudges up the slope, weaving between trees, a gust of wind causes her to lose balance and stumble. She pulls herself up and looks around. She can't see half the distance she could moments ago, but she pushes on until she has a full armload and turns to find the pile she left. Barely able to see her own tracks, she looks down the hill for a glimpse of either man. Beyond the first few trees, she sees nothing but a wall of white. This is where I left the first bundle, she thinks. She looks around for it. She takes a few steps back up the hill and finds indentations in the snow that may be her covered tracks.

"Torstein!" she yells. "Skjervald!" Wind blows her cries back down her throat as soon as she utters them. She looks for her marker. "All right, I know they're close." She says it out loud. She puts down the bundle and pokes several pieces into the snow so at least an arm's length sticks up. Taking the rest, she heads straight down the hill, careful to keep her markers in sight. While they're still visible, she punches another one into the snow, and then moves to the left, keeping both the original and second sticks in sight. She plants a third, and returns to the second, going beyond it to the right this time and plants a fourth mark. From the fourth, she slants down the hill, so it and the second are always in sight. Good, there's the third one, she thinks. Looking back up the hill she sees the second one.

"Skjervald! Torstein!"

She repeats the pattern, forming grids that she knows she's covered as she advances. At the fourth grid she's out of sticks. She has moved no more than a few body lengths, but can't see her first pointers. She turns a full circle, shouting both names so loudly it hurts her throat. By now the wind is screeching and snow covers her tracks almost as fast as she makes them. "Please, God!" she screams.

Inga's fingers and toes are numb, and the pelting snow is making it difficult to keep her eyes open. Tendrils of cold sneak under her clothing and creep up her limbs. Maybe I should follow the marks back up the hill, she tells herself. Try to find the first ones and start over. After a few steps up, waves of nausea pass through her, partly from fear and partly from the throbbing stings of freezing extremities. Falling to her knees, she tucks each hand under the other arm, and whispers again, "Please God, let me see Hakon again. Don't leave me alone out here. My baby needs me."

Then she screams, "Torstein! Skjervald!"

Snow and wind smother Inga's cries for help. She's certain no one hears. Holding her position gives Torstein and Skjervald the best chance of finding her, so she hasn't moved, but it is also the best way to grow cold. Frigid wind and fatigue are robbing her of coordination. Even if she had firewood and tinder and the wind was to stop, she couldn't use her hands to light a fire. Burning pain in her fingers, hands, and feet has wandered off, leaving no feeling at all. She moves a hand up to her nose and feels neither. She pulls off a glove and sees skin as pallid as the belly of a dead fish. Her fingers won't bend. I can't die here, not like this, she thinks. My son needs me. Try once more, Inga! "Torstein! Skjervald! Please!" Somehow, she manages to stand on feet that aren't there, and yell again.

She sees color. Movement. My mind is lying to me now. There's nothing there but walls of snow.

"Inga!"

Was that my mind or did I hear it?

"Inga!"

"*Ja, ja*! Right here! It's me. I'm here." The outline of a man emerges as though he's walking through a wall.

"Inga, are you there?"

"Torstein! Thank God. Is that you?" Her weight topples off useless legs and falls against him.

Torstein grabs her and says, "We're not far from the dugout and Skjervald has fires going. You'll be warm again soon."

Her face is buried in the snow on the shoulder of his bear-skin coat. She can't feel the texture of the snow or the fur, only that her head is against something solid. Lifting it, she looks at the frost on his eyebrows and beard. Icicles dangle there and grow larger each time he exhales. Snow clings to the ice and to his beard and gathers so thick that she can't tell where the hood of his bear-skin stops and his face begins. Two frosted slits trying to blink pelting flakes away from green eyes are the only orientation to his features.

"Are you warm?" she says, failing to see how the face before her could be atop a warm body.

"*Ja.*"

"Then I'm not sure I want to be."

"Come on. Lean against me."

Inga does as he says and watches as his left hand reels in a cord tied around his waist. As Torstein takes up slack, she realizes that he has anchored the cord to the shelter. Later, when they are back in the shelter, she learns that he skied to the end of the tether and back nineteen times, taking a different direction each time.

Three fires puff smoke through holes Skjervald has cut into the roof of the shelter, and the wind makes short work of it. As soon as he pulls Inga into the dugout and sits her between two of the fires, she feels the needles returning to her fingers and toes. Tears well up while she rocks back and forth and folds and extends her thawing fingers, but she's grateful to feel anything. Each man pulls off one of her shoes and puts it on a stick near the flame. Inga watches Torstein's icicles begin to melt as he tears his hood away from frozen hair. Her bear-skin coat dampens and smells like a wet dog.

Hakon is wrapped up near the fire, his hands waving in the air. He looks at his mother. "*Mamma* play inna snow?"

"*Ja*, sweet honey." With painful, stiff fingers she grasps her little boy and hugs him to her.

Fear adds to their frenzy. Ingersson and his three men completed the dugouts. Sveinn and the others collected as much dry wood as they could without losing sight of each other, but it won't be enough.

"We have to go farther from the shelter to find enough!" Sveinn shouts so Magnus can hear him over the wind.

"Too dangerous!" Magnus screams back. "Cut more green and we'll dry it best we can over what we've got."

"It'll be smoky."

Magnus shrugs. Sveinn starts cutting and the others follow until the area in their field of vision is bare. The trees are more like bushes. All of them combined don't yield much fuel. The men keep looking up from their work, looking over their shoulders, making sure they keep one another in sight. Hands stiffen and slow the work even more. By the time they have enough fuel to keep fires going, the penetrating wind has sapped more energy than the day's travel. Exhausted and shivering, they crowd into the shelter to ride out the storm. Through the night and all the next day, the wind pounds. They don't dare try to travel. Several times Magnus reminds the men that their quarry must be stranded also. The green wood burns cleaner than he had hoped, but there's still enough smoke to make them cough. That and the fact that there are eight crowded into this crude dugout makes it difficult to sleep.

Even during the day, there is only the dim light of their fires. The men don't move much, but when they do, to melt snow or pull food from their packs, the motion looks stiff and unnatural as the flickering light reveals part of their movement and conceals the rest. They stand only long enough to exit the

dugout and relieve themselves. Returning makes Magnus—
and the others, he's sure—aware of the odor of wet fur and
unwashed bodies mixing with the smoke. Even muscle spasms
don't provide enough reason to suffer the storm. The men rub
them out as best they can where they sit.

By the second night, the storm has passed. One by one
they emerge, kicking and pushing away snow that reaches
the tops of their thighs. They stretch and twist, trying to feel
their legs under them. Magnus knows that no one wants to
break trail in this, but Sveinn takes the lead and the others
fall into his tracks. One-Ear grumbles something and takes up
the rear. After a while, with each taking short turns breaking
trail, they're able to set a good pace with minimum individual
effort. Well before daylight, they find a single track, already
skied in. Sveinn leaves the trail and skis to the Birkebeiners'
shelter.

"It's empty," he reports, "but some of the coals on the fires
are still warm." He brushes his hands together and wipes them
on his leggings.

"We've gained ground on them," Ingersson says. "We can
catch them on the plateau."

"We've gained ground all right, but have we gained time?"
Magnus says. "They've been climbing steeper terrain."

"And it gets steeper yet," One-Ear says. "Let's push." For
once Magnus believes his enthusiasm.

Using the Birkebeiner's track saves Magnus's men the
effort of breaking trail, and with each step Magnus becomes
more confident that they are gaining. He guesses they've cut
the lead in half, but doesn't say so. With new vigor, the men
press into the hill. It's unusual for the night to be as clear as
it is while the air is warming. For the first time since leaving
Lillehammer, the men peel off some clothing as they move.
They can feel their hands and feet.

"Careful with the pace," Magnus says. He fears a sudden
burst of energy now might increase fatigue later. "Be patient,
steady. We'll run them down." He knows the men sense his

confidence, because he senses theirs. Even against the strain of a steep slope and deep snow, their stride is crisp and steady, revealing no hint of sluggishness. He wonders how long that can last.

Sveinn, a man who tends to keep to himself, continues to emerge as a leader. Although quiet, in his own way he urges the men on. Ingersson and One-Ear stick closer to him than the rest. Ingersson needs to develop a friend after the loss of Nellsson, and One-Ear is a natural follower, but the rest respond to Sveinn for whatever reasons they have. It gives Magnus cause to feel that he'll have somebody besides Sturelsson who can take some responsibility after the two groups reunite. He's encouraged, willing to be patient and watch. Then, with no warning a disturbing realization stops him dead in his tracks. Revulsion for the ultimate goal of this mission mocks the pride he feels in his own leadership.

All night the gale-driven snow pummels the four of them. At times, it blows with such force that all the smoke doesn't rise through the outlets in their snow cave. They cough and soak the sooty stench into their hair and furs. Inga rubs her eyes and squeezes her eyelids together in an attempt to make tears. Skjervald uses a stick to clear the overhead holes while she and Torstein try to clear three frontal vents to create a draft. Inga's sure it's daytime, but can see nothing but blizzard beyond their flimsy refuge. The walls of the cavern have taken on a brownish glaze, the surface slick to the touch, but not quite wet.

"Low on wood," Skjervald says. "I'll go out on the tether and find some. Storm'll last all day." When he moves, Inga can smell his odor mixing into the smoky air. Both he and Torstein smell like unwashed clothes dried in a smoke house. She's worried that she doesn't smell any better. She finds that thought odd, considering the countless, more pressing concerns they face. Part of it, she supposes, is her longing for something normal, like feeling clean.

It would feel so good to pour water on the hot stones in the *badstua* and let the steam rise around her. She can almost feel the heat against her skin, removing the day's grime. She can see Hakon sitting across from her, his skin red and glistening. He would get up, take one of the large gourds full of cold water and empty it over her. She would do the same for him. Maybe they would repeat the ritual. Sometimes they would love each other while they were there. She remembers how good he smelled. She feels an involuntary shake of her head.

Little Hakon stirs. Each of them has slept in short shifts, one at a time. Two have had to stay awake to tend the fire and keep vents and chimneys open. As Hakon takes her breast, she can smell the smoke in his hair and blanket and wants to cry. He's content, though, and feels warm against her, so she's thankful for that.

"Be careful," Torstein says, as Skjervald pushes away some of the brush covering his end of the dugout. The opening sucks air in and up the smoke holes, clearing the charcoal haze. He grabs his skis, slips through the hole and replaces the brush. Smoke hangs in the air again.

"Fresh snow up to my thighs!" he yells.

It's quiet for a moment.

"Got my skis on and I'm still halfway up my birch."

"Don't let go of the rope!" Torstein yells. Gusting wind is louder than his voice.

Inga continues to nurse Hakon.

Torstein stirs the fires and adds fuel. "They can't travel in this either," he says.

"*Tuk*," she says, knowing he says it to ease her tension about being stalled here. "Will the new snow slow them or us more?"

"We can maintain our distance if we don't fight the snow."

"Fight it?"

"Force our skis through instead of gliding through. Even with the skins, we may get a bit of glide in this. "

"So, a slight advantage for us?"

"A little." He shrugs.

Torstein sits at one end of the dugout with his back against the side wall and his feet stretched out toward the fire between them. She sits cross-legged with her back against the back wall, Hakon on her lap. The skins of her bedroll keep her dry and she's warm enough to remove her bear-skin coat. "May I open a larger hole around this vent to keep the smoke down?" she asks.

"Good idea."

She pokes a stick through the brush covering the front of the dugout and chips away some of the inner crust. It feels like snow that has had rain freeze on top of it. The wider vent helps. After a while her eyes stop watering and the dusky smell dissipates.

Inga watches the spot in the wall where the tether is anchored and sees no slack, but she can tell it has moved in a wide arc. For a long time, the tension on the rope and its angle away from the dugout remain constant, except for wind vibrations.

"You there?" It's Skjervald.

"Just waiting for you and the fuel," Torstein says.

"Enough for a while," Skjervald says, throwing in an armload.

"Just in time," Torstein says, as he tosses the last of the original wood on the fire between them. Skjervald wiggles back inside and stokes the fire on the other side of Inga.

Hakon, who is through with his supper, looks at him and smiles. "Skjervi play inna snow."

"That's right, little king. Skjervi was out on his skis."

"Skjervi play inna snow with me?" he chirps.

"When it's a little warmer. You wouldn't like it right now. Too cold. Brrr!" Skjervald wraps his arms around himself and shakes. "We play later, all right?"

"Brrr," Hakon imitates, shaking himself.

* * * *

At least they've had time to eat and drink enough. Inga's view through the vent tells her the meager daylight is fading. Smoke and screaming wind have made it difficult to sleep, so she doesn't feel rested. She hunches her shoulders a few times, stretches her back as best she can in the tight shelter, and rubs each calf. "Any chance we'll travel tonight?" she asks.

"Sounds like the wind is dropping," Torstein says. "Storm ends and clouds clear out, we should be able to. Moonlight for the next three nights."

"I'll try to sleep until it's time to go," she says.

"We all should," Torstein says.

"I'm going to get wood to last the night, just in case." Skjervald says.

Inga's eyelids close before he's gone. Sticks and logs dropping next to her cause a moment's break in her sleep but she doesn't wake again until Skjervald shakes her.

"Time to go," he says. "Bright, clear moon, and it feels warmer."

Inga rubs her eyes and shakes away the sleep. "Where's Torstein?"

"Went ahead to break trail and make sure our 'friends' aren't around. He'll wait for us."

Inga crawls to the hole with Hakon and hears Skjervald throw the rest of the fuel on the blaze behind her.

"I'll carry Hakon for a while," he says. "He's used to me now."

"He likes you."

"You think so? I haven't spent much time around children."

"A playmate is a rank above friend," she says.

Skjervald doesn't say anything, but he looks pleased, like a boy who realizes he's caught the eye of a girl. They punch their way through the face of the dugout and start up the trail. Moonlight filters between the trees and bounces off the bright new snow, casting odd shadows, dark solid silhouettes from the moon's direct light and grayer, subtler imitations from its reflection. Until they get to the trail, Inga dodges several shadows and has her hood knocked off by branches that mimic shadows. When the two reach the trail, they find the extra width forgiving.

Their skis keep them from sinking beyond mid-calf, but they grip their *lurks* high on the shaft because they sink so deep. Torstein's tracks help, and as he said, the soft new snow, over the harder packed, allows for some glide even with the skins. His strides have created a firm base that helps Inga keep her feet flat and on top of her skis, reducing weariness in her ankles and legs.

"Torstein's are the only tracks," Skjervald says.

"Thank goodness."

When they reach Torstein, he's beside the trail, skis across the hill.

"Slow going?" Skjervald asks.

"You break trail for a while and I'll take Hakon."

Skjervald lifts the sling carefully onto Torstein's shoulder. Hakon stirs. Skjervald removes a glove and smoothes his finger across the baby's cheek and forehead, pushes back wisps of hair and watches him settle to sleep again.

After Skjervald has led for a while, Inga moves up and takes her turn. Pushing the skis through the deep powder is more work than following a track. She remembers Torstein's caution against fighting the snow, and doesn't make any extra effort to kick her skis forward. She tries to let momentum do the work, and anticipates her turn at the back of the line. Branches suspended over the trail, while fewer now, hang lower, weighted with snow. Moonbeams pierce the surface crystals and flash rainbow colors. Inga knows that it's Ull and Skade at their work again. Of all the gods and goddesses her ancestors revered, she wishes that her people still kept these two winter smiths. If only she had time to stop and gaze. This is the kind of snow Hakon and she loved to ski. Its silence and beauty made skiing in it feel easy. She can't think of anything now that was difficult when she was with him.

Both men pass her and Skjervald takes up the lead. Inga's glad for the rest, if that's what it is. The trail rises so sharply that a fall forward would not be much more than an arm's length. Her thighs begin to hurt again and she can feel the tight stretch of her calves and ankles. Soon she'll begin to feel that burning in the back of her legs, between the knee joint and buttocks, and have to slow or stop to let it subside.

"How far to the plateau?" she asks Torstein.

"Daylight, at this rate, maybe longer. Tired?"

"Like to stop and take off my vest if I could."

"Me too. Skjervald, let's rest for a moment."

By comparison to yesterday, the air is warm. Skjervald and Inga peel off their parkas, remove their beaver-skin vests and put the heavier coats back on. Inga pinches at her shirt to see if it's damp. It isn't, but it smells like the *røkt laks* smokehouse. Torstein puts the baby's sling back on Skjervald and makes his changes. Readjusted, they turn their skis back up the hill. It feels steeper than ever and Inga doesn't believe it's just the resistance of all the new snow.

Without warning, from a sound sleep, Hakon wakes, screaming. Skjervald tries to swing the sling as he moves along. Neither the rocking nor gentle talk soothes what is becoming a tantrum. Skjervald slows, and Inga skis forward to see what she can do, but he continues to scream.

"Did I do something?" asks Skjervald. His face is a mask of bewildered apprehension.

"No, no. I don't know what it could be, except a bad dream. I just fed him."

"Poor little fella. He's been so good till now. Maybe it's just time to be a little grumpy."

"I hope he's not getting sick. Or maybe all the smoke hurt his eyes. He almost never does this." Inga strokes the child's forehead, but he only yells more. "He doesn't feel feverish," she says. "He'll be all right. Why don't I carry him for a while and see what happens?"

Skjervald nods and transfers the sling. Inga watches him. Skjervald's eyes are fixed on Hakon. His lips are taut across his teeth and clamped on the tip of his tongue which protrudes to the left side of his mouth. His brow is the battle mask of a soldier on a mission. His transfer is awkward, almost missing her head at first.

"There, that wasn't too difficult, was it?" Inga says, as she smiles and adjusts the placement.

Skjervald's face relaxes and he shows her a self-conscious smirk. "I'm beginning to think they can smell fear."

"Just like a wolf," she says. They both chuckle.

They push on, and after a while the screaming changes to

crying, finally mellows to whimpering and then he's asleep again. Inga knows that's good and she's thankful, but as they climb, she experiences other, more troubling thoughts. What if that happens at the wrong time? What do I do?

Shadows of small trees become shadows of scrub growth, and first light reveals a landscape of nothing more than hummock and brush peeking above the snow's surface. Before Inga and her escorts left the woods and the last abundant supply of fuel, each of them gathered a large bundle of dead limbs and branches and strapped it to their packs. They still climb, but the pitch is shallower. The extra burden doesn't help. Inga's body aches from the uphill trudge, her legs most of all. Breathing is in gasps, as if she's been underwater and has struggled to the surface.

"Just below the boundary of the snowfields." Torstein wheezes the comment and gestures with his head.

When she looks up, Inga sees the edge of a broad, flat curve of white. The slope creates a looming horizon that unfurls above her. The colorless terrain stretches left and right as far as she can see. The higher she and her comrades climb, the broader and flatter it becomes. The sun rises from behind her and its reflection looks like white fire consuming the earth. With each step the snowfield grows, until as far as Inga can see in any direction, except to the rear, lies stark, pallid flatness.

"Hope there's no wind while we're up here," Skjervald says.

"Look behind, so you'll know what you'll face this afternoon," Torstein says.

Inga looks back at the intensifying orb that warms her in the still air. Unlike the blandness ahead of them, the sun sparkles off the snow, reflecting colors, like tiny red, green and blue stars. She can enjoy the glitter only for a moment. Reflexes force her eyes closed.

"Can we travel into that?" she says. Black, red and blue spots drift before her long after she turns away from the glare.

Skjervald removes his ruck basket and draws the length of rope from it. They back up in their tracks until they're a good distance from the hole.

Torstein secures the line around her waist with a knot that won't slip. "Stay about a body length away from the edge," he says, yanking on the rope. "The cornice should hold there. Be deliberate. Keep a steady weight on your skis and shuffle. Don't apply enough pressure to glide." As he throws a loop of rope over his head and one shoulder, he adds, "We'll be out there, holding on."

"Out there. Where it's safe." Inga gives him her best imitation of a smile.

"Right." He returns it.

Torstein lowers his face and pretends to wipe his mouth.

They all start forward in the same track. The men follow the old line, a safe distance from the crevasse, as Inga nudges closer to it. As they creep forward, they spread out, stretching the line to its full length. Inga's heart bounds between her stomach and throat as she gets near enough to peer over the brink. Sunlight creeps over its boundary and turns shadowy, and then dark, and she tells herself that the darkness never ends. She sees herself riding a huge chunk of snow cornice into that void and being jerked to a sudden stop by this flimsy piece of twine between her and finality. Then, with alarming clarity, she envisions her body dangling in the blackness until she begins to experience a sensation of slipping. More and more, faster and faster, she slides down into the abyss, out of control, pulling Torstein, Skjervald and her child behind her. She says a silent prayer. Oh, God, please don't. And if you do, please let Hakon be waiting for me at the bottom.

"You're more than halfway there, Inga." Skjervald's voice comes from somewhere else, like a vision during sleep.

Sucking in a breath, Inga forces herself to stop looking over the edge and concentrate on staring straight ahead to the end of the chasm. After several more strides, out of the corner of her right eye, she sees a crack the width of her little finger. She doesn't know if it was there when she started or just forming now, getting ready to travel the depth of the cornice and plunge her into eternity.

"*Heia*, Inga, *heia, heia*! Go! Go! Go!" Both men yell, urging her on. Inga can't tell whether it's because they see the crack, or because she's so close to the end. She points her skis to the right and scrambles away from the crevasse, crossing the chink and then racing for her companions, throwing herself at the last stride into the safety of their arms. As soon as she gets her breath back, they all ski, in one track, away from the crevasse. Inga takes the child and rests, while the two men travel back to define the outer track, parallel to the one she made. It looks very clean, innocent. Were their pursuers not trying to kill her baby, she could feel pity for the ones who take the wrong path.

As they resume their trek, Inga realizes, more than before, how weary she is, as if the anxiety of her trip along the edge has sapped what reserves she had. Even though the terrain is flat, her breathing is labored. Fatigue's sharp teeth gnaw at her lower back and cause a dull pain that travels down the back of her legs to her knees. Her arms hurt, more on the hind side than the front. She's inefficient with her *lurk*. Although she tries to drink often, stored water quickly freezes, reducing them to eating ice or snow as they move. It's the seventh morning of a journey she hoped would be over in six days. Skjervald shot two snow hares before they left the trail, but they won't last long, and other food is running low, meat in particular. The men's shoulders sag but neither complains.

When her shadow is no longer in front of her, Inga puts a hand to her forehead to deflect the light. Maybe it's the flatness of the terrain or perhaps she's distracted by the growing intensity of the glare, but her fatigue recedes a bit, or at least doesn't increase. The sunlight provides warmth compared to the numbing cold of the storm. She can feel her toes and fingers again. They sting as the warmer air and the exertion thaw them.

They eat and drink without stopping to rest. The nourishment helps. Gnawing *røkt laks* and letting snow melt in their mouths is all they can manage on the move. Between the three of them, they are able to get enough food in little Hakon and keep him warm, so he is quiet and sleeps a lot.

The closer they get to sunset, the easier it is to look above the sun and avoid the reflection from the snow. Inga is two body lengths behind Skjervald and catches a whiff of him sometimes. It reminds her how long they've been on the run, and that, here on the plateau, there is nothing else to smell.

"Moon rises early tonight," says Skjervald. "Should we stop after sunset and cook a meal?"

"Probably all we have time for," Torstein says. "Inga?"

"I could eat again, and it'll give me a chance to really fill Hakon."

"We can start a fire in the dark," Skjervald says. "Let's use all the light we can."

Almost as he says it, the sun drops below the horizon. Shadowy gray transforms to black, freckled with stars. Torstein takes Inga's bundle of wood and lights a fire as Ull and Skade throw one of their stars across the sky. Inga watches its orange tail break the blackness around it and disappear. Hakon begins to whimper and she nurses him while the men roast the last piece of reindeer meat. All of them drink as much water as they can melt, and don't leave a morsel of the meat. Inga boils some of the lentils and shreds some of her reindeer into it to give to Hakon. He eats it all. How he can be so good when he's so hungry is a blessing. She kisses his forehead and strokes his face as the moon rises.

"Moo' *Momma*," he says, pointing skyward.

"Yes, sweetie. The moon. It's pretty isn't it?"

"Erty," Hakon says, as she rocks him in her lap. He's so beautiful and he reminds Inga of his father. She watches his face until his eyes droop. Torstein takes him again and they're ready to go.

Silver fingers of moonlight spread themselves over the

crests and cornices of snowdrifts, but are unable to wrap their light around, and leave stark contrasts. Black against white, light against dark. Inga wonders if that's what the moon is. She wonders if their winter world is nothing but another moon, if life would be better there. Fairer. Or is it black against white everywhere?

With the clear skies comes the bitter, numbing cold again. Even without the wind, the frost bears down and hurts, biting deep into places on Inga's body that never have been cold before. Her knees, at their core, not just the skin, her stomach, even shoulders begin to feel the ache. While dinner still sits in her stomach, this iciness probes beneath her skin. This chill moves within, deep and abiding. Flesh and sinew feel it, but it is also capable of freezing the mind…with fear.

All of them hate to waste the light, but they stop before moon-set and dig into a snowdrift for insulation. They have no choice.

"Torstein, can we light a fire?" Inga asks. She struggles to keep her teeth from chattering.

"Better not. They see it, might spur them to keep moving. And I need the darkness to see if they start one. Moon's about to set."

"I don't see anything. You?" She says.

"No."

"Is that good?"

"I don't think they'll move in the dark," Torstein says. "Too easy to lose direction with no trail or trees."

Inga looks up at the silver Troll's face staring down at her from the darkness, balancing on the horizon, mocking her black-and-white world with his.

"If we build a fire, they can use it as a beacon." Torstein pauses. Inga's close enough to see him squinting, as if straining to see something tiny. "Wait. There. Can you see that pinpoint of light?"

"Where?" Skjervald asks. Torstein raises his arm and aims it. Skjervald and Inga both lean in to direct their line of sight.

"Yes...yes." Both in unison.

"They're that close?" Inga whispers.

"Probably just cresting the edge of the snowfields, still a quarter day behind us."

"Does that mean they've stopped?" she asks.

Torstein recognizes the hope in her voice and hears in it an unspoken question. "Perhaps, but they may be hoping we will think that, so we'll build a fire that they can move toward. And they may have built a fire and left it for us to see while they march. We just don't dare take the risk, Inga. He puts his arm around her shoulder and throws the side of his furs over her. "We'll rest a little, and then start out again. The exertion will warm us till the sun rises. Put your hands inside my coat and vest. You can feel Hakon sleeping, warm against my chest."

She does, and it helps to know her child is warmer than she is.

Skjervald presses against her from the other side and she warms up enough to sleep. When Torstein wakes her, her eyes feel like they never closed. She's stiff, colder than she was when she went to sleep, and not a bit more rested.

Now her effort, as Torstein promised, is purging the deep chill, and for a moment, she prays again. Thank you for keeping Hakon warm tonight. Help me protect him. Keep the two men leading me strong and resolute. Slow our enemies' pursuit so that we may reach Nidaros and the warmth of your church.

Inga looks ahead at Torstein and Skjervald. The modified contrasts of an inert landscape surround them in dim morning twilight. Their shadows are gray, gray and moving. She looks behind her. Hers is, too. A stark truth occurs to her. We are the only difference between this and the moon. Always? Maybe not, but tonight we are. She scans the darkness behind her where she senses the horizon. The speck of light is gone.

*　*　*　*

The three cover a lot of distance in the long twilight before the sun rises. So much time is sucked into the perpetual nights of winter that they must use any available light to travel. At least the group will move away from the morning sun, or have it quartering to their left. They'll be able to see better than they could if it came from in front. Still, moonlight offers greater definition than this shadowless gray time that precedes and ends each period of sunlight. Feeling the snow support her weight is the only way Inga can tell she's on land. In these high snowfields above the Gudbrans Valley, the undulating snowdrifts, void of color in the morning twilight, are indistinguishable from waves rolling on the *fjord*. Over her shoulder, Inga sees a thin horizontal line of light fading to gray. If she didn't know they were at the top of a mountain, that gray could be sea or sky instead of land. The long sliver of light begins to broaden and, for now, it alone marks the passage of time.

Up here they will have more daytime than on the narrow woods trails, where the sun struggles for recognition, and twilight doesn't exist. If the sky remains clear, at this elevation they will spend one third of their time in either sunlight or the long predawn and long afternoon twilight. Moonlight provides additional travel time. The rest of their time is shrouded in black and is not time at all, except to rest and eat.

Ahead, Inga can discern the silhouettes of Skjervald and Torstein. They are the puppet shadows her father used to make for her in the light of a candle before he would snuff it and bid her sweet dreams. The only way she can tell which man is which is that the top of Skjervald's spear, carried in his right hand, and the top of his bow rise above his right shoulder and splice onto his puppet. What distinguishes Torstein's puppet, further ahead, is the curve of his shield where it rises above his shoulder. He holds it high to protect Hakon from what little wind there is. She knows his battle-axe is there because it always is, but he carries it too low to project any outline against the dimness. Inga wonders for a moment if their pursuers are close enough to see their back-lit figures. She looks over her shoulder and sees only the blackness of Eystein's soul, and the sun trying to pierce it.

Seeing the arc of Torstein's shield protecting Hakon reminds Inga of another way she marks the passage of time in winter. It should warm as the sun moves toward its peak and cool as it sets. But today that fails. On this high plateau, the movement of time guarantees nothing except that the weather will change. The sunrise hues she's beginning to see as they trudge into their eighth day, remind her of the ones Skjervald pointed out two days ago, and tell her another storm might chase them today. She prays that they are clear of the snowfields before it arrives and that their enemy is not.

The line of light behind her thickens now and darkness surrenders enough to confirm that she's on land, snow is white, and the outlines in front of her are men and not puppets.

Not much more time passes before they are outlined again, this time by a blinding corona. Inga looks down at the snow to avoid the glare she knows will stalk her eyes and poach on her vision until the next twilight, or until they are in the woods on the far side of this crest.

When the sun is above the horizon, Torstein stops and lets Inga catch up. Hakon is awake and starting to fuss. Inga fumbles with layers of wool and fur so she can feed him. Torstein drops his shield and axe and lifts the blanket sling, baby still in it, from his shoulder and hangs it over hers. Then he steps on the backs of her skis with the front of his and adjusts the knot, pulling Hakon higher on her. The baby feels like a spring day against her, warm and pure, and she lets him nurse. After a time she looks up from Hakon's head to notice Torstein still facing the other direction. Skjervald has turned around, too, and both men's eyes are fixed, unblinking, on the eastern horizon. She steps forward so she can turn her skis, and tries to pick up the object of their concentration.

"What?" she says.

"Croziers," Torstein says.

She squints to focus on the distant dot. "Any way to tell who?" she asks.

"Not from here. Knowing Eystein, I'd wager Magnus is either leading a group trying to get in front of us or," he juts his chin in their direction. "that gang, trying to catch us."

"How far behind, you think?" Skjervald asks.

"Hard to say. I don't think they'll catch us today if we keep moving."

"Can they see us?" Inga asks.

"If we can see them, they can certainly see us. Can you feed him on the move?" Torstein says.

"Think so. I'll try." Her heart pounds so loud that it drowns her words.

"Let me know. Skjervald, you lead for a while. I'll follow Inga and Hakon."

Skjervald pivots in two steps and heads northwest. Torstein pats Hakon's head and looks at Inga. She knows he can read the fear in her eyes, because she can feel it coursing through her body like it's looking for escape. Torstein bends to pick up his axe and shield. When his face comes up even with hers, he smiles and says, "Tell me when he's full and I'll take him again."

Still in the Birkebeiners' tracks, Magnus and his men reach the top and enter the vast snowfields just before sunset on day seven of their pursuit. A strained grimace covers each man's face. One-Ear and Sveinn stand, doubled at the waist, hands on bent knees, drinking in as much air as they can find. Ingersson kneads the back of his calf. Magnus squats on his skis in an attempt to stretch the front of his thighs. Thorvald Ericsson has removed his pack and is sitting on it. The other three, Ulf, Egil the Thin, and Askell, lag and exert to catch up as they come over the crest. Sveinn encouraged and urged the men on during the climb, continuing to display leadership. Since Nellsson's death, the soldiers have consoled each other, particularly Ingersson. Olaf One-Ear is less boastful, probably the influence of Sveinn, whom he shadows now. As the last three reach the rest, they fall in behind Sveinn, and assume their own postures of recovery.

Sveinn scoops a handful of snow toward his mouth, looks at Magnus and says, "We going to use the rest of this light before we eat?"

"Not much left. Let's build a fire and continue as soon as we've eaten."

"Before the moon rises?"

"By the time we eat, we won't be long without the moon."

Two of the men unload wood they have carried from the last campsite and get a fire started. The sizzle of fat dripping into the fire and the smell of roasting meat puts a ravenous edge on their appetites. Two shanks of mutton and boiled lentils fill them, and all of them drink as much water as they can hold. With Nellsson gone, they should have more than enough food.

Only the stars break up the darkness as they prepare to leave. Cold drops on them like a pouncing beast, so they warm their hands over the fire, then leave it to burn itself out. Later, Magnus looks back, sees it still burning, and wonders if the Birkebeiners can see it. He hopes so. Knowing that he and his men are closing in could cause them to set too great a pace and expend precious energy, he thinks. Or maybe they'll relax, thinking we've stopped.

Sometime later, just after moonrise, Magnus is near the end of the pack. Only Sveinn and Ingersson are behind him. The men rotate the lead often and stay in the Birkebeiner tracks to increase their speed and conserve energy. Out of the corner of his eye, Magnus notices that the two of them have drifted to the left and are parallel to him. "Stay in the track," he calls.

"We are in the track," Ingersson yells back. "Head was down. Thought we were right behind you."

"Two sets of tracks?" Magnus says. "Why would they do..."

"Stop!" Sveinn screams. "Don't move!"

"God, no!" Magnus says. Agony crosses his face as though he's been hit between the shoulder blades with a club.

Ingersson looks back at Sveinn, several strides behind, but doesn't stop. Sveinn breaks to his right, skiing toward the others with every ounce of strength he can muster. "This way! This way, Ingersson!" he screams.

In front of Magnus, the others now look to their left. Ingersson steps right, realizing something is wrong. Sveinn's tone bellows danger as much as his words.

The muscles in Magnus's neck tighten all the way to his chin and he recoils as the sound rips into him. A sharp crack followed by a low-pitched grinding. "No, no! Jump Ingersson!" Watching him sink, Magnus has the sensation that Ingersson is floating, that if he could just get a stride or two, he'd float all the way to him. And then the scream begins as Magnus watches the jagged, icy edge of the crevasse rise up the length of Ingersson's body until the last thing he sees is the soldier's hands flailing over his head, clawing at broken, falling chunks of snow like a drowning man splashing to stay afloat. When he disappears, the scream continues. Magnus pounds the snow with his fists, willing the horror of that scream to stop. It won't. It fades, dimmer, dimmer and more distant, until he no longer hears it, but it never stops. Never.

In the same moment, Magnus sees Sveinn, still running toward him, just ahead of snow breaking up at his heels. Magnus can see the tail of one of Sveinn's skis hanging over the edge before he rips it forward and strides, the precipice widening behind him, like a living thing chasing him, determined to suck him in and swallow him. Four body lengths from Magnus, Sveinn throws himself forward, turning sideways in the air to keep from catching his ski tips. Magnus lies flat, extending his spear at arms' length toward his soldier. A desperate grab and Sveinn finds the shaft just below the point, as his legs disappear into the hole. Hanging over the edge, he begins to pull himself hand over hand toward Magnus. The others have turned and started in his direction to help pull him out.

"No, no!" Sveinn shouts. "Stay back! You'll kill us all!"

They stop. All they can do is watch as he pulls himself up over the edge. At least for now, the cavern is not growing under him. When he's within reach, Magnus's hand clasps his and he backs away, digging the edge of his skis into the snow and contracting his legs while Sveinn pushes with his own edges. The two men flop and undulate well past Magnus's set of tracks before they stand, neither saying anything, trying to catch their breath. They look at each other and embrace, two comrades who have survived. The others join them, slapping backs and shoulders, celebrating.

Magnus remembers his conversation with Ingersson. This is what I meant, Ingersson. We didn't have time to prepare, and now we're glad to be alive. We're sorry you're dead, but glad we are not.

There's not much time between moon-set and the beginning of morning twilight. Magnus greets the gray shroud as insulation from the decisions he grapples with. In so dim a light, his face can't reveal his doubts. Dealing with Eystein has taught him to conceal his feelings under any circumstances. No sooner is he comfortable with this mission than he begins to suffer qualms again. *What of my soul? This isn't a soldier's mission. It's a tyrant's pursuit.*

"Let's go," says Sveinn, pushing the last of his fish into his cheek to gnaw on as they move. Without hesitation, each gets back on his skis and into the rhythm of the rotation. While the sun rises behind them, the colorless plateau turns to sparkling white, and shadows shorten. As the light moves, Magnus moves his eyes back and forth across the horizon, squinting. When he rotates into the lead, he sees a speck ahead of them, too far ahead to tell if it's them. *That's the only thing it could be,* he thinks. *When the sun gets a little higher, he'll be sure.*

"Magnus, look back." It's Sveinn calling from the end of the line.

He looks over his shoulder. On the horizon, just behind the sun, is a wall of angry clouds. "Easterly storm?" he shouts, as Sveinn pulls out of line and surges to the front.

"Looks like."

"How long?"

Sveinn doesn't answer until he catches his breath. "Sun'll be overhead before the clouds are. They start slow out of the east, but we may have to dig shelter."

"Move on," Magnus says. He focuses on the speck. It begins to pull him forward. His nostrils flare as he sucks in breath and pushes other thoughts away.

With the sun overhead, there is less glare when Inga looks back to the east. The speck on the horizon hasn't changed size, but it's impossible to tell if the Croziers have gained ground. Inga sees that they are there, and they're moving. Worry enough, but not the only menace she sees. An ominous collection of clouds also stalks them. Several shades of gray look like they are trying to roil into one dark mass and march to surround the sun.

Skjervald sees her staring. "Look angry, don't they?"

"Worse," she says. "What should we do?"

"If you set your gaze straight ahead, you can make out the first hut. We should run for it."

"How long to get there?"

"Wind behind us helps. If we beat the storm, won't be by much." Skjervald looks at Torstein. "Run for it or dig in?"

"Hut'll be better shelter. Firewood there. Let's push."

Before she turns her head back to the west, Inga sees the men's hair beginning to waft out in front of their faces, and feels the breeze beginning to lift her own. They pick up the tempo, and she watches small whirlwinds of snow swirl off their ski tips and skitter unhindered across the barren landscape. Her breath starts to come in rasps, and she can hear Skjervald puffing behind her. His breathing doesn't sound as labored as hers, but she knows the men are letting her set the pace so they don't outrun her. Stay within yourself, Inga.

No sooner does she issue this self-warning then she hears Torstein say, "That's plenty Inga. No faster."

She backs off a bit, pulls her hood up and keeps her head down. Blowing snow doesn't reflect much light and it's only a matter of time before clouds bury the source. Snow pelts her eyes like blown sand. She rejects the urge to look around for the Croziers. If the snow is starting to whip around her, it has already obscured the enemy.

By the time the edges of the clouds intersect the rim of the sun, the wind whips her hair out of her hood and snaps it against her cold face. Chill steals through every stitch in her clothing, but the level of exertion generates enough warmth to hold it at bay. Inga's breath is a cloud itself, and she feels it freeze on her face each time she exhales.

Through short breaks in the wind's intensity, she sees the hut grow. The closer they get, the more often the angry wind blurs their view. Clouds begin to drop huge, driven flakes. If they don't reach the shelter soon, the wind, even though behind them, will turn the storm horizontal and create a shroud their eyes can't penetrate and their bodies can't withstand. Torstein and Skjervald come next to her on either side. Torstein grabs her right hand and tucks it into the leather strap around his waist. Skjervald has his line out and puts a loop around Torstein's right wrist. Letting the coils slip from his hand, he skis ahead of them to the full length of the tether.

"When Skjervald can't see us any more from his end, he'll stop until we catch up, then surge forward again until we reach the hut," Torstein says. He has to shout so that Inga can hear him above the wind.

"We're close, aren't we?" she asks.

"What?" He moves his head till his ear is close enough for her to bite it.

"We're close, aren't we?" This time she shouts.

He has to turn his head and lean toward her. Even with that, he screams, "Very. Two or three times and he should find it."

Inga watches Skjervald's figure at the far end of the tether, its outline fogging with each new gust, until it's only a blur. After each foray, he stops and waits. When he presses away from them again, his image fades until all Inga can see is a rope that disappears into a wall of snow. As Torstein reels in the cord for the third time, Inga sees the outline of the hut before she sees Skjervald leaning against it, smiling. If the shelter were a dead reindeer, he would have his arms crossed and a foot on its rack. The wave of relief is palpable, but she lacks the energy to be euphoric.

Well-established snow banks rim the tiny building, so it should offer sturdy shelter from the wind. Skjervald lifts the wooden latch without resistance and the woven alder door swings inward. As soon as they loosen their bindings, they step in, single file, carrying their skis. Both men lean against the door to close it against the wind and blowing snow. Spots flitter about in front of Inga while her eyes grow accustomed to the dark. Dirt as hard as stone makes up the floor and offers a sweet, moldy aroma. Frozen thatch the depth of a man's forearm on the roof and sloping sides of the building carries a whiff of hay.

"Whoever built this built it to last," Inga says.

"*Tusen tuk*," Skjervald says.

"What?"

He repeats, "Thanks a lot."

"You built it?"

"Most of it. Hakon and Torstein helped."

Torstein smiles at his comrade. "Since you did so much to provide us with this shelter, you may have the honor of building the fire, Great Wilderness Builder."

Moments later, Skjervald is feeding well-cured logs from a stack in the corner onto a crackling blaze in the center of the floor. Smoke, what little there is, draws through a hole in the roof that he cleared of snow. Now Inga can see the reindeer and wolf skins lining the interior. Even the lattice of the alder door is covered top to bottom with fur. There is room for each of them to spread bedrolls. She fetches snow to melt, and feeds Hakon while the men cook the last of their supply of meal and mix it with the remaining *røkt laks*. For the first time since they left Lillehammer, Inga feels that they'll be truly warm.

Magnus and his men underestimate the speed of the storm. Before the sun reaches its apex, the wind howls around them. Snow pours so thick that the first man can't see the seventh and they link themselves together with a line. Even with that, they can't continue to move for long under this white cascade. With the wind out of the east, the men begin to dig out a west-facing cave in the biggest drift they can find. Each time they paw away snow or scoop it with a ski, half falls back into the hole and the sky drops billowing layers to slow the process. Fingers, stiff with cold, drop skis and fumble at the task. An easy chore requires utmost effort, but they finally manage to carve out enough of a burrow to hold them.

One by one, they crawl under the makeshift snow roof and spread their skins. Askell and Ulf still have some firewood atop their ruck baskets and are able to kindle a small fire and melt some snow. Two men at a time warm their hands. All of them line skis across the center of the cave's opening and sit cross-legged around the flame, trying to protect it from the weather. As hard as they try, they can't keep the dense cascade of snow from suffocating it. After that, all they can do is allow the swirling torrents to blow in and cover their bear-skin-wrapped bodies with a measure of insulation. It falls so thick that it blocks out the light. Sun sets somewhere behind the white blanket.

In the darkness, Magnus hears One-Ear and Sveinn rummaging through their baskets. When the sound stops, he smells *røkt laks*. The smoky fish scent prompts him to find some of his own and gnaw on it, as much to pass the time as for nourishment.

In spite of the snow's insulation, the shelter is too shallow and exposed to provide adequate warmth. No one attempts conversation. After a long time, Magnus is able to get some fitful sleep. Gudrun and Jorund visit first, then Einar and his prophecy. Magnus sees the eagle swoop down at the raven, but this time, flowing yellow locks stream back from her white head. There's a child in the bird's talons, held gently, not showing a scratch. As the eagle gets closer, the raven can see that the child is happy, smiling and healthy. At first the raven sees that it is Sverrisson's son. The huge black predator attacks and suddenly the baby's face changes to Jorund's face. The raven veers off and the face again belongs to the bastard pretender. The raven turns and dives again, his talons thrust forward, gleaming sharp and menacing. As the winged razors slash into the child, and its blood streams back in a crimson trail, the eagle screeches. At first the sound is furious, the enraged shriek of the Valkyries. Then it softens to a forlorn weeping, sadder than Magnus has ever heard. The bleeding child's face becomes Jorund again, and both raven and eagle keen. "No!" Magnus hears himself scream as he pitches upright, wide awake, the sweat clammy and cold on his face and chest.

"What is it?" a shivering voice asks. It's Egil.

"Nothing. Never mind," Magnus says.

"Magnus, I can't last here," Egil says.

Magnus feels Egil's trembling, and the man's teeth chatter so, he can hardly get the words out. "Here is all we have until this storm passes."

"I think I can make it to the hut. At least the movement will warm me."

"If you leave here, you'll die. Even if you don't lose your way, the wind is strong enough to knock you down. You'll freeze." He grabs Egil's shoulder through the snow and squeezes it hard.

"Please, Magnus. I'll freeze here. I know I will. I can't stay. Please."

"No. You stay! At least here you can share what heat our

bodies generate. Storm breaks, we'll get warm again. Out there, you die. We'll find you frozen, if we find you at all."

"But I…"

"No more! You're staying." Egil doesn't answer. Magnus knows that it's not discipline that silences him, but fear that a response will deteriorate into hysteria. When he's certain Egil will argue no more, he allows himself to drift back into restless sleep. The prophecy doesn't return but wind wakes him several times. If this storm lasts beyond tonight, he says to himself, I don't think we will all survive it.

* * * *

The storm vanishes like the flame of a snuffed candle. Light filters through the snow that covers Magnus and his men and the roar of the wind moves west. Quiet fills its space. Magnus shakes his head, brushes his face with gloved hands and watches the snow scatter in billows. Quick sweeping strokes push a layer thicker than the length of his arm off of lap and legs. The flakes are dry and light. He folds his legs until he can lean forward onto his knees to get more of it off his chest. In the same motion he pushes up and out of the drifted shelter and continues to brush.

A few feet away, Sveinn shakes like a wet dog, producing a haze of white dust. Magnus walks toward him, sinking to his thighs with each step. When he reaches Sveinn, he extends one finger and makes a circular motion from his wrist. When Sveinn turns, Magnus brushes the snow from his comrade's back, and then turns to let him do the same. Three arms probe through the long drift, followed by heads Magnus can't identify. He reaches for one of the hands, grips it and leans back, pulling Ulf from his wintry cocoon. Sveinn drags out two more, Askell and Olaf. Olaf lifts One-Ear and they both help Thorvald.

"Where's Egil?" Magnus asks.

Shrugs and grunts follow. Everyone shuffles in circles and

pokes skis or *lurks* through the loose fluff of the shelter.

"I hope the fool didn't disobey my orders," Magnus says. "Cold and fear had him last night. He wanted to try to run for the hut."

"No!" says Sveinn. He kicks at piles of snow as if he expects to unearth his missing friend. "If he did, he's dead."

The men look at Magnus and at each other, the distress of losing yet another comrade carved on their faces. When it's obvious no one has a better answer, Magnus says, "We'd better go. Pack up."

"*Ja.* He's probably waiting for us at the…" One-Ear's voice trails off, and he shakes his head.

Magnus has his pack on his back as the others get ready. He scans the western horizon and the back side of the storm.

Sveinn joins him. "Moving away fast."

"Not clear of the plateau yet." It looks like a wall across the world. There is nothing between him and that moving barricade but a vast sunlit snowfield. No creature, not even a plant, breaks the drifting white expanse.

"So the Birkebeiners are still in it?" Sveinn says.

"Not for long," Magnus says. "Soon as it clears, we'll see them."

"We see them, we can run them down," Sveinn says.

"Surround them. Remember, Sturelsson and his men are somewhere to the west of them. If he sees no sign of them at the base of the southern trail, he'll move to the northern one and wait at the bottom."

Sveinn frowns and studies the snow. Magnus lets him process the image. After a moment, he looks up and says, "Perfect. The Birkebeiners will run right into them with us close behind."

Turning to the others, Magnus yells, "Let's go!" Sveinn, Thorvald and he ski west. The others fall in behind. They quickly gain speed and rotate the lead. The sheer depth of the new snow offers resistance, but not enough to overwork them.

No sooner do they establish their rhythm than Sveinn says,

"What's that?" He points ahead at something sticking out of the snow. After a few strides they can tell that it's a spear with the tip pointing skyward. When they reach it, they see, just above the surface, a bare white fist clutching the shaft. Sveinn twists the shaft, but the bloodless appendage refuses to yield its grip.

Askell bends forward to start digging, but Magnus grabs his shoulder to stop him. "He's better off left under," he says.

"But maybe he's not…" Askell stares.

Magnus imagines the young man has never seen a hand that color. He shakes his head, his hand now resting on Askell's shoulder. The soldier looks to the others, hoping for a different answer. Each nods or shakes his head, either gesture confirming the same reality. Then Askell, still staring down at the hand, says, "*Ja*. Let's go." There's no fear or bewilderment on his face now, just sadness dabbed with a trace of anger.

By the time they have their speed and rhythm back, the storm has moved far enough west that Magnus can see a speck on the horizon. "The hut," he says.

Not long after that Sveinn says, "There. Look there." He points with his free hand. "It's them. See them?"

"Where?" One-Ear says.

 "Right of the hut. Tiny. See it?

"I see them," Ulf says.

"Yes," Askell says. "See them, Magnus?"

"We've got them," he says.

Frustration is obvious in One-Ear's voice. "Where?"

Sveinn drops behind him and gets close, so that one of his skis is between One Ear's. He sights over his disciple's shoulder with the handle of his axe and grasps the back of Olaf's head with his free hand, pointing it in the right line. "Right there. Look down my axe handle."

Squinting and grimacing, One-Ear says, "Oh. *Ja. Ja*. Now I see them."

Magnus is not sure he does, but if not, he's decided to take their word for it.

The running line forms and Magnus senses the men's urgency. As the pace accelerates, he begins to think about his vision. And wonder about the nature of his soul and how many ways he can damn it.

After they finish the last of their food, at least the meat and *røkt laks*, Inga tries to sleep but can't despite her fatigue. Her mind drifts back to Borg and Sundays there. After her family returned from their tiny church, her sisters and she would help their mother prepare the morning meal. Her father, if it was spring or summer, would split wood for winter. If it was *Ylir* or later, he would build up the fires in the *soverom* and *stue* and feed the animals. Chores took most of the morning, but the meal that followed was always the best of the week. If they had meat, Inga and her mother prepared it. The night before, they rolled dough and let it rise until morning, so the bread was always fresh and warm and made the whole house smell clean and sweet. As soon as they could pull from the garden or fields, from *Midsommer* on, they had bowls of fresh vegetables, greens first, then potatoes and carrots and later corn and lentils. It was the only day the family table held both milk and butter. Her mother would mix cream and the juice from the meat with the potatoes and carrots.

Inga can taste the memory.

When they had eaten all they wanted and cleaned the *soverom*, her sisters and she would run to the mill pond and jump into its cool water. It was the same pool she told Hakon and Torstein about when they visited Borg for the first time. They and some of their soldiers accepted her offer to go there after that dinner. The three girls led them from the house, showed them where the bottom was firmest and left them to swim. Halfway back to the lodge, the youngest of her sisters said, "Let's go back and spy on them." Inga's hand went to her mouth in her best imitation of shock. "You know you want to," her sister said. "I saw you talking with him while we cleaned the pots. Rather, looking at him while he talked to you." Inga slapped her on the arm. She slapped back and the three of them began to laugh. "*Ja*," Inga said, and they crept back to where they could see the men. They arrived in time to see the men run into the water. They lay in the high grass looking down at the pond.

"Look," her sister said "a King's rump looks like anybody else's!"

"How many have you seen?" Inga said.

"Enough to know," she said.

"Ha!"

When the men came out of the pond, Inga and her sisters covered their eyes. At least most of the time. Then they sneaked back to the lodge and talked and laughed about their adventure. Inga talked most about Hakon.

She dabs at a tear, and falls asleep smiling at those memories.

* * * *

She's awakened by a bright ray of sun beaming though a chink where the wall meets the roof on the east side of the hut. Faster than it started, the storm has transformed to a delicate flurry. All night, the fury pounded around them, and now in an instant, it is gone and replaced by sunlight filtered through sporadic flecks of white. Like a lamb stepping out of a bear.

For some reason, the wind did not wake Hakon, but Inga's grateful that he slept through the night. As soon as he wakes, he cries until she gives him milk. Skjervald makes a paste of warm meal, the only food they have left, and all of them eat some. Inga believes that Hakon's tummy is full, but knows the men must be hungry. She puts a hand on her own stomach and presses.

Skjervald says, "Looks as if we can get started."

"Pack up," Torstein says. "Quickly." He opens the door and

a pile of fluff spills to the floor. "Looks soft," he says. "Going to ski a bit. See what kind of headway we can make." With his skis in one hand, he steps out, pulls the door closed with the other, and stomps down an area around the entrance. Inga hears him struggle to tighten his bindings, then the soft swish of skis pushing through fresh powder. Torstein hasn't skied far when the cloak of airy snow absorbs every sound.

She and Skjervald pack and hoist their ruck baskets onto their shoulders. "Lighter now, aren't they?" he says.

"Not much food left," she says.

"Two more days should get us there. Once we're back in the woods, we can hunt if we need to."

"That takes time."

"Keep your eyes open. Something easy will come along."

From outside, they hear the soft brush of Torstein's skis returning. Through the door, Torstein says, "It's soft and deep. Up to my knees, but easy to glide through. Let's go."

Skjervald has Hakon's sling over his shoulder and a pair of skis in each hand. Inga opens the door and he hands them out to Torstein, who is tramping down more area around the door. It would be easier to put the skis on in the hut, but Skjervald waxed them during the storm and he knows that dirt on the bases will slow them. While they draw the thongs tight around their feet, Torstein says, "I can't see any sign of them. Storm would've moved past them before it did us."

"They've had a rough night out there." Skjervald's eyes sweep the eastern horizon.

"How rough?" Inga asks.

"Had to dig in. If they waited till the storm was on them, they've had problems with exposure. Couldn't cook or melt snow."

"Slow them down?"

"Should. Let's hope."

Bright morning sun feels warm on Inga's back as they set off toward the northwest. Small flakes drift from nowhere, lazy in their effort. Each crystal seems to have its own personality in a silent conversation with the sun, reflecting instead of talking, sparkling instead of gesturing, and then lying silent amongst its brothers and sisters. Watching them causes her to slip out of Torstein's and Skjervald's track, and she stumbles. The soft snow offers no support and she thrashes until she untangles her skis and pushes herself upright with her *lurk*. She's able to shake most of the powder off, careful to clap her mitts against each other so no snow sticks to melt later. She scolds herself. I'd better concentrate on following them or I'll end up wet. She catches Skjervald looking over his shoulder at her fumbling. She scowls at him, but it doesn't wipe the smirk off his face.

By the time the sun is overhead, it's warm enough to peel off the heavy bearskin and ski in their *vadmel* and the beaver-skin vests. While they shed the parkas, each turns to the east, hoping to see nothing but endless snowfields. But there it is, the black dot on the horizon, closer now than before. Close enough that they can distinguish more than one dot.

"I count five," Torstein says.

"At least," Skjervald says. "Probably six."

All Inga knows is that she can discern movement. Arms swinging. Legs reaching out for the next stride. Can I see that? Are they even close enough to make me imagine that I can? Her chin trembles, not because of the cold, and the tremor travels the length of her spine and settles in her stomach. She wishes she could build a wall right here. One so high, nobody could scale it. One her child and she could hide behind. She knows, as she thinks it, that her only choice is to run. Stay ahead of them. Keep Hakon away from them. Run until we reach Nidaros or they kill us.

"We can beat them to the first trail down to the Gudbrans, even the second," Skjervald says.

"If there are five or six in that group, I'd wager there are at least that many already in the Gudbrans, waiting for us," Torstein says.

"Or climbing one of the trails we must descend," Skjervald

says.

"But which?" Torstein says.

"Hakon said the northern trail is the easiest," Inga says.

"It is," Skjervald says. "But we've had two storms. Likely worse in the Gudbrans than here."

Inga looks back and forth between the two. "So if weather slowed them, they won't come up the first trail and risk being behind us. They'll go to the second and wait for us at the bottom?"

"They go to the second, won't matter which route we take. We'll have to go through them," Torstein says, finishing her thought.

"We can ski the tougher trail faster than they can," says Skjervald, brandishing his spear toward the specks. "Let's run for the first trail, get the protection of the woods and our skill advantage."

Both men look at Inga. She nods.

"*Dra,*" Torstein says.

Skjervald takes the lead and holds back little. Inga struggles, but with Torstein encouraging her from behind, is able to keep pace. After a long stint, Skjervald drops to the rear and Inga breaks trail for a while. Even though it's soft, the depth of the new snow offers resistance. Her stamina is good, but she lacks the strength of the men, necessary to sustain speed under these conditions. As soon as the additional burden of breaking trail begins to slow her, she yields the trail to Torstein. They continue to take turns at the front, the men taking longer shifts and Inga shorter ones. Their speed doesn't suffer, but Inga wonders how long she can sustain such a pace.

Glare from the sun is ahead of them and angled from their left. It doesn't blind them, but it distorts landscape, hinders concentration, and obscures some of their field of vision. Not being able to see the horizon makes it feel as if there is no destination, no end point they can see and say, "That's where we'll rest." When there's no visual reference, weariness becomes the most prominent signal. Inga's thighs ache, and the small of her back feels close to spasm. Her throat grates from sucking in cold air and her eyes alternate between burning dryness and freezing tears.

For the first time she can hear the men's breathing over her own and understands that if they labor that much, then she is well beyond her capacity. She fights to keep her ankles from falling to either side of the skis in this deep, soft snow. It's hard enough to do when fresh. Right now, weariness wobbles her legs like an infant's. When she takes the point again, her instinct is to slow the pace, stop the hurting. What the Croziers will do if they catch them overrides her exhaustion. Only one thought drives her. I will not see my child in their grasp, no matter what.

Torstein shortens Inga's turn even more and she flashes a grateful smile as he passes her. She looks into Hakon's precious face. He's smiling and wiggles his fingers at her over the edge of the blanket. "Hakon go fast, *Mamma!* Go fast." Could she spare the energy, she would spend it laughing.

By now, they're losing daylight again. Torstein points at something. "There," he yells. "Straight ahead."

For the first time since they reached the plateau, Inga sees scrub again, the far edge of the snowfield. She manages to gasp out, "Will we make it before dark?"

"No, but we'll keep going."

She wants to ask what his plan is, but lacks the wind. And she doesn't want to tax his energy by making him answer another question. Besides, there aren't many choices. Either they start down the trail in the dark or hide in the shadow of the woods and wait for moonrise.

One-Ear's stride is inspired, the hardest Magnus has seen him work since they set out. He begins to think Olaf does actually see them, and the thought of confronting Torstein Skevla puts strength in his legs. Plumes of soft snow, lifted by the tips of One-Ear's skis, splash against his shins. Residue swirls away in white puffs. Much of it sticks to the hoarfrost formed from sweat that penetrates his leggings, until he looks like a creature rising from snow to form a man.

The others keep pace with him. Alternative explanations of Olaf's sudden fervor elude Magnus, but he's pleased with his speed, whatever the motivation. One-Ear is drawing their quarry back to them.

The speck on the horizon has grown steadily larger, and now Magnus can make out three specks and discern motion.

No sooner does Sveinn take the point, than he yells back, "I can see the scrub!"

"Are we going to run in the dark?" shouts Askell, as he drops back beside Magnus.

Magnus opens his mouth but before the word leaves his tongue, it echoes from One-Ear, Sveinn, and Ulf. "Yes!"

Magnus knows that his men remember how they lost Ingersson and would fear an all-out pursuit in the dark. He's also aware that they know they must push if they are to succeed in their mission. "Moon'll be up early tonight." Magnus says it quietly, an attempt to console the others and perhaps himself.

Anger is what fuels him now. His disdain for Eystein grows with each stride and yet he exerts every fiber of body and will on a mission without honor.

Already the sky grows dim, that stark, cold gray just before the sun plunges below the horizon. Then they'll lose sight of the Birkebeiners and have to be satisfied with hope that they're gaining ground. They stride on, each thrust of the ski resolute, purposeful. They're gliding well. The snow seems to part for them before their skis drive through it. For a while, there is no sound but their breathing and the swish of six pairs of skis through soft snow.

Ulf says, "How do we know which trail they'll choose?"

"Stay in their tracks," Magnus says, his tone suggesting that the answer is obvious.

"No, I meant should we follow or take the other trail?"

Magnus thinks about it for a moment, more to catch his breath than to form a response. "We'll follow them," he says. "If they take the southern trail, we trap them between us and Sturelsson. If they take the northern trail, we're no worse off." There's no discussion and Magnus is glad, as he needs all his wind to keep pace. For the first time, he's certain they will overtake the infant king and his protectors.

Now barely able to distinguish between land and sky, Inga finds it impossible to discern a shape, a tree or a rock. Outlines of small pines and brush merge with descending shadows. The three still have a considerable trek to the end of the snowfield as the horizon blends into the dark gray above it. In moments, the sky won't part from the ground and somewhere in that stark blackness the trail will drop like an eagle swooping on prey.

Skjervald and Torstein tow Inga along between them. She has the impression that Skjervald is always on the verge of pulling away from her, but senses her capacity and measures his pace. If not for the terror of facing steep, narrow, downhill corridors, blind and on weary legs, Inga would welcome the chance to descend.

Her breathing is labored, but steady and rhythmical. Branches begin to brush by arms and legs, a signal that she is in the small trees and undergrowth. Sometimes the outline of a small pine is a shade darker than the surrounding night. At first she's surprised that they reach the plateau's perimeter in such a short time, but then realizes that darkness clouds perceptions, including time and distance.

Skis offer less resistance and the blackness closes tight, warnings that she's back in the woods at the crest of the long, winding downhill. Her rhythm and concentration break when the first branch slaps across her cheek. When the men show no signs of pausing, her hope dwindles that they will stop to rest before they accelerate.

"Keep your eyes down," says Skjervald. "The snow will be lighter than the woods."

Inga fails to see any contrast, but makes no attempt to

slow. She can distinguish between Skjervald's body and the trail, and focuses on his vague outline for guidance.

"Stay low on your skis," Torstein yells.

Already, she's bent at the knees with her weight forward from the ankles, holding her *lurk* in front of her to fend off branches before they gouge an eye or break her nose. A loud crack, followed by several smaller ones, startles her as the pole pushes through resistance. She refuses to slow down, desperate to keep touch with Skjervald.

"Big right!"

Unseen forces pull her body to the left. She pushes her hands into the force and drives her knees hard to the right as she slides her left ski out ahead of the other. Her skis snap her around the turn on their right edges. Whips of her hair, long since sucked out of her hood, snap behind her and the wind whistles past her ears. Fear for Hakon and the harm that pursues him suppress any anxiety about injuries at these speeds, and she accelerates. It's as if something has dug a hole in her mind and she has thrown any self-concern into it and kicked the dirt back in.

Skjervald yelps and three branches whip across Inga's face, causing her to echo his pain. She hears the limbs bang off Torstein's shield like thrown rocks. The sound tells her Hakon wasn't hit, and that takes some of the sting from her cheek.

"Left!" yells Skjervald. Inga reacts. The tail of her right ski careens off a solid mass. All her strength pulls the ski back under her, and she escapes upright. Shaken and terrified, she makes the next turn by the narrowest margin, certain she feels the rough brush of bark against her left hip and the tail of her left ski. Her thighs threaten to fail under the weight of one more turn just as the pitch modifies and skis slow for a blessed instant of relief.

She hears Torstein behind her. "Try to relax on this shallow section."

"There's more?" For a moment her spirit hurts worse than her legs and face. In less time than it takes for her question to reach him, she knows the answer. Only the sudden acceleration keeps her from pitching forward as the ground drops from under her. "Thor's *fyr!*" she screams. Back and forth she bounces from one ski to the other, fighting to keep her balance. Each time her weight lands on one leg, the throbbing ache of fatigue increases and recovery in the free leg diminishes. Fatigue is winning the battle.

Why she's aware of the scent of pine, she can't imagine, but it tells her that they are well below the tree line in their descent, that the steepest terrain is behind them. As if her mind is trying to repel hope, she remembers that most of the mountain is below the tree line. Long way before we reach the valley, she thinks.

Darkness magnifies speed and obliterates reference. A tree you can see is orientation. One you can't see is an obstacle careening toward you to tear skin and crush bone. Each bump in the trail is a snow snake trying to entangle your skis and throw you to the ground. And the bumps of darkness find their way under your skis with much greater frequency than the bumps of daylight. If she rode a reindeer blindfolded, Inga would have more control over her destiny.

Once again she senses deceleration, a suggestion that the terrain no longer falls away at the severe pitch of the top. Skjervald's outline has a little more definition now. There's still no light, so she attributes his more distinct silhouette to the slowing. She wonders how he does it with no one in front of him. At least I have someone's turns to mimic, she thinks. She hears the thwack of a limb and his grunt in response. She bends her knees at the sound and the branch glances off the top of her hood. Torstein's skis are the only sound she hears behind her, so she assumes he ducked the obstacle.

Speed varies but never reaches the runaway acceleration of upper sections as the three continue the gauntlet of face whips and body blows toward the trail below.

One-Ear does not relent. The Birkebeiners have disappeared into the blackness and it's a long time from when the three specks meld with the night until Magnus and his men arrive at the top of the trail. "We've closed half a day's lead to having them in sight," Magnus says. "Don't lose them now."

"Let me charge into Thor's sword before that happens!" One-Ear screams, and he plunges down the trail.

"I believe Thor has possessed him," Sveinn says, leaning toward Magnus.

Magnus hears a smile in Sveinn's words. The two of them race side by side behind their fervent new leader. As they slide into the trail, the silver edge of brightness creeps over the horizon.

"Arrgh!" Olaf yells, as he reacts to the slash of a branch that is now in Magnus's face. Several others yelp with their turn at nature's whip. The moon vaults high over the woods, like it has hit the valley floor and bounced off, its light transforming murky obscurity to contrasts and shadows as distinct as daytime. Moonlight offers advantages in negotiating the downhill turns, and increases Magnus's confidence even more. Now he has no doubt.

Reaching the valley offers no rest. One group of the enemy closes fast and drives Inga and her companions headlong toward the pack they are sure awaits. But feeling flat trail under her, having forest around her to block the wind, smelling the scent of pine again relieves some anxiety, and before they have traveled far in the Gudbrans, the moon breaks the horizon. In moments it's bright enough to cast their shadows against the silver trail.

"*Mamma* look," Hakon says. His hand juts from his *vadmel* cocoon with a tiny finger extended skyward. Inga drops back beside him. "Yes, Hakon, the moon."

"Ertty moo, *Mamma*."

"Pretty moon," she agrees. She peels off a mitt and strokes his face. Torstein slows so she can tuck the baby's hand back into the warmth of the blanket. She looks up at Torstein's face. Dried blood mats his eyebrow and the top of his beard and there is still a crimson trickle from a gash that cuts across the old scar and another on the bridge of his nose. "Do those hurt?" she asks.

"What?" Moonlight reflects off his teeth.

"Never mind."

"You look like you lost an argument with a lynx," he says.

Still skiing hard, she pulls off her right mitt and touches the parts of her face that hurt, which is most of them. Rough scabs dotted with sporadic stickiness turn her fingertips red. "Glad I can't see it," she says, and decides to leave it alone.

"Not too serious. Looks and feels worse than it is," he says.

She doesn't think he's just trying to comfort her. "Good," she says. "What now?"

"Get past whoever is waiting for us."

"Sure somebody is?"

"*Ja.*"

"Can't we go around them through the woods?"

Torstein shakes his head. "Even if we didn't get lost, we'd be too slow. Trail's faster. They'd stay ahead of us without any effort."

Inga bites her lower lip. Torstein's right, she knows. Moving through the woods off trail is difficult and sluggish, even in summer. Navigating around every tree, pushing through tangled branches, is slow on foot, and even slower on skis. "So they'd get us wherever we come out."

"Right."

"And we'd be easy prey."

"Very." He leaves her and dashes the short distance to Skjervald's side, where the two of them converse for what seems a long time. Neither yields speed, but the conversation appears intense to her. The men have their heads as close as balance will allow and their hands are busy with conversation.

Inga wonders what they're discussing, probably some kind of defense, but she doesn't dwell on it. It's never easy for her to keep pace with them, so it's rare that she gets the chance to study her surroundings. Use by animals and man has pushed the trail wider here, turned it into the Old King's Road. On the slopes, tight paths forced them to stay single file, but here they can travel three across if they choose. There's room for her to see the trees, branches laden with fresh snow that sparkles in the moonlight like ripples on a vertical lake. Her motion creates the illusion of undulation as the higher boughs flow into the lower ones and back again, waves of snow cresting and troughing between them. With each breath, the rich scents and sights of the forest, missing as they crossed the high, barren plateau, flood back into thirsty senses.

After a while, she looks again at Torstein and sees Skjervald touch his face and say something. Torstein shakes his head and drops back toward her. Skjervald continues to lead.

"When we get near the second trail from the plateau,"

Torstein says, pausing to get his wind, "Skjervald will race ahead and attack with his bow. One, maybe two arrows and retreat." He breathes again. "Before he leaves us, we'll conceal ourselves in the woods and wait."

"For what?" She wants to give him another chance to catch his breath.

"For them to chase him past us."

"And when they do?"

"I'll get the last one with my axe. Skjervald will turn and loose another arrow. You'll be behind me with Hakon, ready to run for Nidaros. Once we get past them, it's only the rest of the night and half a day."

"I want a weapon."

"You'll have Skjervald's spear. And a knife if you want it."

"Good." She thinks for a moment. "Will we have enough time before the ones behind us catch up?"

He nods.

It doesn't convince her. She prays. God will that we have enough light left before the moon sets.

Skjervald reduces the pace for the first time since they started the run on the plateau. She knows he's trying to conserve energy for his attack and a speedy retreat. All of them will need an extra surge when the time comes.

* * * *

Anxiety twists silence into thunder. No words pass, but Inga can hear the men's breathing like hammers on an anvil. Even her own panting doesn't conceal theirs. Fatigue makes it seem a long time before Skjervald signals a halt. Torstein and Inga creep toward him. For the first time she sees how battered his face is from leading the way in the darkness. When they reach him, he puts a finger to his lips, lips split and bleeding, and whispers, "Trail is just beyond the second turn. Hide there." He points to a boulder surrounded by brush and alders.

Inga and Torstein turn in their tracks, follow them back beyond the line of sight and push into the woods a few feet, then work their way back to the boulder, leaving no tracks into the woods near the ambush point.

Torstein gives Skjervald a wave and he's off, bow poised and arrow notched. Inga hopes the raw bloodiness of his face looks fierce and savage to the Croziers. Her hand quivers around the shaft of his spear. Her chest tightens and her throat goes dry. Her legs are sore and heavy as stone. She fears they may cramp without warning.

Torstein pulls his hunting knife from the leather scabbard at his waist and hands it to her. His axe dangles from his wrist by the rawhide loop through its handle. With rapt concentration, he adjusts the knot on the loop to reduce the slack so he can snap the heavy weapon back into his hand should an enemy blow knock it loose. While he checks the straps on his shield, he orients it and his skis so that he can slip out of the woods without snagging limbs or undergrowth. "Cut those away," he says pointing to low branches. With a few quick swipes, she gets them out of the way. One of the branches brushes against Hakon's face, waking him from a long nap. He begins to whimper.

"Oh, God," she whispers, and strokes his face. He starts to cry. "Please baby, not now. Shhhh, shhhh." Panic pounds at her temples. If she puts her hand over his mouth it could make him hysterical. She can't move deeper into the woods because the men might need her. Singing, soon even whispering, is out of the question.

From down the trail comes a shriek that tells her Skjervald's arrow has found its mark. Shouts follow. Torstein's eyes don't leave the trail. Inga slides the knife into her birch leggings and with both hands rips open her parka and vest. She pulls Hakon out of the sling and pushes him under her shirt. She takes the back of his head through the garment and guides him to her breast. His crying returns to a whimper and then a contented sigh. Thank God for instinct, she thinks.

She hears the clamor of the chase rush closer, a cacophony of screams and shouts. "Get him! Take him alive!" someone yells from a place she can't see. Skjervald charges past them at full stride, notching another arrow as he runs. Torstein's eyes hold the trail like a dog holding a bird for the flush. Two Croziers pass and Inga wonders if they are too close to Skjervald for him to turn and get a shot. A ski length behind comes a third and right on his tail, two more. A sixth soldier follows, farther back. When the trailing Crozier is two strides from the rock that hides Inga and Torstein, Torstein hooks his axe blade around a sapling and yanks on the handle with all his might, propelling himself into the astonished enemy with enough might to knock him down. No sooner has the Crozier hit the ground than Torstein's axe completes its powerful arc through the man's ankle. Agony reverberates off the trees, and a crimson plume spurts onto Torstein's birch leggings. Before the echo dies, the Crozier does, as a second blow, this one to the head, thwarts another scream.

"*Dra*, Inga! Run!"

Two steps out of the woods, she's at full speed. From the corner of her eye, she sees the last two Croziers change direction to face Torstein. Skjervald turns across the trail and she hears his bow string twang. Zfft! The lead Crozier staggers and falls face down. She doesn't try to see more, but puts her head down and concentrates on speed. As she approaches the second bend, she can still hear the ring of weapon against weapon and the thud of shields absorbing blows. Desperation such as she has never experienced stabs her like forged, honed iron. She and Hakon are alone, and all that lies between him and death is her speed and what little endurance she has left. When she rounds the second turn, she crashes from maximum speed to a dead stop in one stride as desperation turns to horror.

One Crozier has stayed back as a rear guard. Their eyes lock for a long moment. He's as startled as she is. With a grimace, he brandishes his sword and charges. There's no time to think, and she can't be any more terrified. His charge assumes the quality of a sleep vision as Inga's mind shrinks his speed so that she can see his food-stained beard and the froth of saliva at his rabid mouth. She hears no noise. Not from him. Not from the battle behind her. Not from her own breathing.

She bends and puts Hakon at her heels to position herself between him and his murderer. Both hands tighten on the spear shaft as she lowers it to the level of the Crozier's chest.

The threat brings him up short. "I have no quarrel with you, woman. Stand aside and let me do the king's bidding."

"You and your king can burn in Thor's *fyr*, Crozier." She takes a stride toward him, brandishing the spear as she does.

"As you wish," he says. His expression blends annoyance with scorn as he crouches to the posture of a predator confident of its kill. With measured steps, the caution of a stalking beast, he approaches. Inga matches each of his advances with one of her own and another thrust of the spear. When he is close enough for their weapons to overlap, he swings his sword, catches the spear tip just above the shaft, and knocks it aside. Before she can recover, he steps in, grabs the middle of the shaft with his free hand and drives his fist and the hilt of his sword into the side of her face. The power of the blow causes numbing pain, and the woods begin to spin in a cluster of black and white flashes.

When she shakes her head, all she can see in front of her are drops of blood in the snow between her hands, and the tails of his skis passing beyond her field of vision. Dazed and in pain, she manages to pull herself to her feet and draw the knife from her leggings. She turns and sees him hovering over her baby. Hakon's terrified shrieks rip through her pain.

"No!" She screams as the dizziness causes her to stagger and fall toward the soldier. As she lands on the tails of his skis, she thrusts her arm over her head and drives the blade into his right calf. He tries to pull away from the source of pain, but her weight on the back of his skies makes him stumble and fall forward on top of Hakon. The enemy rolls, screaming, onto his side, trying to untangle his skis and reach the knife. Each movement of his leg must cut new flesh, for he cries out several more times before he's able to arrange the skis so that he can extract the blade. As he gasps and curses, Inga's head clears enough for her to grab Hakon and begin to back-step toward the spear lying in the snow where the fight began. She puts the baby down, picks up the spear and turns to face her marauder again.

Before she can rise to a full defensive position, he has driven into her, his skis to the left of hers, the knife in his left hand and the sword in his right. With his left he pushes the spear down and slashes toward her head with the knife. She's able to throw her left forearm up to block his wrist. He grunts as his forearm smashes into hers, and his rancid fish breath swamps her senses. At the same time she drops the spear and uses her right hand to wrap his wrist and try to pull the dagger away from her face. Too powerful for her, he pushes the point closer to its goal. She jerks her head to the left and lets the blade come up. As it tears her hood and pushes through the hair just over her ear, she opens her mouth as wide as she can and like the most ferocious she-wolf ever to defend her pups, she clamps her jaws on his forearm where the grappling has pushed back his sleeve. She bites until she feels teeth against bone. His cry, so close to her ear, deafens her on that side, and its foul odor makes her want to vomit. Even when she feels the knife slip and fall from his grip, she doesn't let go. He screams and flails his arm, throwing her head around like it's part of the appendage. He's too close to reach her with the blade, but he raises the hilt and swings a glancing blow into her head. As she goes down, she feels his flesh rip before she releases and falls stunned.

Inga lifts her skis and twists onto her back. She rubs her eyes to stem the dizziness which darkens and blurs her vision again, but she is able to see him holding and shaking his stricken forearm. She reaches to her left and feels the shaft of the spear there. With her right hand she claws a fistful of snow and presses it to her forehead. It's enough to give her some clarity. She looks up the length of his body to mean eyes, full of pain and hate, glaring down at her. He takes half a step back, grits his teeth and raises the sword. In his rage he fails to notice her right ski sliding across both of his. As his sword reaches its highest point, ready for the arc to her skull, she pulls the spear up and to the center. When he contracts at the waist to begin his swing, Inga thrusts her leg into his ankles and sends his skis out from under him, so that the full weight of his body crashes against the tip of the spear. It sinks into his chest until she can feel it wedge between ribs. A startled gasp gurgles through lips void of color. A look somewhere between confusion and terror molds his face. He fights to get his feet back under him. Blood trickles from the corner of his mouth, then gushes in an exhaled foam. Inga pushes herself out from under the stream of bubbling blood that splatters her parka, and kicks again. This time his feet fly out behind him and he slides the full length of the shaft and lies still as the snow on both sides turns crimson.

With trembling limbs that have suddenly chilled, she pushes herself further away from the dead Crozier, toward Hakon, who is hysterical with fear. Her vision is still blurred and splotchy. "Don't cry sweet baby. I'm here, Hakon. *Mamma's* here," she says, trying to soothe him as she crabs her way in his direction, dragging skis splayed to her left side. She kisses him and puts the unhurt part of her face next to his and he relaxes a little, gasping and sniffling, trying to catch his breath and stop the sobbing. She warms him with her body for a moment. Her head begins to clear and she feels she can get to her feet. Wrapping her arms around him, she pulls herself to her knees, where she rocks him a little. She gets one ski under her, then the other, and rises. She wobbles with each tiny motion, struggles to keep her balance. Every instinct she has pushes her to move toward Nidaros as soon as she can.

Hakon's crying diminishes to an occasional pitiful gasp. Listening to him breathe makes her aware that that's *all* she hears. Screaming and battle sounds from down the trail are gone. Quiet. There's no wind. Everything is still, hushed. She takes a tentative stride, loses her balance, and forces herself back on to her skis. The next few steps are steadier until a wave of nausea takes over. She gags and vomits onto the trail. Afterwards, she scrapes some snow into her mouth, straightens, draws a few deep breathes, and skis off, determined to lengthen and quicken her stride. She's not far beyond the trail where Skjervald attacked the Croziers, when she hears him calling behind her.

"Inga! Inga, it's me!" She can't see him by looking over her shoulder, but she's so glad to hear his voice, she stops to wait. When he and Torstein round the bend, she sees no sign of wounds, except the bloodied faces from the plunge in the dark. "Thank God!" she says. "I've never been so glad to see anyone."

As they pull alongside, Torstein says, "We saw your friend back there. Sorry we weren't with you, but it looked like you didn't need us."

The blood-stained spear rests in Skjervald's fist. Inga turns her face toward them, so they can see where the Crozier hit her.

"On *Odin's* eyes! How did you stay conscious?" Skjervald says.

"Almost didn't. Luck, I suppose."

"Wasn't very lucky for that Crozier," Torstein says.

She starts to smile, but winces instead. "How'd you do?"

"Skjervald killed one with his sword after he got the first two with his bow. I dropped the one in the ambush, and then caught another one across his shoulder. Doubt he'll live. One other, Magnus's lieutenant, was able to get beyond us and run with the man I wounded. May have been a third ahead of them."

"One or two able-bodied and one wounded. What will they do?"

"Wait for Magnus, or whoever is leading the other bunch,

to come down from the plateau."

"So there will still be seven or eight pursuing?"

"Looks like it," Skjervald says. "We'd better keep going. You all right?"

"Yes," she lies, shaking her head. She turns to Torstein. "Can we stay ahead of them?" It's more an appeal than a question and begging eyes betray her doubt. Torstein puts a hand on each side of her face and lifts it until she can look nowhere but into his eyes.

"Of course," he says. Kindness and understanding fill his voice. The resolution comes from his eyes. "Now, let's go." When she nods, she drops her eyes. That's when she notices a stain the size of her hand seeping through the *vadmel* fiber of Torstein's left legging.

"You're hurt."

Skjervald turns at the words, and Inga realizes that Torstein had hoped they would not notice the wound.

Torstein reads the concern on their faces. "No matter," he says, waving them off with a dismissive flick of the wrist. "The Crozier I wounded managed to get the tip of his spear in me, but he was falling away to avoid my blow. Thrust had no weight."

Neither replies, but they all look at each other a bit too long.

"Let's go," he repeats, and Inga and Skjervald fall in behind him.

Flooded with moonlight, the trail offers little resistance, though One-Ear displays caution in the steeper turns. It's been some time since they passed the tree line and the terrain has moderated, allowing them to sustain a safe pace. Shafts of silver bleed through the trail canopy and light the forest floor. Only the air stings Magnus's face now and Sveinn confirms his suspicion.

"Getting colder," he says. "Much colder."

"Pick it up. Get some distance out of the snow before the cold makes it slow," Magnus says.

Sveinn nods and they pull past One-Ear, who grunts either protest or appreciation.

"If Fortune is fair, we'll push them into Sturelsson and trap them between us," Magnus says.

"And if Fortune's the ungrateful beggar he usually is?" Sveinn asks.

"Pursue, destroy."

"All?"

"The Birkebeiners and the heir. The woman if she resists."

"All, then."

Magnus ignores the comment, leans down the hill and lets his skis run. A branch reaches out like an old woman's hand and slaps his shoulder as he rounds a turn. He thinks about the Birkebeiners' descent. *In the dark that would have been in my face. We're lucky the moon is up. Skiing this trail in the dark would be teasing the trolls.* Before he finishes the thought, he's dodged three more limbs. It occurs to him there's no snow on any of them. *Knocked off,* he thinks. *All the way down. They must not have slowed at all.* He shouts over his shoulder to Sveinn. "May not catch them before they reach Sturelsson."

"Why?"

"Never mind. Pick it up!" He hears the snow rushing under the base of Sveinn's skis and his own, a sound like water rushing through narrows or wind pushing through a ravine. Branches whip and crack off of parka sleeves and mitts held up to protect faces, and again Magnus imagines what a terrible gauntlet this must have been in the shroud of pitch darkness.

Before long, the terrain levels again, this time to a gentle slope, and he sees it. "There. Gudbrans," he says. Within moments, the narrow mountain trail has merged into the much wider valley trail, the Old King's Road, and they have turned to their right with Sveinn, One-Ear and Magnus skiing abreast. Ulf, Thorvald, and Askell, side by side, follow. Snow still clings to the trees along the new trail and they can see three sets of ski tracks.

Sveinn stops and squats over one pair of tracks. Stretching forward, he pinches the edge of one of the tracks, then stands, moves forward and repeats the sequence. "Fresh, soft," he says, and squeezes the lump of snow in his fist. "Wouldn't take long for these tracks to set firm in this cold. Can't be far ahead."

Each of them hears the sound before they see anything, something between a moan and garbled speech, like someone waking who doesn't want to. Weapons scratch from sheaths, and arrows rustle from quivers. Shields rise, and muscles tense while they strain to see. At first, it's a shadow, and then moonlight reflects from skin and something metal. A helmet? Sword?

As two forms congeal out of the forest shadows, One-Ear says, "Skevla." He says it like he found something he lost, something he knew he would find someday, but maybe not so happy to recover. He raises his axe and moves forward.

"No, wait." Magnus's sword blocks his way. "It's Sturelsson." He slides forward. "Sturelsson!" he yells.

"Magnus!" Both figures stop. "Help me. Gunnar's hurt."

As they scramble toward them, they can see Gunnar

hanging on Sturelsson's shoulder. His left arm is stained red from shoulder to fingertips, some of the crimson already turning dark and beginning to freeze. He's slumped, head hanging as if his neck bone has dissolved. Magnus and his men can see he won't last long. When Magnus gets close, he slides his hand under Gunnar's chin and lifts a head that would fall the other way if he didn't steady it. Even in the dimness of moonlight, he can see that if it weren't for the blue in his lips, he would have no color at all. Gunnar's eyes wander from Magnus's without settling on anything, and he moans again, a slur his tongue doesn't govern. Then his eyes roll back in his head and the air around them fills with his stench.

One-Ear and Sveinn help Sturelsson and Magnus lower the dead soldier to the snow. For a few moments they look at him, until One-Ear says, "Skevla?"

"Skevla and the younger one, Skrukka, ambushed us," Sturelsson says. "When we pursued them, we left Vegeir behind to guard our rear. I haven't seen him since and the others are all dead. I think Gunnar wounded Skevla, but I'm not sure. It was all I could do to keep Gunnar and myself alive."

"They killed all but you?"

"Lost Flat Nose to a birch-leg snare, and we lost Hrolf in the last storm. Never found him. Vegeir...?" Sturelsson's voice fades. He looks down at his feet.

"The woman? The woman and Hakonsson?" Magnus asks.

"Never saw them." He shrugs. "Last I saw, the two birch-legs were heading in the direction of Nidaros. No sign of the woman or her son."

"Must still be alive or Skevla would have tried to finish you. She must be ahead of them with the child. How long has it been?"

"Moon had just risen when they attacked."

"Moments, then. We can still catch them. You hurt?"

Sturelsson hesitates, like he's ashamed that he's not. "No. Let's go."

"What about Gunnar?" One-Ear says.

Magnus shakes his head. They turn, single file, and gather as much speed as they can sustain, each taking short turns at the front.

Inga used to think, as she climbed from the head of the Gudbrans Valley and crossed the high snowfields, that the Croziers would not be able to catch them. She thought that she and her child, with the help of their protectors, could descend the other side to the Oster Valley and put distance between the Croziers and themselves. But now her legs feel the weight of her body as if it were a millstone. Beyond the ache of fatigue, her thighs burn and calves cramp. Twice the pain has tied up Inga's legs so that she has had to stop and let one of the men massage the knots. Her heart hammers, using her ribs as its anvil. Her pulse flaps against her temple like the wings of a startled bird. Her mouth is dry and her throat sore from drawing the frigid air in gulps. The insides of her nostrils are frozen together so that even the pine has no aroma.

Perhaps the painful protest from her body causes her to imagine things, but she fears she can hear them. Can they be that close, she asks herself? "Torstein, do you hear them? Skjervald?" She wheezes out the words through rigid and tender air passages.

"No, what you hear is fatigue. We'll see Nidaros over the next rise," says Torstein.

Skjervald grunts agreement.

Both men reveal signs of physical stress. Arms hang lower than usual, and scrapes and cuts bleed or darken to hideous, frozen scabs. Torstein favors the wounded leg, and his stride appears erratic, even labored.

Hakon, thank God, still shows good color. The heavy blanket sling and Torstein's body heat continue to keep him warm. Of the four of them, he alone has been able to get adequate sleep, and Inga's milk has been enough to nourish him three or four times each day. Slowing or stopping to feed him is probably the reason the Croziers have closed ground.

Inga turns her head so her ear faces back down the trail. I'm not imagining it. They are close. I hear them urging each other on.

Snow begins to fall and Torstein covers Hakon's head and face with the blanket. Inga watches and is glad that this fearsome warrior has a gentle and nurturing way with her child. As he tucks the corners of the *vadmel* around Hakon's chin and forehead, careful to leave tufted pockets for breathing, she notices how huge his hands seem next to the baby's face. Hakon is comfortable with his protector and reaches a hand out of the blanket and wraps a baby fist around one of the thick, scratched fingers. Torstein tickles his chin with it and eases the hand back into the blanket, then pulls the blanket corners close together over Hakon's nose and mouth, talking gently, so it's a game.

Skjervald has dropped behind Inga, she thinks to make sure she doesn't falter or faint. I won't faint. I won't hold these men back. We're too close now. In less time than it takes to prepare supper, my son will be safe.

Torstein drops back beside Skjervald. They must fear that she'll collapse and want to allow her to find her own pace. They talk for a while, like before, heads close together. Inga hears them, but can't distinguish their words. Makes no effort to. Doesn't even turn to see what they're doing. After a while, Torstein comes forward again and surges toward a rise in front of them. When he has crested the hill, he waits for the other two.

Compared to what they've done, the climb is small, but Inga struggles to reach the top. When the knoll flattens, she can see the dark gray steeple of the cathedral, the Shrine of St. Olaf, as it reaches for the clouds. The spire appears to pass through the huge Nidaros *fjord* that sprawls beyond the city wall and forms a natural moat where it closes to a narrow isthmus between the *fjord* and the Nidelva River. Even from this distance, Inga sees the scaffolds of new construction on the west face of the huge church. She knows it will bear the carved images of Christ, the Apostles and saints. Visions of angels would not announce as merciful a welcome. Between the three Birkebeiners and the cathedral, sit hundreds of thatched-roof dwellings on both sides of the *Nidelva*.

"Mostly down hill now," Skjervald says as he reaches the high point. He puts a gentle hand on Inga's shoulder. "We'll rest a while."

"I dare not stop," she says. "My legs will seize." He doesn't respond. She watches his eyes as they lose her and concentrate on something behind them, something down the slope. Inga looks to Torstein and sees the same concentration.

"What...?"

He snaps his hand up, palm open, to silence her. Then they all hear it. Men's voices, several, labored and urgent. There's no mistake. They're too far away to make out words, but the sense is obvious, "Faster. We're gaining on them."

Skjervald says, "Run for Nidaros. I'll make a stand here to slow them."

"No," says Torstein. "Even without my wound, you're faster. Inga, take Hakon and go. Skjervald will follow." He turns to Skjervald, who looks at once both very old and very young to Inga. "Stop for nothing but death."

"But..."

"We don't have time to quarrel. I know you're brave and you know I'm right."

Skjervald nods and pulls his parka tight at the neck, his shield held near his throat.

Torstein removes the blanket sling, turns to Inga and puts it over her bowed head, positions it on her chest, the baby's head and face covered.

"Leave your bow and arrows," Torstein says to Skjervald. "And run with your king and his mother."

Skjervald drops his bow and quiver, then grasps Torstein's forearm to his. "Never fall in flight, my friend."

"Those who do never gain renown, Birkebeiner."

Both men smile. Skjervald turns and plunges into his descent.

Inga leans and kisses Torstein's cheek.

"*Dra!*" he says. "Stay close to Skjervald. If they get past me, give Hakon to him, and stop. They won't hurt you. They'll go past you after him."

"They won't pass me without killing me."

Torstein looks at her and says quietly, "I know."

Inga turns and doesn't look back, her concentration on Skjervald and trying to ski with him. Something inside of her. Fatigue that was oppressive retreats. Energy? No, but something has reduced the pain in burning and cramping sinews. Something gives her speed. Even with the surge, she senses for the first time in their journey that Skjervald is trying to pull away from her, *is* pulling away from her. He's making no effort to keep me in tow, she thinks. Bewilderment, then fear, wrap her like a plunge into freezing water. "Skjervald, wait! Stay with me!"

"Stay close!" he shouts over his shoulder. "Don't fall off."

"Can't. Can't go any faster," she gasps. "Wait!" She hears a death cry, a man's scream that can be mistaken for nothing else. Risking a glance back, she sees Torstein fire an arrow, drop the bow, and stand ready with his axe as three men attack him and three others slide by him—slide by him to chase her down and kill her baby. None, she can tell, has a bow, and she is beyond its range if they did. Then they have to catch me, she thinks. "Skjervald! There are only three! Wait!"

But he continues to pull away, this time without any response.

"Skjervald!"

Nothing.

Another glance tells her the three Croziers are closing ground. Her charge is desperate now. The energy of moments ago is spent. Sore legs can move no faster. Exhausted arms can push no harder against her *lurk* and the fatigue is back, worse than ever, gnawing into her body like a starving animal on a bone.

"Halt now and we spare your child!" one of the Croziers yells.

"Thor's sword strike you," Inga screams back. "Skjervald! Skjervald, please! Don't desert us now!" But he doesn't turn. And she knows she has no strength left, none at all. "Skjervald, you coward! *Odin* curse you!" she screams, a scream that rips her throat raw. She pulls Torstein's knife from her birch-bark leggings and turns to face her child's murderers, screaming profanities at them through tears of rage.

A she-eagle without talons," Magnus says to Sturelsson as they approach the woman carrying the Birkebeiner heir. Never has he seen a woman look so spent, or so ferocious. And he hopes he never does again. He looks into a twisted snarl that makes her young face look hard enough to cut stone. Sandy hair that would otherwise have served to soften her features is tangled and matted with blood and sweat. Dark circles make the glare from her green eyes seem as savage as a mother wolf's. A swollen and bleeding lip, facial cuts, including a gash across the bridge of her nose make her look fearsome and much older than her years.

"Come feel my talons, Magnus," Inga challenges, as she removes Hakon's sling from her chest, sets it carefully behind her, and brandishes her dagger at her enemy. Neither fear nor defiance show, rather a ruthless determination, which makes Magnus hesitate. He remembers the rest of Einar's prophecy that warned the raven not to get too close to the eagle's nest.

Sturelsson says, "Let's finish what we came to do," and strides toward the woman. When he is within an arm's length she thrusts the knife from waist height toward his chest. With a quick sidestep, he parries the thrust by grabbing her wrist and twisting back and away with cruel force, causing her to drop the weapon and shriek in pain. A second twist causes another cry and she drops to her knees. Magnus skis past them as Sturelsson tosses Inga aside. Before Magnus reaches the blanketed bundle on the ground, Inga has spun around and is clawing her way toward the blanket, dragging her skis, like a ravenous and wounded animal scrambling for its survival. Sturelsson steps on one of her skis, which are splayed sideways, stopping her short and twisting her ankle.

There's a grunt, but instead of another painful scream, she shrieks, "No, Magnus, don't! No!"

He looks at her and feels a pang of regret for her pain, and then in one motion raises his sword and brings it crashing down on the blanket.

*P*inned and rendered helpless by his henchman, the one he calls Sturelsson, I can do nothing but watch Magnus's sword follow its arc toward my precious Hakon. My own scream reaches my ears from another place, like the echo of a sound I made long ago. A thousand times in that arc, my mind sees the sword stop, but each time my eyes see it crash downward until it smashes through the blanket. I feel the edge of the blade as surely as if it was against my own skin, and sicken to the sound of its impact as if it sliced through my own midsection. And then all I can do is lie there and sob, my world gone, nothing I value left, nothing I want or feel or recognize.

And just before I sink into a bog of grief from which I will never pull free, I hear Magnus curse. "Hva faen?"

And then Sturelsson repeats it. "The hell? He's with the other one. The child is with the other Birkebeiner."

Slowly, still fearing the worst, I raise my eyes from the snow. At first I see only the surprise on Magnus's face. Then I see the blanket sling hanging limp from the tip of his sword. My eyes snap back to the ground where the blanket had been. There sits a log of birch, a terrible gash in its middle. Confused, not trusting my eyes, I look down the trail toward Nidaros, and see Skjervald, now too distant for a deer to catch him, skiing as hard and fast as he can. Beyond him, I see dozens, perhaps a hundred men gush from the city gates and cross the bridge over the Nidelva. They carry the banner of Arne, the Birkebeiner Prefect of the Nidaros *Lagting*.

My spirit soars and my energy returns. "Skjervald has him! Torstein put Hakon in Skjervald's ruck basket while they were behind me!" It pours out with a gust of laughter and I can't help but wonder if Magnus and Sturelsson even understand

what I'm saying. "My son is safe!" I beam into Magnus's scowl.
"Smile, Magnus. Your king is safe." And I laugh out loud as my
tears turn to joy.

Sturelsson skis toward me, his face a mask of fury, and
raises his sword. I continue to laugh, not flinching from him or
looking away.

"No!" Magnus screams. "Leave her! Our fight now is with
her son. And I've spent enough of my soul for one day."

And I watch until they disappear over the rise, skiing back
toward the Oster. I hope their return trip is as difficult as the
journey here.

*A*rne has provided Hakon and me with a comfortable lodge, smaller than the one in Lillehammer, but I don't need a stue. Such a room is the territory of a leader, a place where he and his lieutenants can assemble. Just a dry, warm place to sleep and prepare our meals is plenty. Over the winter, Arne did all he could for us, even assuring me that he would act as prefect and guardian for Hakon until he comes of age to assume leadership, if the Lagtings elect him.

Skjervald lives with Arne's soldiers now and has gained great respect among them. When Skjervald returned to me after assuring Hakon's safety, I threw my arms around him, and said, "Skjervald, I'm so sorry. Forgive me. Please, forgive me. I never should have doubted you."

"Inga," he said, smiling. "that was Torstein's plan. 'If you can fool Inga,' he said, 'you will fool them for sure.'"

"Thank you, Skjervald the tall." I touched his cheek and made him blush. Since then, I've seen him often. He comes by to play with Hakon or I stop to see him when I go from my lodge to the great cathedral that overlooks the fjord. The skihytte is on the way, and I know that's where I can find him more often than not, laboring over a new pair of skis. We talk about Hakon and his future, about his father and Lillehammer, and Torstein.

When Skjervald and the troops from Nidaros came to take me into the city gates after Magnus and Sturelsson fled, we returned to where Torstein made his stand to slow the enemy. There were two dead Croziers there, but no sign of Torstein, except for his battle-axe wedged between the shoulder blades of one of the dead. Skjervald laughed when he saw the slain soldier.

"What?" I asked.

"Look at his head," he said.

A thick crust of blood covered the side of his face and matted his hair. "He's missing an ear," I said.

"Both ears."

I looked again and saw, on the side not bloodied, a lump of scar tissue where an ear once was. Skjervald leaned forward and yanked the axe away. Later, on one of his visits to play with Hakon, he told me the story of One-Ear.

* * * *

The day we reached Nidaros, there were those who wanted to chase down Magnus and the remaining Croziers. None of Arne's Birkebeiners had had time to prepare for a trek of any length, and the western sky was threatening another storm. But each day after that, until the next blizzard, Skjervald and I and several others went out to look for signs of Torstein, but we found none.

When spring came and the snowpack left, we started to look again. One day, we had traveled far from Nidaros on the muddy trail back toward the Oster, when we heard the voices of a large number of people coming from the other direction. We hid in the woods and waited for them. Men, women and children, about forty in all, trod the crusty remains of winter. Most carried heavy packs or pulled small pulks laden with their possessions.

"From Lillehammer," Skjervald said. "I recognize some of them."

"Me too."

We stepped from our hiding place to greet them. We passed amongst them, grasping hands and hugging old friends. Near the end of the line there were two boys whom I recognized as Heiki's grandsons. They towed a pulk. On board was the shell of an old woman, swathed head to toe in blankets except for her face. Her skin was as pale as the vadmel that wrapped her, and about the same texture. If there had been two holes burnt in her covers, they would have been difficult to distinguish from her eyes. I reached down to stroke her forehead and her darkened eyelids peeled themselves open.

Her eyes fought with her in an effort to focus, until I saw a flicker of recognition, a drop of clarity in a lake of bewilderment. "Inga?" she said. The word barely escaped dry, shriveled lips.

I bent closer, and then knelt over the long sled.

"Inga, it's me, Heiki."

"My God," I said, and then wished I could reclaim my astonishment and suck the words back past my tongue. "It's you. Oh, dear Heiki, it is you." And I bent and kissed her. I looked up at her grandsons and the older one, Per, shook his head.

"Inga, I want to talk to you," she croaked.

"Oh, ja, Heiki. We'll get you to Nidaros and we'll spend all our time in wonderful conversations."

"No, kjeare deg. I mean, I need to talk to you. Now." She could barely get the words out. "Was so afraid I might not get the chance." A deep, crackling cough rattled through her throat from some sick place deep inside.

I leaned closer, reached under the blanket and took her hand. Twigs I had fetched out of winter's snow were warmer and less brittle. "Ja, Heiki, let's talk."

"They overran us, you know. The Croziers. The day after you left."

I nodded.

"We heard rumors, but weren't sure till now that you made it," Heiki said.

"We made it, thanks to Skjervald and Torstein. Hakon is safe," I said.

I guess it was a smile that creased her face. "Thank goodness. Such a beautiful child." She made an effort to clear her throat, but each word grated like pebbles in the grist. "They killed most of the young men, gave quarter to few. Left the women, old men and youngsters with no animals and little food. Per and Sigurd and a few others hunted or we all would have died." I looked at the two boys. They were dirty and tired. Neither smiled. Both looked older than boys should.

"Do you know of Hakon's fate?" I didn't believe I had the courage to ask what I was sure I already knew.

She moved her head side to side. "Not sure. Some say his men carried him to the gate and propped him up to fight them as they broke through and he took an arrow from Erling's bow. Others say that in the melee, a half dozen Birkebeiners swept him onto a horse and made it to the woods. I wish I could tell you more, dear."

"That's all right, Heiki. Rest and we'll talk for a long time when you're comfortable."

"No. There's one more thing." She drew a shallow breath. "Hakon summoned me before the battle. Gave me a message. 'If I don't survive,' he said, 'tell Inga that my last thoughts are of her and our son.'"

I held back tears, stroked the brittle skin of her face, and said, "Sleep now, Heiki." She closed her eyes and that was the last I spoke to her. I've made some friends here, but none like Heiki. Often, when I miss her, I pick up Hakon and give him an extra hug. Heiki was right. He and I will always have a bond and I will cherish it beyond all else.

How often I think of Torstein, too. I hope, without hope, that he fought his way through the Croziers on that last day of our long struggle. Seeing us safe, maybe he slid off the trail to avoid confrontation with Magnus and his two lackeys. But why wouldn't he then join us in Nidaros? Could the strength of his loyalty to Hakon have propelled him back toward Lillehammer? I suppose I would like to imagine that, to see, at least in my mind, the two beautiful brother wolves together, back to back and side by side, protecting each other. Ja. That is what I would like and that is what I shall dream.

As I read of the birth of the Birkebeiners, I also witnessed the emergence of a novelist I'd strap on my skis to follow anywhere. Jeff Foltz deftly informs and definitely entertains and we are helpless but to follow the characters, including heroine Inga on her harrowing eight-day ski through forest and over mountain, all to keep safe her infant son the prince. The author reaches back to 13th-Century Norway for the spark of this story, but the selflessness with which his characters attempt to protect family and homeland ring familiar even in this very modern age.

—**Suzanne Strempek Shea**, author of *Becoming Finola*

There are very few authors who could make me care about Thirteenth Century Norway, but in his masterful historical novel, Birkebeiner, Jeff Foltz does exactly that. Brilliantly researched, fully imagined, and finely written, this story examines both the tenderness of family relationships and the viciousness of war—a mix of human extremes that is achingly timely. Here is a book that cannot be described in a line or two. Let Foltz immerse you in his fictional world; the scenes and relationships will linger long after you've come to the end of his sweeping tale.

—**Roland Merullo**, author of *Breakfast With Bhudda*

Jeff Foltz's *Birkebeiner* is not only a raging, action-filled Scandinavian war saga, it is also a damn good novel. The inner actions of his characters—particularly his female characters like Inga—are every bit as captivating as the external world of war and conquest, of bloody battles and mayhem. If you like your novels packed with action *and* psychological insight, this is the one for you.

—**Michael White**, author of *Beautiful Assassin* and *Soul Catcher*

eff Foltz received a B. A. in history from Marietta College and an MFA in creative writing from the University of Southern Maine (the Stonecoast Program). He has three grown children and seven grand kids and lives with his wife, Sue, in Camden, Maine.